THE ONLY WIZARD IN TOWN

HEIDE GOODY

IAIN GRANT

1

DAEDAL

Priest Daedal hurried as fast as he could.

Six bells sounded from the calendarists' tower, the bells oddly dulled as if they were struggling in the hot wind. Night was falling over Ludens. Daedal would be expected in the temple for daily Summation soon enough, but he wanted to put a question to the imprisoned wizard. However, progress was slow: the crowds around the corn market, even as the market was closing, were irritatingly dense. The city folk of Ludens seemed perversely blind to his urgency. Also, there was the hopping.

Daedal was not an old man – he still had all his own hair and teeth, and even some residual acne – but even he couldn't move at much of a pace while hopping solely on his right foot.

He glanced down to check he *was* still hopping on his right foot, and not his left. He had attempted *Hop all day on one's right foot* some weeks before discovering shortly after lunch he had inexplicably switched to his left. There was no *Hop all morning on one's right foot and all afternoon on one's left* on the *List of Things to Be Done*; at least not in the sections he had read. It might appear in the Esoteries which only the high priests and Hierophant were permitted to read, but he didn't feel like speculating on the matter and gave up.

Today, it was right foot all the way. The guards bowed as he hopped through the great gopherwood gate of the temple, round to the lesser courtyard and the entrance to the Hierophant's cells of justice. He brushed clumsily against the stone arch as he came to a halt. Ancient loose sandstone powdered against his robes; it didn't matter. Everything in Ludens was the colour of sand: the stone, the clothes, the people, most of the food.

As he got his breath back, a dirty youth – one of the jailer's helpers, a nephew perhaps – backed out of the jailer's cubbyhole office, bumped into Daedal and almost sent him tumbling.

"Watch where you're going!" snapped Daedal, swinging his left leg wildly to keep balanced. "You almost had me over!"

The dirty creature regarded him thoughtfully. "Have you ever tried standing?"

Daedal huffed. "Today is the day to hop on one's right foot."

"Is it, now?"

"Tell me: *What will you do today?*" asked Daedal, quoting Hierophant Foesen's era-defining question to the faithful.

The lad scratched his face. He had fine child-like

features, quite feminine under all the filth. "Dunno. I climbed a tower. Ate some fruit."

Daedal had doubts. He wasn't aware of either of those being on the *List of Things To Be Done* but, if they were, he would have completed them many lifetimes ago. Each strata of society had its own list to be completed before ascending in the next life.

"Then they are done," intoned Daedal formally, "and will not need doing again. Where is the jailer? I wish to see the wizard."

The lad shrugged and gestured down the stairs. Giving the young fool another peevish huff which Daedal was sure said more than any lecture, the priest hopped slowly and somewhat painfully down the steps to the cells.

Daedal stopped at the bottom to rest his ankle, giving the jailer time to spot him, waddle over and remove his fat ring of door keys ready to open the wizard Abington's cell. Ludens was a small (albeit religiously significant) city. It did not warrant a large jail and most cells were occupied – for good or bad – only briefly. Daedal paid regular visits to one prisoner, and one alone.

"He's in good spirits today," said the jailer, unlocking the door.

"I am not!" roared Abington from within. "I'm in bloody prison!"

Wizards were not a local phenomenon. Certainly, Ludens and the plains around had their fair share of conjurers, magicians and sorcerers, but wizards...? They were an entirely foreign affair. Daedal had met only one wizard, this Abington, and therefore, as far as he knew, all wizards were tall, cantankerously loud pipe-smokers in the habit of growing beards which were not merely long, but bushy enough to conceal a small troop of monkeys.

"Ah, Abington," said Daedal warmly, hopping into the cell.

Abington's fierce eyebrows waggled as the wizard glared at Daedal's dangling left foot.

"*Buqit demands there is a time for everything*," Daedal quoted.

"Hmph! And does your blasted goddess demand there is a time to bring a wizard a cup of beer?"

"Yes," said Daedal. "We did that last month. Remember?"

"We could it again."

"Buqit remembers all. Repetition is redundant, insulting even."

"But that was a barley beer, yes? No hops. Do you have beer made with hops in the city?"

Daedal tried not to glance down, wondering if the wizard was trying to be funny. "Maybe."

"Then maybe there's a time to bring a wizard a cup of that."

"I will give it some thought." Daedal made himself comfortable on the bench beside Abington's little table, making sure his left foot was elevated. The remains of a meal was scattered across the table top. The wizard's papers covered much of the unoccupied floor.

Abington's cell was as pleasant a place in which one could hope to be imprisoned. Light and dry, it would have served as a decent wine cellar. It was better furnished than many a sea captain's cabin. The bed was soft and superficially free of vermin. There was a wash stand, a chamber pot, quill, ink and paper, and even a shelf of little jars in which Abington was permitted to keep his magical powders and herbs.

The wizard was accorded the comforts of a beloved guest; perhaps one who might lose his head to the executioner's blade within the week, but a guest nonetheless. This degree of hospitality was all Daedal's doing; Abington was a wizard and Daedal valued his knowledge and insight.

While Abington harrumphed amongst his papers and magical apparatus, searching furiously for something or other, Daedal got straight to the point of his visit. "I saw a magician today."

"How interesting," said Abington, entirely uninterested and peering into the chamber pot.

"In the Upgate market."

"Did you?"

"He had an assistant. Do all magicians have assistants? I don't think he paid her very much. She certainly couldn't afford many clothes. Bangles, yes. Clothes, no."

"Is there a purpose to your wittering, Daedal?" Abington irritably moved a grimlock skull he was using as a paperweight from one shelf to another and back again.

"Before our eyes he, the magician, produced a trestle table laden with enough food to satisfy a Hierophant's banquet. Glazed ham. Dates in syrup. Pigeon, pineapple and pomegranate."

"I see," said Abington, hefting the skull again.

"You do?" said Daedal.

"You've come to torment a man who's had nothing to eat today except steamed artichokes."

Daedal paused a moment to compose himself. Abington was not only irritable but sometimes quite irritating. "There is a time for eating artichokes," he said, piously.

"I had artichokes yesterday too."

"Maybe the kitchen has a surfeit of artichokes." Daedal wished the wizard would put the skull down. "The point of my story is this: did he do it?"

"Do what?"

"Did the magician actually magic up a whole banquet?"

Abingdon finally placed the skull on a shelf and left it there. "I wouldn't know. You were there, not I. *Blast it all!*" This last was directed at the room and general, and the mess of Abington's papers in particular. Whatever he was looking for refused to be found.

"My concern," persisted Daedal, "is that he performed this feat of conjuring and the people threw him coins. Coppers all."

"You think he was overpaid?"

"I think it was pointless. He had conjured up an entire feast, enough for him, his poorly-clad assistant and a dozen others. If he was capable of that, why not simply cast such a spell every day and eat like a king. Better still, why not open up a tavern and make a grand living selling the best food in the city—"

Abington had begun ransacking his bed.

"—And," persisted Daedal, trying to ignore the wizard, "if this is the case and magicians can produce food so effortlessly, why do we have farms at all? Why send the peasants to toil in the fields when we could just train up a score of magic users to conjure all the food the city needs? It all seems so horribly illogical."

"Illogical, hmm?" Abington stroked his beard, as though it were some sort of chin-dwelling pet cat. (It was certainly big enough). His eyebrows abruptly shot up. "I've got it!"

"Have you?" said Daedal hopefully.

The wizard bent, picked up a slipper, and fished around inside. His hand came out holding a bundle of matchwood, which Daedal recognised as fire-making sticks of Abington's own devising. With great satisfaction, the wizard struck one of the fire-sticks against the bars of the high cell window and put flame to the oil lamp on the wall. The light produced was a sickly yellow, but very welcome. Night had all but fallen outside.

"There," said Abington. He looked at Daedal properly for the first time since the priest's arrival. "It was a trick."

"The magician?"

The wizard nodded. "Just a trick. Does that mean the man will be punished? Your goddess is none too fond of liars."

"Only if he claims to have done something and fraudulently asks Buqit to strike it from the *List of Things to Be Done*."

"You're pretty keen on punishing magicians, too," said Abington, holding up his hands, displaying the iron manacles which symbolised his imprisonment and prevented him casting any spells of his own.

"Your crimes are of an entirely different order," said

Daedal as kindly as possible. "How do you know it was a trick?"

"For the reason you very eloquently give." Abington picked up a clay pipe from among his papers, struck another match and put it to the already weed-filled bowl. He puffed gently until the weed was glowing and its pungent smell filled the room. "Casting a spell, or indeed getting any task accomplished, is like a journey."

"Is it?"

Abington nodded and took a deep and deeply satisfying toke. "Imagine one had to transport an army from, say, the Amanni stronghold in Hayal to Ludens."

"Why an army?"

"It's just an example. The road across the plains would take a matter of weeks. Hiring boats in Carius and sailing round would be a longer journey distancewise but, with a fair wind, take about the same length of time."

"Yes?"

"It's all a matter of time and effort. Same result, different path. So it is with magic. Look at this pipe." Daedal looked. "How much time and effort would it take to produce such a thing."

Daedal gave it a moment's thought. "A few minutes to roll out the stem. The same for the bowl. An hour in a kiln, perhaps? It would take hardly any effort at all."

"It would require some small skill," said Abington, charitably. "But, yes. A meagre wizard could conjure up more than a dozen of these in a day. Same result, different path."

"Ah," said Daedal. "So what's the use of magic?"

Abington harrumphed, expelling a mighty cloud of

smoke. "The *use* of magic is threefold, you unimaginative dolt. Firstly, I can use it to access skills which might naturally be unavailable to myself. I can no more fashion a pipe by hand than you can, let's not pretend otherwise. Or if we did it would be a very sorry affair and more closely resemble a sausage than a pipe."

Daedal had no idea what a sausage was but nodded anyway.

"Secondly, those skills might be skills which no human has access to," continued Abington. "Flight. Clairvoyance. Speaking to the dead. And thirdly, whereas a mere human has to expend the effort at the moment of performing the act, a wizard can prepare far, far in advance. Even now, while I'm indulging you in fatuous conversation, I could be galvanising my internals and generating the effort required to produce a pipe in an instant."

Daedal scrutinised Abington as much as he dared, in the hope of observing the wizard galvanising said internals. He wondered what spells the wizard might be storing up inside them.

"The banquet-making conjurer you mentioned," said Abington, "would either have had to spend the past week mentally preparing himself – which seems unlikely, don't you think? – or he would have to dredge up the necessary time and effort in the instant. You would have seen him frozen, immobile and insensible, for hours or days before the feast was produced. Certainly, to him, it would have felt as though no time had passed, but the crowd would have wandered off long before he was done."

"Oh, I see."

"He could have theoretically used his assistant to, indeed, assist. A wizard's touch at the moment of casting: the holding of hands for example. In this way, a *willing* participant can add their vital energies to the process. Halve the time with two of them. Cut it to a third with three, and so on."

"I knew you'd have the answer," said Daedal, nonetheless feeling oddly disappointed. He leaned back, almost putting his elbow in the remains of the wizard's artichoke dinner. "Your explanation makes perfect sense, and yet..."

"It seems quite unmagical."

"Yes. Yes, it does."

Abington smiled. At least, the form of his moustache and beard shifted into a shape which might indicate a smile somewhere beneath. Daedal had no reason to assume it was a nice smile. "There are few true wonders in the world," said Abington, "and those few are worth risking all to possess."

Daedal knew exactly what the wizard was referring to. "You should be grateful we arrested you before you even entered Foesen's Tomb."

"You have said."

"But it's true. To die in Foesen's Tomb is to suffer indescribable torture. Do you know how many levels of traps, deadfalls, mazes and doors – locked, false and secret – Kavda the Builder put in the catacombs and dungeons beneath the temple?"

Abington's gaze was stony. He placed a hand on a collection of scrolls. "The collected works of Kavda the Builder." He slapped it down on a bundle of parchment. "The commentary by Kavda's nephew and my own notes on that." He slammed a fist on an untidy sheaf of papers. "The blood-stained diary of Handzame the Unlucky." He swept the sheaf to the floor. "And months and months of my own notes! Of course I know how many bloody traps and doors are in the tomb!"

Daedal coughed uncomfortably. "It was a rhetorical question."

"Curse your rhetoric, man! This is my life's work, a hymn to the wonders of Buqit's temple, and your Hierophant would have me executed for daring to delve into the tomb; to stand before the final resting place of Hierophant Foesen; to gaze upon its awful majesty."

"And take the Quill of Truth from Foesen's grave and keep it for yourself?"

Smoke billowed from the wizard's nostrils. "Slanderous rumour!"

"Well, that will be for the Hierophant to decide," said Daedal. "But, in truth, even entering the tomb is a crime against Buqit. I am one of her priests and even *I* am not allowed to enter. Buqit willing, I may be interred there upon my death – my most heartfelt desire – but until that day, no. Still, I do not intend to second-guess the Hierophant's wisdom."

"And when do you expect him back?"

"His grace returns from the pilgrimage to Qir before the week is out, barring any obstacles or incidents."

"I should think there will be precious few of those with the entire Ludens army as his escort."

"True."

"I'm surprised the city guard have been able to cope in

their absence," said Abington, trying to draw on his pipe. It had gone out.

"Ludens is a peaceful city," said Daedal. "They have coped. And we have no enemies who could reach us without coming through Qir first."

"Ah, well, then," said Abington, once again patting his pockets in search of matches.

"Your slipper," said Daedal helpfully, pointing.

"Ah. Indeed."

The cell door opened and a serving girl entered. Without a word of apology or any consideration for Daedal's station, she brushed past him to collect Abington's dinner things. She was as filthy as the jailer's boy and, under the grime, had similarly fine, child-like features. So the jailer had a niece as well as a nephew, Daedal surmised, and had been short-changed both times.

"Girl!" said Abington and beckoned her over.

She approached dutifully. The wizard leaned in close to her ear. "No artichokes tomorrow or I will turn you into a newt."

The girl hurried out wordlessly. Daedal had no idea what a newt was but got the gist of the threat. He stood to go (slowly and on one foot only). "Please don't make idle threats against the staff, wizard,"

Abington struck a match and relit his pipe.

Outside a bell tolled. It was full dark now, but surely too soon to be seven bells. Another set of bells joined the first, and then a third. Bells rang out across the city. Daedal fancied he could hear shouting some way off. A cry went up in the lesser courtyard.

"What's happening?" he said.

"That?" said Abington lightly, cocking an ear and pretending to listen. "Oh, that would be the sound of an Amanni army attacking the city."

"What?"

Abington tilted his shaggy head. "At least five hundred of them, I'd say. They sound very fierce. Angry even."

Daedal's mind spun. "What? Why? How do you know?"

Abington grinned. There was flash of teeth among the whiskers. "Because I invited them."

"You what?!"

Towering over Daedal, the wizard put a commiserating hand on the priest's shoulder. "I'm sorry for the lies."

Daedal's mouth was dry. "You can't do this ... you can't have."

"You know that old thing about wizards being unable to cast magic while bound with iron."

"Yes?"

Abington banged his wrists together. His manacles fell to the floor. "Lie," he said.

"Goddess, save me," Daedal whispered, knees sagging.

"If it's any consolation," said the wizard, "I suspect you will be receiving your most heartfelt desire before the night is through." He grabbed his pointy wizard's hat from a shelf and jammed it on his head. "Now, I'm off to find a tavern and a cup of beer. I welcome you to try and stop me." He wiggled his long fingers mystically and left.

Daedal stared after him for a long time. He then looked down. Both feet were firmly on the floor. "Bugger," he said.

2

LORRIKA

"Pictures" Bez sits in the belfry of the calendarists' tower, his back to the great bell, a bottle of beer at his side, his legs dangling over the long drop to the corn market below.

Bez has his drawing board on his knees, held upright with one hand as he sketches in charcoal with the other. It is a picture of the temple to Buqit. The sun has just set and now Bez is racing against the fading light. With economical strokes, he draws in the broad ziggurat and the giant bronzed statue of Buqit, complete with eagle wings, which stands on its very top. The temple is the tallest building in Ludens. It beats the calendarists' tower by a head, maybe a head and a wing.

There is little grandeur to the city of Ludens. It is not prosperous like Sathea. It is not a beacon of civilisation like Carius. It is not burdened with a magnificent history like Qir. Its location, in the flattest, scrubbiest part of the plains, is a constant cause for complaint by the residents. It is almost as if a holy man with an edict from his goddess and no grasp of geography, trade, farming or city planning had simply wandered out from a more civilised and prettier part of the world, stabbed his staff into the ground and declared, "Here! Build it here! This will do!" The nearest waterway is the sluggish Yokigiz river delta which winds down to the coast. The fish there, like the water, are brown and tasteless. Ludens is famed for two things and two things alone: the temple to Buqit and the hot dry foehn *wind which blows down from the mountains, sets everyone's nerves on edge and drives men mad.*

Bez is handsome and, yes, he is mad after a fashion. But he's an artist and madness is therefore expected. As an artist, he's understandably poor. There's little money in pictures of a temple which people can look at for free and less when he spends most of it on ale. His clothes might look fine but they're an actor's trick – all embroidery and no substance – and they can't disguise the smell of dried dung and booze which hangs about him. If he just had a bath and bought some new clothes, he might be worth—

"YOU *DO* KNOW I know you're there," said Bez, without looking round.

There was a pause. "No, you don't," she said.

"You've been there for quite some time."

Another pause. "Prove it," she said.

Bez looked round and up. He pointed. "That's you, there."

Lorrika dropped from the dark ceiling, slid silently down the great bell and landed equally silently on the stone floor. "I am a shadow," she said, defensively. "You couldn't have heard me."

"Didn't say I heard you," said Bez and sniffed, returning to his work.

"You didn't see me."

"Babe, you're a shadow, but a predictable one. This is the third day on the trot you've come here, drawn to my irresistible presence."

Lorrika stuck her tongue out at the back of his head and took out the nectarine she had stuffed inside her tunic.

"And speaking of predictable shadows..." He got up, whipped off the raggedy blanket which also served as his cloak, and wrapped it around the clapper of the great bell: folding it round and tying it up as if it was a pudding to be sold at market.

"Six bells soon." He looked her up and down. "You've got dirt on your face."

Lorrika rolled her eyes. "I'm in disguise."

"What as?"

"A dirty person."

"Where did you pinch the nectarine?" he asked.

"I never steal," she said.

"Oh, bought it, did you?"

"No, it was mine anyway."

Bez raised an eyebrow. "How'd you reckon that?"

Lorrika, swallowed the mouthful of fruit and licked her lips. "I remember, very clearly, once eating a nectarine which looked just like this one."

"Most nectarines look the same. I say that as a man who's known a good few nectarines in his time."

"I didn't say it looked a bit like this one. It looked *exactly* like this one. When I saw this nectarine on a stall in the corn market—"

"Ah, ha!"

"—When I saw it I was stunned. How could this be? Two nectarines entirely alike? And then I remembered. I distinctly remember eating that nectarine and dropping the stone on the ground." She spread her hands, her story told.

Bez thought about it. "So," he said slowly, "you think that nectarine grew from the stone of the one you once dropped on the ground?"

"Only explanation," she said cheerfully, and took another bite.

"But you still pinched it."

"How can I have stolen it? It was already mine. My nectarine, my stone and, with a little sunshine and rain which no one can begrudge me, my new nectarine. I put it to you that, somewhere out there, there's a whole nectarine grove which belongs to me."

"You're a shameless liar, Lorrika," said Bez.

"I never lie," she said.

LORRIKA WASN'T LYING. She had a clear and specific relationship with the truth. Rather than tell things which were true or not true, she found it easier to make the truth what it ought to be and then wait for the world to catch up.

She had a sound philosophical basis for this viewpoint, one she had learned as a child when she had been sold in apprenticeship to the philosopher Rabo Poon of Carius (a city where philosophy was less an occupation than an endemic medical condition). Rabo Poon had given her the first of the many names she'd since owned, and the giving of that name was the first lesson she learned in the nature of truth: that truth was only what everyone agreed it to be, just as names were only what everyone agreed to call each other. That's what *received wisdom* and *common knowledge* were: commonly agreed truths. If enough people believed it, it was true. That's why it was definitely and certainly true eating bread crusts gave you curly hair, what doesn't kill you makes you stronger, and a good bleeding will cure any ill. All definitely and certainly true, despite the evidence of Lorrika's straw-straight hair, the fact her fall from the Carius market wall on her first illicit night climb had smashed her leg and left it unable to bend fully, and the fact that the doctor who came to treat her leg with a good old bleeding, when Rabo Poon feared he was going to lose his investment, was very nearly the death of her. In what Rabo Poon described as an *entirely subjective universe* ("For if the moon rises and no one sees it, does it truly rise?"), truth was what people agreed it was.

Lorrika's own personal relationship with truth and reality was cemented by a second insight gained from observing her philosopher master. When he was laughed out of the council hall for daring to suggest they could defeat the approaching Sathean war fleet by all pretending *really hard* it didn't exist, Rabo Poon left knowing his tactic was perfectly sound. A man in a minority of one, he complained that night, wasn't wrong.

And so Lorrika's personal philosophy was born. Accepting truth as a matter of consensus, and starting with a consensus of one (her), she bent the reality of the world to her needs. She was not a thief: she was a material goods redistributor. She was not a burglar or housebreaker: she was a rooftop traveller and amateur lock enthusiast.

SHE MUNCHED down the rest of the sweet sticky nectarine flesh. "I'm a very moral person, me," she told Bez. "Will you be in the taverns later?"

"My adoring public demands it," said Bez and jiggled the near empty bottle. "And my hungry belly. Have a look at this." He held up his drawing board. He'd sketched in a vast winged creature over the temple.

"There was no dragon," she said.

Bez tilted his head. The fact he was poor and smelly didn't seem to matter so much when he tilted his head and looked at her like that: his ragged mop of hair curling round his cruelly beautiful (if slightly ruddy) face.

"Artistic licence," he said. "I offer the chance for mere mortals to share my frankly astonishing vision of the world. I bet someone did see a dragon today."

Lorrika sucked the last juice from the stone and tucked it in her tunic. Bez, like Lorrika, was a dabbler in presenting the world as something other than it might traditionally appear to be. However, he'd not had Lorrika's philosophical training, so he was just a bloody liar.

"Oh," she said, pointing at the fastidiously drawn figure in the foreground of Bez's picture. "And Chainmail Bikini Woman was there too? She's in a lot of your pictures."

Bez grinned. "Yeah. That's right. She gets about a bit, that girl."

"Never met her in the flesh."

"She's very busy."

"Because I've got some questions for her."

"Yes, well..."

"I mean, it must chafe. The chainmail. Cos it's chain, isn't it?"

"I've always considered chafing a matter of personal taste. Besides, I'm pretty sure they don't make woolmail."

"And there's those," she said, indicating a bosom any adventuring woman would find unbalancing, to say the least.

"There are always those," he agreed.

"Yes, but they're not always that size."

"I assure you they are within what would be considered the normal range."

"Everyone says you have a problem with perspective," she said.

"Well, everyone can go to hell." He tipped up his bottle to drink and received only dregs. "I do not have a problem with — Look, if you don't mind, it's been a slow News day, but I've got to get this finished if I want to eat."

"You want some news?"

"I could be persuaded to listen if it means I get to eat."

Lorrika took him by the shoulders and steered him round the great bell to the other side of the belfry. She pointed towards the north gate.

"Not listen: look. In that direction."

Bez peered. Shadows were deepening and the north wall was becoming indistinct from the sandstone plain beyond.

"I'm not exactly unfamiliar with the view, so if that's all your news...."

The rope pull which ran all the way down the tower twitched and the great bell began to rock. The clapper struck the bell and, even muffled by Bez's cloak, it was tremendously loud. Six bells.

"Just watch," Lorrika shouted over the noise and stepped off the edge of the belfry. She dropped twenty feet to a narrow ledge, bounced and jumped to the buttress, which she slid down to a narrow roof. Foot over foot along the roof edge and then a jump, a swing, a dramatic pose for no one's benefit but her own, and it was just a hop between roofs to the wall of the temple courtyard.

She scrambled down a stack of empty barrels to the lesser courtyard and nipped through the archway to the cells of justice. There were no guards in the lesser courtyard. A trio of holy men in their silly robes were hurrying towards the temple itself, too blind and preoccupied to notice her. She slipped through the arch and tried the door to the jailer's room. It was locked. This did not present a problem. Whoever had built these cells had clearly been of the mind that locks should be big and sturdy rather than difficult to pick. Lorrika could have picked this lock with a bent spoon. Not having a spoon handy, she contented herself with a sturdy lock picks instead.

The jailer's room was a mess. A filthy cot of a bed, piles of unwashed crockery, baskets of cruddy odds and ends. The prisoners' cells couldn't possibly have been much worse. As she searched (Abington's description of the required key had been precise and unambiguous), she wondered if the jailer's poor housekeeping was an unconscious attempt to create a cell of his own. Perhaps he had a guilty conscience and didn't think he deserved any better than his charges.

Or perhaps, the jailer was suffering from what Rabo Poon called *rude particulates*, gained from too much contact with prisoners. Poon's theory was when two objects came into contact with each other, rude particulates would rub off from each and onto the other. Thus, a cup regularly placed on a table would become increasingly *table-y* and the table become ever more *cuppish*. Rabo Poon cited this theory in explaining how seasoned warriors developed resistance to pain and injury from their constant contact with armour, why fishermen were the best swimmers and why consorting with the poor and needy was bad for one's wealth. As Rabo Poon grew older his beard thinned and he'd blamed this on regular and unwholesome contact with his obviously beardless wife and banished her from the bedroom.

The last Lorrika heard of Rabo Poon was he had been sentenced to death for corrupting the young, this by rubbing himself against them in the city street to soak up some of their youthful particulates. He had elected to face trial by combat in the city arena, preparing for this by wearing a suit of solid armour day and night for a week before entering the arena: confident he now needed no external armour to protect him. Lorrika recalled Rabo Poon was fond of saying, "A philosopher, in search of truth, is always happy to be proved wrong." She was comforted to believe he died a happy man.

The key was underneath a small cage containing a furry lump which might once have been a pet or a piece of food, but was now definitely neither. The key was finger length, reed thin, and made for a lock that would be a challenge to any lock-picking enthusiast.

She slid the key up her sleeve, left the room and immediately collided with a priest who wasn't watching where he was going.

The priest was unapologetic. "Watch where you're going! You almost had me over!"

The stupid, moon-faced man was, for no discernible reason, wobbling around on one foot rather than the customary two.

"Have you ever tried standing?" she asked.

"Today is the day to hop on one's right foot," said the priest grumpily.

"Is it now?"

"Tell me: what will you do today?" asked the priest, as though there could be nothing more important than hopping.

"Dunno," she said. "I climbed a tower. Ate some fruit."

"Then they are done and will not need doing again," said the priest pointlessly. "Where is the jailer? I wish to see the wizard."

Lorrika pointed down the steps to the cells. It was as good a guess as any.

The priest, persisting with the hopping, struggled down the stairs, grunting on every step. Maybe today was also the day to break one's neck doing something stupid. The priest was certainly going about it the right way.

Lorrika locked the door again with her picks and considered her next move. With the priest and the jailer down there, it wasn't going to be easy to just sneak past. A disguise was in order. She was sure Abington would be content to wait a few minutes more.

"No, I am not!" came Abington's shout from below stairs. "I'm in bloody prison!"

Tough, she thought and stepped outside.

In short order, Lorrika liberated a pie from the kitchens, borrowed a skirt and apron from a cupboard and fashioned a headscarf from a tablecloth that clearly nobody wanted. She walked back to the cells, down the stairs and bobbed a clumsy curtsey to the fat jailer before entering Abington's cell.

Her master, Abington, was in conversation with the stupid moon-faced priest and had a look of crabby consternation on his face: his natural expression. Lorrika found serving under wizards and philosophers equally tolerable. They were similar in many ways: both had a very poor understanding of the real world, despite claiming unique insights. As far as Lorrika could tell, the significant difference between the two professions was when their beliefs were at odds with the world, philosophers bent their beliefs to match the world, whereas wizards blasted the world with magic until it learned to conform.

Lorrika went to collect the dirty pots on the table.

"Girl!" snarled Abington.

She turned. The wizard crooked a finger to call her over. There was a scowl upon his face but Lorrika could see a twinkle in his eyes. It was a tiny twinkle, hidden behind layers of impatience, exasperation and general miserableness, but there nonetheless.

She approached and leaned in close.

"No artichokes tomorrow or I will turn you into a newt," he muttered as his fingertips found the manacle key hidden up her sleeve.

Lorrika nodded and, her job done, left. She heard the idiot priest berating Abington for his manners as she dashed up the stairs.

Any person wandering through the temple grounds might have later found an apron, a skirt and a tablecloth discarded on the ground and pondered why they were there. However, before Lorrika had scaled the lesser courtyard wall, alarm bells were sounding across the city and the folks in and around the temple had far greater things to worry about than incongruous textiles.

3

There was chaos in the streets.

There was, as everyone kept shouting, an Amanni army beyond the wall or, quite probably, inside it. Ludens had been taken entirely by surprise. The Amanni had appeared from the plains almost entirely unseen while the city's own army was hundreds of miles away. The city and temple guards were torn between either going forth to meet the threat or defending the walled temple grounds and, subsequently, did neither. Likewise, the general populace didn't know whether to run to the city's aid, run away or simply bury their valuables and hide.

As people thronged the streets dithering, Lorrika walked entirely unheeded. She fell into step beside Abington as he strode down Mercer Row. He didn't acknowledge her for several minutes and then simply held out the key to his manacles to her by way of a thank you.

"Aren't we meeting General Handzame in the temple?" she asked.

"In good time," said Abington. "I have a wretched thirst upon me and I will see it satisfied."

And that was that.

By eight bells (although no one was actually ringing them), it was essentially over. The Amanni had flooded into the city, driving all before them with steel, exquisitely fashionable armour, and battle cries. They had swept Luden's meagre forces inside the temple and then flooded into that. Within two hours of the alarm being sounded, Ludens was taken and a strange quiet had fallen across the city, broken only by the tramping of occasional Amanni patrols going in and out of the temple complex, the furtive noises of the wealthiest citizens trying to find fresh spots in which to bury their remaining valuables, and the sound of Abington loudly demanding another beer.

The tavern on the corner of Mercer Row and Kidgate was doing a brisk trade, mostly to men who were drowning their sorrows, or those who were enjoying an evening on the ale to demonstrate they weren't intimidated by no upstart foreign invaders (although they might also have been drowning their sorrows too, quiet-like). As Lorrika fetched Abington his fifth cup of beer, Abington sat back to observe the entertainment.

"Pictures" Bez and "Words" Stentor, fresh from a whirlwind tour of the city's other drinking holes, stood on a pair of fruit crates they had brought with them: otherwise known as the stage. In his hands Bez had a number of picture panels which he had sketched out and painted during the day and now held up in turn as Stentor, wearing his floppy orator's hat, struck his little gong and announced the doings of the day.

"Tonight in News of the World..." boomed Stentor.

BONG.

"Five thousand Amanni warriors seize Ludens in surprise attack."

BONG.

"A special report on the bloodthirsty Amanni horde."

BONG.

"Dragon sighted over Buqit's temple. Priests ignore portent of doom."

Lorrika picked up a cup of beer from the bar. As she turned away with it, a hand gripped her upper arm. She looked at the hand and then the owner.

"That's mine," he said.

"No, it isn't," she said.

"I bought it. I saw you take it, thief."

"Thief?" she said indignantly, earning a shush from a couple of old duffers who were trying to pay attention to the News. "I am no such thing. You say you bought it. You can only buy something if you plan to keep it. The same goes for stealing. Were you intending to keep this beer?"

"I intend to drink it," he snarled and reached for the cup which she held away at arm's length.

"Drinking is not owning. It's an ephemeral transaction at best. A matter of transmuting one substance to another. You might as well try to buy sunshine."

"Listen, girl—"

"Here." Lorrika put the cup down on a table, lifted a full pint pot away from another patron and gave it to the arm holder.

"Oi!" yelled a little man.

"It's okay," said Lorrika, took a third man's drink, gave it to the second, swapped over three drinks between a table of other drinkers, temporarily gifted the original fellow with two further beers (neither of which were his but it forced him to release her arm) and put a final drink before a man who had never had one before.

By the time the drinkers had recovered from their surprise and were contemplating whether they were a drink up or down, Lorrika had wandered off. She put the cup of beer in front of Abington.

"We have money, you know," said the wizard, dipping into one of the many pouches at his belt and pulling out a pinch of weed.

"I don't hold with having money," said Lorrika. "It leads to greed and violence."

There was the sound of a pot smashing and of a fist connecting with a face and a strangled cry of "But that's my beer!" from a little man at the bar.

"See?" said Lorrika.

"*If* I may continue!" said Stentor, waggling his gong-stick threateningly at the rabble at the bar. "And – lo! – as night settled over our fair city like dark treacle – like *burnt* dark treacle – the Amanni horde launched their vile and cowardly attack."

Bez held up a picture board featuring a black night sky, the nearly black plains and the mostly black cityscape of

Ludens. The audience peered closely to try to make out the details, any details.

"Can't see them," muttered a bloke with his beard so neatly and closely trimmed it tested the very definition of beard. "It's too dark."

"Wearing their fearsome and fashionably *black* armour," said Stentor, "they fought their way into the city. Like doomed but well-armed spinning tops, our outnumbered city guards fought bravely against the well-disciplined and fearless Amanni."

"Excuse me." It was the neat beard fellow again. "The Amanni were both fearless *and* cowardly?"

"Will you please be quiet!"

"Just saying..."

"The individual Amanni are entirely fearless, yes," said Stentor petulantly, "but the attack itself was cowardly: skulking around on the plains until nightfall before coming out from their hiding places and—"

"What hiding places? The plains are flat. I mean they're ... plains. They'd have nowhere to hide except behind each other."

"Who knows the arcane ways of the Amanni? They are as cunning and as cowardly as a fox in the grip of a particularly bad dream."

Lorrika was momentarily taken by the notion of an army which managed to remain concealed by hiding behind itself. Some sort of circular formation...?

"Bravery then," offered neat beard, "would be attacking in broad daylight? And providing the city with decent forewarning perhaps? A letter for instance?"

"Shut your jabber, fool!" snarled Abington as he lit his pipe.

"Yes. This is not a public discussion," said Stentor. "We do Questions and Answers on alternate Wednesdays at the White Horse; this is the News."

Lorrika watched neat beard as Stentor struggled on with his news report. She hadn't seen him in Ludens in all her weeks here and, in a city like Ludens, you got to see everyone soon enough. And neat beard definitely wasn't a local. For one, he had the pink-white skin of a northerner and there were few of them in these parts. He also had a young girl with him – six, maybe seven years old, as pale-skinned as him – and they made a rather strange couple. Father and daughter? But who took their child into a tavern? His clothes were also considerably finer than the girl's. Master and servant? Slave even?

"But who are the Amanni?" declared Stentor. "What do they want? And why? Descended from the ruthless tribespeople of northern Hayal, forged in the unforgiving ice mountains and, like giant man-wolf-bear hybrids baptised in the blood of war, the Amanni found their true purpose under the mad demagogue Nirage. Nirage led a campaign of conquest which saw the Amanni empire extend from sea to sea. City after city fell to their savagery, hundreds slaughtered in their bloody rituals. Hearts plucked from chests! Brains scooped out with spoons! Nirage proclaimed a republic which would last a thousand years but he was ultimately defeated at the Battle of Oopons by the brave people of the plains. Snikiter Jelly, a Ludens resident who, as a boy, was present at the battle—"

"Tha's me! Tha's me!" crowed an old codger from the back of the tavern.

"—told this reporter the Amanni were 'right frightful devils' and 'not right in the head' and he helped the plainsfolk attain victory with a spot of quick thinking."

"Tha's right!" called out the old boy. "I confiscated all the spoons in the camp. Can't scoop out our brains if they don't have no spoons!"

"Defeated and contained, the Amanni horror has hidden within its borders for a generation. Until now! Who knows what the Amanni want, now they have taken Ludens?" asked Stentor portentously. "What horrors will be unleashed by these beastly, degraded and uncivilised—"

The tavern door slammed open. A huge figure filled the doorway. Black plate armour bristled with wicked spurs and swam with diabolical decals. A heavy gauntlet rested on the pommel of a sheathed longsword. If dark vengeance had a form, it could do far worse than this.

"—and welcome visitors to our city, home to many historical sites and charming markets," finished Stentor meekly, giving the intruder his most obsequiously grovelling grin. "It wouldn't be Ludens without 'u'."

The figure stepped inside. There was a weird collective gasp-squeak as the patrons saw this Amanni warrior, despite her short hair and manly armour, was a woman. The gasp-squeak concluded with a curious tone as patrons realised that, despite being a woman and possessing an expression so genially open it would make an village idiot jealous, this woman was still the tallest and burliest individual many had seen in their lives. Lorrika could almost hear the grinding of cogs as some of the men present had to rethink their attitudes towards women. Lorrika knew Cope Threemen from her many errands to General Handzame's camp, and pitied any man who didn't get their most fundamental attitudes towards women rethunk. There was a peculiar breed of man who reacted oddly to strong and powerful women, although, in the general vicinity of Cope Threemen, they were generally a dying breed.

The giantess waved a hand at the News team. "Why? What would it be?"

Stentor gurgled and gave Bez a wild-eyed look.

"Continue with your business," said the warrior as though her presence was nothing out of the ordinary.

Bez shuffled rapidly through his boards to find something non-contentious.

"In other News: a dragon was seen over the temple of Buqit today," said Stentor, struggling to find his voice. "Gliding over the city like a mountain, a gliding mountain, many saw this as an omen of doom." He glanced at the Amanni woman. "Or ... an omen of good times, peace and new friendships. Yes, um, that's right. Long has the dragon been a symbol of the basic unity between all peoples..."

As Stentor struggled on, Cope Threemen walked to Abington's table. The crowd simply melted around her, treading on each others' toes in a bid to melt the quickest.

Abington drained his cup and looked up. "Aren't you meant to be in the temple, Cope?" he said.

"I am," said Cope simply. "And so are you. The general sent me to fetch you."

"And fetch me you can," said Abington, suppressing a

belch for a second. "After I've got a few more of these inside me."

"Only idiots drink to excess," said Cope.

"I've been on enforced sobriety for over a month and currently operating at a deficit. This is just me bringing myself back into balance."

"The general sent me," repeated Cope. From the occasions Lorrika had met Cope, she wasn't sure if the hulking great woman had a tiny brain with room for only one thought at a time, or if her mind was a big empty cavern in which the same thought echoed again and again before finally fading.

"Hey, I'll get you both a drink," said Lorrika. "I'll even pay with actual money."

Cope gave her a suspicious look, reached under her armour and extracted a bundle of yellow cards. She sorted through them, until she found one she apparently liked, read it and declared, "Yes. One drink and then we must go."

Lorrika looked to Abington. "I mean, I'll need some actual money in order to do so," she said.

Jamming his pipe in his mouth, Abington located his coin purse and passed it to Lorrika, who weaved her way to the bar.

"One eyewitness to the dragon's appearance," Stentor was saying, "was intrepid adventuress and long-standing friend of the News of the World, Chainmail Bikini Woman." There was a ragged cheer from the audience (although more ragged than usual tonight what with there being an Amanni warrior woman in the audience) and many craned forward to get a better look at Bez's rendering of the local folk heroine. Bez jiggled the picture board enticingly.

"My cousin Youshan says she came into his shop last week," one drinker at the bar told his neighbour.

"Lucky bugger," said the neighbour. "I've never seen her."

"Me neither but, you know, she's a busy girl."

"Red haired Chainmail Bikini Woman, who is twenty-three years old and comes from the city of Ludens," said Stentor to another cheer, "told this reporter she too regards dragons as a definite omen of peace and amity between all people and one day hopes to tame and ride a dragon of her own. Here's hoping her dream comes true and she will soon have the massive beast between her thighs."

There was a third and final cheer. Lorrika rolled her eyes and signalled to the barman.

"That was the News of the World," declared Stentor. "Thank you!" and leapt off the stage to pass his cap around the crowd.

The barman put two beers in front of Lorrika. "She can't stay here," he said, nodding towards Cope. "She'll drive away business."

"Do you want to tell her?" asked Lorrika.

Bez pushed his way to the bar, took one of Lorrika's beers and downed it in a single gulp.

"You're welcome," said Lorrika and gestured to the barman for a replacement. "That was a good show."

"I'm not sure we wowed our audience as much as we might have," said Bez with a doubtful pout. "Look at this stuff." He held up a board. "I might as well have dipped it in tar."

She looked at the black-on-black cityscape. "It's moody and atmospheric."

"*Pff!* What self-respecting army invades at night? Is there no consideration for an artisan trying to capture the historic moment?"

He nodded to where Cope and Abington were sitting. The neat bearded northern chap had joined them at the table, his little girl vanished off somewhere. "I might ask them," said Bez, "if they'd consider restaging it."

"What?" said Lorrika.

"Invading again. Tomorrow morning, like. Just imagine, that magnificent specimen of womanhood striding through a smashed breach in the city gate, the rising sun appearing over her padded shoulder like a benediction from the gods themselves."

Lorrika's mind was stumbling over the phrase "magnificent specimen of womanhood" and took a moment to get to the end of the sentence. "Smashed? They didn't smash the gate in. They took the city before they could close it."

Bez shrugged. "We could smash it for them. The whole thing needs sexing up, and I'm just the man to help."

"They're not going to invade again." Lorrika was adamant.

Bez was crestfallen. "No consideration for the charismatic artist and historian." He licked his lips. "You think you might be able to put a good word in for me with the warrior maiden?"

"What?"

"You're clearly on speaking terms."

"And you want her to ... model for you?"

"She wouldn't regret it. Just some reference pictures, I assure you. For a re-imagining of the spectacle as it should have been."

"Re-imagining?"

"Truth through the artist's gaze. Is that my beer?"

She slapped his hand as he made to take another one from her before leading the way back to the table. For some reason, Cope had her gauntleted hand clamped fearfully over her mouth.

"It doesn't work like that, Cope," Abington was saying irritably. "This man is no wizard."

Neat beard tugged at the lapels of his outer coat proudly. "I am the finest wizard you'll find in a month of searching. I have letters of recommendation from the king of Yarwich and the merchants' guilds of Aumeria to prove it but—"

"Wizard? You don't even have a hat," Abington scoffed.

"*But* I was actually talking about my primary occupation: oral hygiene and innovative dentistry. For example – Cope, was it? – by looking at just one of your teeth I could tell all manner of things about your diet, your history, your very soul which mere magic could not."

"Calumnious codswallop!" spat Abington angrily and then saw his pipe had burned low and gone out.

Cope clearly wasn't going to let this man anywhere near her teeth. The wizard looked up at Lorrika. "Or you, miss," he said.

"Me? Um—"

Bez coughed lightly behind her.

"—Oh, yes. Cope: this is Bez. He does pictures. He wanted a chat."

"About what?" said Cope.

Bez bowed low. "A request. A commission, if you will."

It was probably the fear of having her teeth interfered with rather than interest in Bez's proposition which got Cope out of her chair, but stand she did. As Bez guided the warrior woman away, beginning to make his pitch, Lorrika sat.

"Do me then," she said and gave Wizard Neat-Beard a smile.

"Sorry? Oh, yes, indeed," he said. "Open wide." He peered in closely. "Fascinating."

"Is id?" she said, mouth open.

"Yes ... sorry, what's your name?"

"Lorrigka."

"Lorrika, eh? I'm Pagnell. Well, I must say you have very fine teeth."

"'ank you."

"A lot of fresh fruit and possibly even fish in your diet. Hardly any grinding down of the milling teeth. No chewing on tough breads and grains for you. And here—" he tapped a tooth in her lower jaw. "—Your name's not Lorrika at all, is it?"

She drew back and gave him a sharp look. The wizard Pagnell spread his fingers wide to demonstrate he meant no harm. "It wasn't the name you were born with, at least," he said.

"How could you possibly know that?"

"Ignore him!" snorted Abington, scraping out his pipe with a short knife. "The man's a charlatan!"

"You're from Carius, Lorrika, or thereabouts," said Pagnell. "Someone has tried to use beeswax to cure a rotten tooth. Failed, but tried."

"I'm amazed," said Lorrika.

"Then you're a fool!" muttered Abington.

"As I said, we're all fools until we work out how it's done," said Pagnell.

Pagnell began to pontificate on the differences between magic and trickery and such. Lorrika would have listened, but there was some sort of commotion in the corner, a crash of metal, the banging of furniture. She turned to look but there were too many people about and it was over too soon.

Pagnell had exasperated Abington to a point where his face was red and his great beard quivered with anger. Lorrika wasn't surprised; all manner of people, even those who were just standing there, minding their own business, were capable of infuriating Abington. She was surprised he didn't snap his pipe in half, the way he was violently stuffing it.

"So, what else can you tell about me?" said Lorrika. "What do my ears say? I've been told I've got ears like a fairy."

"That I wouldn't know." Pagnell smiled at her. This wizard appeared to be master of the charming smile: that of a salesman who was confident of making a sale. "My experience of fairies is limited, and dentistry only extends to teeth, gums and the whole apparatus of the mouth. What would we be without our mouths and our voices, eh?"

"Quiet, perhaps!" snapped Abington and felt around for his matches.

"Show me another tooth and I will speak all manner of truths," said Pagnell.

Cope leaned over and placed a tooth in the centre of the table. It was small, chipped and bloody.

"Well, I didn't mean quite like that," said Pagnell.

Cope Threemen had a face like a winter storm: dark, angry and full of threats. "We're going now," she said.

Lorrika looked around for any sign of Bez.

"Ah!" declared Abington, finding his fire-matches up his sleeve.

Pagnell picked up the tooth and leaned back to inspect it. "At a guess – and it is a guess – I'd say this is the tooth of an idiot."

Abington harrumphed. "Toss a stone in this place and you'd hit a dozen brainless idiots." And then his head exploded. One moment, he was a wizard with a head and the next he wasn't. This came as a surprise to everyone, perhaps Abington most of all.

4

In the small dark hours, they entered Foesen's Tomb, five of them in total: Rantallion Merken, Cope, the wizard Pagnell, "Pictures" Bez and Lorrika herself.

Merken was the leader of their expedition: General Handzame's right hand man and a seasoned soldier. In fact, he was so seasoned a soldier, Lorrika suspected he was all seasoning and little else. Lorrika had nothing against the old. She had known Rabo Poon as an old man and he could unpick the universe with his mind alone. Abington had been a grey haired old geezer, and until a few hours earlier had not only enjoyed rude health but also being healthily rude. Rantallion Merken – ash blonde hair of handsome youth now turned bone white, a thick brush of a moustache dominating a face like beaten leather – looked as if he had gone through old age and out the other side, transformed into some sort of unkillable, post-old creature. Lorrika reckoned the wiry walnut of a warrior could not only take on an army but probably give Death a sound thrashing any time He had come to claim him.

There were stories. It was Rantallion Merken who turned the tides of battles with deception, brought the bandit king Lothwar to heel with a vastly outnumbered force, and had famously felled the island fortress of Abrelia with a mere handful of words painted on a banner. Merken was brains and brawn; or at least he had been.

By comparison, Cope was nothing but hired muscle. Handzame certainly hadn't selected her for her intellect. She was a soldier like Merken, but she and Merken were as different as their blades. Cope's was huge, obvious, lacking any subtlety, and could probably fell trees with a single swipe. Merken's knives were small, whisper sharp and, Lorrika reckoned, only ever seen when it was far too late.

Bez, though. Lorrika wasn't sure why Bez was there. He had a pack on his back, stuffed with Abington's many books and notes, and a wad of sketching paper in his hand. He also had an expression of bitter indignation on his face.

Pagnell was a last minute stand-in for Lorrika's former master. The wizard was supposed to be clever – he would need to be – yet Lorrika somehow doubted he was going to be clever enough.

She picked at the bandage on her left hand. "I wish Abington was here."

"So do I," said Pagnell with feeling, holding up his iron manacles.

"Oh, I'm sure he's here in spirit," said a sullen Bez.

Pagnell raked fingers through his hair and inspected a crumb of something. "Not just in spirit," he said, casting the crumb aside in disgust. Lorrika had, in the madness of the moment, gathered up what she could, but the tavern staff would be sweeping up bits of Abington for weeks to come.

They stood in the great under hall of the temple. Millions of tons of fine stonework, statuary, altars and the gubbins of worship were above their heads. Below the hall lay the fabled tomb, perhaps equal in size. Behind them stood the tomb's stone arch entrance, constructed to appear like the open mouth of an eagle. Its upper beak hung ominously over their heads. Before them was an honour guard of soldiers and General Handzame herself.

Handzame didn't look much like a general. She didn't really look much like a soldier at all. It was as though Cope's giant frame and Merken's battle-scarred experience had soaked up all the soldierliness in the room. If not for the dark Amanni plate Handzame wore, people might have looked upon the jowly woman of middling years and hazarded she was perhaps a greengrocer's wife, or maybe some sort of nurse, or governess. In an effort to remedy the soft and inoffensive nature of her appearance, Handzame had had some extra spikes added to her exquisitely-tailored armour, and her helmet was decorated with a thick black crest of stiffened horse hair. The helmet was probably intended to give the general some additional height and gravitas. Unfortunately, it simply made her look like she could be flipped upside down and used as a broom. A very spiky broom.

Of the five tomb-raiders, only Cope was wearing her Amanni plate. Merken had discarded his in favour of lighter, more comfortable clothes. The five looked less like agents of a fanatical military horde than run-of-the-mill grave-robbers. Four grave-robbers and an artist. Three grave-robbers, an artist and a dentist.

Handzame fixed all five with a glittering gaze.

"Glory!" she shouted and looked to them all for their responses. Lorrika had no idea how she was expected to respond; from the looks on the faces of the others, she reckoned they had no idea either.

"Glory!" shouted Handzame again, in case they'd missed it the first time. She had a thin, weak voice and her shout carried little power. It occurred to Lorrika that Glory was Handzame's dog and she was calling him to go on a nice walk. It was that kind of shout.

"Glory! Some are born to glory. Some seize glory. Some have glory poured upon them. You, my fine men! You shall wear glory from head to toe. I want you to lap it up. Down there!" She pointed viciously at the entrance to the tomb, nearly taking out her eye with the spikes on her arms. "Down there is glory! Can you taste it? Are you ready to lap it up?"

"Are these rhetorical questions?" Pagnell whispered. "I've very confused."

"And down there is death! Horrible gruesome death! Unspeakably horrible and prolonged deaths!" Her glittering gaze had taken on a deranged edge. "The tomb is your enemy and would have you dead! But there can never be glory without a side-order of death!"

"I reckon she thinks glory is some kind of pudding," whispered Bez.

"You will find the Quill of Truth. Bring it to me and your plate will overflow with glory!"

"Some sort of custard?" suggested Pagnell.

"Shush, you damned fools!" hissed Merken through yellow teeth. Aloud to Handzame he added: "Ma'am. I'm afraid we must be off. Time is against us. The most pessimistic assessment puts the Hierophant's returning army at the gates of Ludens three days from now. We will need to have retrieved the Quill of Truth by then."

"Indeed!" declared Handzame. "Time is the enemy!"

"I thought the tomb was the enemy," said Bez.

General Handzame made no indication she had heard him. "Go now! To death or to glory! Or both!"

"Yes, ma'am," said Merken. "Stirring speech. Inspiring." He faced the rest of them. "You heard her, chaps. In we go. Success or death. Pipsqueak and Sparkles, lead the way. I'll take rear guard."

Pipsqueak and Sparkles apparently meant Lorrika and the wizard Pagnell. Lorrika picked up her lamp and stepped into the tomb; the wizard followed close behind. Soon enough they were beyond the torch light of the under hall and the two lamps they carried were their only illumination.

"I don't get it," said Bez facetiously. "Is the glory down here? Are we fetching it to bring it back so she can give it to us? Can't we just get it and keep it?"

"I think glory is meant as an ineffable concept with no physical existence," pointed out Cope.

"So, it's a bit like exposure?" said Bez.

"Exposure?" asked Lorrika.

"Didn't you know? We artists get paid in exposure all the time. 'Can you paint a mural on the wall of my tavern? I can't pay you but it will be great exposure.' Apparently exposure's great, but try buying a round of beers with it and you'll end up with a slap in the chops. I've tried." Bez took out a sketchpad and began drawing as they walked.

The chamber they passed through was longer than their lights could illuminate, maybe twenty or thirty feet in height and lined, top to bottom on both sides, with alcoves containing the mummifying bodies of priests, wrapped in their mouldy robes of office. The high spaces echoed with the sounds of footsteps and the charcoal scratchings of Bez sketching as they walked.

"I don't understand," said Lorrika, looking up.

"A natural state for most of us," said Pagnell. "Always good to recognise it in oneself, though."

"Why do they put all the bodies on these little shelves?"

"It's a crypt."

"I know what it is! I just don't get why. You put cups on shelves. Ornaments."

"Books."

"Exactly." Lorrika poked a grey and dusty priestly cuff as she passed. Her finger went straight through it, like it was cobweb. "You put things on shelves either because you want to use them later, or because they look nice."

"Neither of which applies here, true. I think this is a sign of respect. It's considered a great honour to be buried here."

"I should think they would be glad for a damned lie down after a life of service," said Merken gruffly. "I'm certain I would."

"Serve Buqit all your life and get your own shelf?" mused Lorrika. "Think I'll pass,"

Close behind them, Cope said, "These were great men. Holy men. You should be awed to be in their presence."

"We're working on it," said Pagnell.

"When I was in Yelzun on the Aklan Plateau," said Cope. "I was fortunate enough to visit a temple which held the skeleton of the High Shepherd Vos which the monks had preserved and protected for centuries. The skeleton was only tiny, but one could feel the mystical power in those bones."

"Tiny?" said Pagnell. "Vos was said to be stronger than an ox and more imposing than any king. Why was it so small?"

"Ah," said Cope. "This was his skeleton from when he was boy."

There was a considerable pause before Pagnell murmured, "Right. Okay."

"Hey," called Bez from behind. "Shouldn't you two be scouting for traps or something, not chinwagging like fishwives?"

"There aren't none until we pass the first threshold," Lorrika replied. She looked at Pagnell. "Right?"

"Er, yes," said the wizard, thumbing through the smallest and most expensively bound of Abington's journals. It was the easiest to hold, and filled with the most useful information. Abington's handy guide to tomb raiding, in fact. "There are no traps or pits or anything until we enter the tomb proper. These are just the catacombs for the regular priests. Wouldn't want the unwary spiked or diced in the middle of a funeral."

"Spiked?" said Cope.

"Or diced, yes," said Pagnell, flicking through the book. "According to this there are at least five levels to the tomb complex. Mazes, the *Mouth of Torments* – whatever that is – the *Pathways of the Righteous*, *the Surprising Pit*, magical traps, terrible monsters, spikes and—" he tried to do hand gestures "—dicey things. Hierophant Foesen was buried here over a thousand years ago, and his followers immediately built a series of dead ends and traps to deter tomb-raiders. And then, of course, along comes Kavda the Builder – this was about four centuries later – who laid the framework for the tomb we have now. He devoted his life to the rebuilding of the temple above and the tomb below. It took thirty years alone for the builders to excavate the—"

"That's fascinating," said Bez, decidedly bored. "Great background detail. Thanks muchly."

"I thought you might be interested in a little bit of the tomb's history."

"Yeah?" said Bez. "No. The problem with history is it tends to be long. And that's fine for some people. You know: boring people."

"I thought you were a painter of historical events," said Pagnell.

"Sure, but I'm more interested in the history of the now. Yesterday? That's gone. Last year? Who cares? History? Pah. If I paint something from ancient times, I don't want to get bogged down in unhelpful details. History is totally impressionistic, yah?"

"What does that mean?" asked Cope.

"It means what I think historical events looked like is more important than what they actually looked like."

"Lies then," said Cope.

"Artistic truth. People romanticise the past," said Bez.

"You think the *good old days* were actually good?"

"Better than today, boy," called Merken from the rear. "Where is this first threshold?"

"Through, down, along," said Pagnell. "The catacombs are big."

They passed through an archway and down a dozen steps or more to another, essentially identical chamber. The indefinable sense of depth, of being far below ground, started to weigh on Lorrika. Not in a fearful way: more like being tucked tight into bed under a heavy blanket by an overzealous grandmother. Lorrika never had a grandmother but she was aware of the concept.

She wasn't afraid of depths or the dark or the horrible traps ahead but, nonetheless, put her hand inside her tunic and touched – next to the nectarine stone from her own personal nectarine tree (or possibly grove) – the comforting mass of soft hair she had bundled there. She felt strangely guilty about having it.

For reasons she couldn't fully explain to herself, she took it out to show Pagnell. "Is it okay for me to have this?"

The wizard looked. "What is it?"

"I was confused and shocked and I was scratting on the floor. I don't know what I hoped to do. But I found this and it was all singed at one end but I picked it up anyway and..."

"That's Abington's beard?" said Pagnell.

"Yes. Is it weird?"

"As beards go, I've seen weirder."

"I mean me taking it."

Pagnell had the decency to give it some thought. "Were you planning on wearing it?"

"No."

"Then it's not weird," he said, gently. "He was dear to you?"

Lorrika shrugged. "He was better than some I've known. Okay, there was that thing with the plague in Dalarra."

"I heard he saved hundreds of lives."

"You could say that. Anyway, I've served him for over a year. Met him in Aumeria."

"Was your name Lorrika back then?"

She looked at him suspiciously. "We're not friends, you and I. You know that?"

Pagnell licked his lips and glanced over his shoulder. "I'm not sure many of us are friends, here."

Lorrika grunted. "I was Aisel," she said.

"Aisel in Aumeria. Lorrika in Ludens. Is that how it goes?"

"I find life easier that way."

"And what will you be in Trezdigar?"

Lorrika chewed her lip. "Is Trumpet a name?"

"Not really," said Pagnell. "Best think on it."

Cope tapped her on the shoulder as they walked. "They say an earthworm, if split, can regrow from the tiniest fragment," said the warrior woman.

"Um—" said Lorrika.

Pagnell's lips twitched as he thought. "Are you perhaps suggesting we can regrow Abington from his beard?"

Cope made a meaningful expression, which was quite a sight on a face which was mostly devoid of meaning and expression. "And the great wyrms are said to heal themselves no matter how many pieces they are cut into."

"Wizards are just people," said Pagnell. "We're not earthworms or ... the other kind of wyrms."

"I've heard it said wizards cannot be killed by mortal weapons," commented Bez.

"Yeah. That's just a clever lie we tell people." He moved closer to Lorrika and jerked a thumb back towards Cope. "Is she ... is she normal?" he whispered. "I mean ... regrowing wizards?"

Lorrika shrugged. "She's a bit literal-minded."

"Is she?"

"She believes pretty much anything she's been told. I think there's a lot of empty space in her noggin for any nonsense you'd care to put in there. If you get chance, ask about her sacred mission for the High Shepherdess."

"Sacred mission?"

"Ask. She's harmless really."

"Oh?" Pagnell looked doubtful. "That thump she gave your artist friend..."

"Bez? Ah, he probably made her an offer she had to refuse. I wouldn't be surprised if the words *chainmail bikini* came up somewhere in the conversation."

"Ah."

Up ahead, the chamber ended at a solid rock wall, and a gateway which grew clearer as they approached with their lights.

"Is this the first threshold?" asked Merken.

"Possibly," said Pagnell.

The gateway was formed by two fat stone uprights and a massive lintel. These were plain and unadorned, but the closed double doors within crawled with seriously unpleasant imagery. Contorted, screaming faces, cast in grubby bronze, thrust from the surface of the door. Hands or sometimes just fingers, reached out, frozen in the act of grasping at the air. Here and there, elbows, sword hilts, spears and feet protruded.

"Wow, that's so ugly it's almost beautiful," said Bez, sitting down to sketch it.

"Not very lifelike," added Merken critically.

Pagnell knelt to run his fingers over the semi-circle of symbols carved into the floor in front of the doors. "Mmmm. I think it's probably very lifelike," he murmured. Loud enough for everyone to hear he added, "No one is to touch the door. At all."

"Then how do we get through?" asked Cope.

"The first threshold is a riddle," said Pagnell.

"I am the guardian of the gate," said a voice as cold and dead as the grave, which seemed to come from everywhere and nowhere at once. "Those who wish to enter must answer my riddle."

"See?" said Pagnell. "Tedious things, riddles. *I have eyes but cannot see* and all that nonsense. It will sound superficially profound but end up being trite and really obvious. The answer will be *Death*, or *Nothing*, or the letter *e* or something. Bring it on, guardian."

"My riddle is this: Forever changing, drawn through taverns and mines the same, we go to ancient times and join those with no name. To arches far and the butcher's block, seek the forests of tomorrow and undo my lock."

Pagnell was nodding to himself. He kept nodding.

"What's the answer then?" asked Bez.

"I'm thinking," said Pagnell.

"Is it *Death*?" suggested Cope.

Pagnell shook his head.

"*Nothing*?"

"No."

"The letter *e* then?"

"No!" he snapped. "It's none of them." His face twitched. He looked up at the door. "Could we hear it again?"

"FOREVER CHANGING, DRAWN THROUGH TAVERNS AND MINES..."

Pagnell muttered along as the tombstone voice recited its riddle. When it was done, Pagnell made a thoughtful noise and then stepped inside the semi-circle to give his answer. "Is it *Death*?" he hazarded.

"NO."

"Can I have another guess?"

"NO."

"What? Not now or not ever?"

"NOT EVER."

"Oh." Pagnell turned to the others. "Well, at least we tried. Time to tell the general, eh?" He took a step; suddenly there was a curved sickle of blade against his stomach.

"It is incumbent on me to remind you," said Merken, "that your little girl's life is dependent on you helping us. Cope, if he tries to run before we get to the Quill of Truth, you damn well kill him."

"Sir!" Cope responded.

"And you said she was harmless," Pagnell hissed at Lorrika.

"But obedient," Lorrika observed.

"Can't you pick the lock, thief?" asked Cope.

"Who are you calling a thief?" said Lorrika. "I'm a professional lock enthusiast."

"And even the most amateur lock enthusiast can see this lock is impossible to pick," added Merken. "No keyhole."

"Can't I guess the riddle?" said Lorrika.

Pagnell shook his head. "It said—"

"EACH PERSON MAY MAKE ONE GUESS," intoned the guardian of the threshold.

Lorrika stepped inside the semi-circle. "Is it *Nothing*?"

"NO."

"Are you sure?"

"YES."

"What if I said it was *Nothing*. Can you disprove it?"

"I DO NOT NEED TO."

"Spoilsport."

"The letter *e*?" said Bez, stepping up.

"NO."

"No!" squealed Pagnell. "It's none of those!"

"You said it would be."

"Yes. I meant, something *like* those. Not that but *like* that!"

"The letter *a*?" suggested Cope.

"NO."

Pagnell clutched at the air. "Why?" he cried.

"It's like the letter *e*," said Cope, "you know, *a*."

"Just everyone shut up and let me think!" said Pagnell.

"Is it *man*?" said Merken.

"NO."

"Shame," said Merken. "I was thinking you find men in

taverns *and* in mines and also—"

"Oh, you blithering idiot!" spat Pagnell. "That was our last chance!"

Merken turned unhurriedly to Pagnell. One second and a knobbly knee to the groin later and Pagnell was on the ground, curled up in a ball and regretting his life choices.

"As I was saying," continued Merken, rubbing his knee, "you also find men working as butchers and, I suppose, underneath arches. I thought it a good answer. Oh, well."

Cope squared up to the high double door. "Maybe we should just smash through it," she said and turned an armoured shoulder towards it.

"If there are no more to give answers, you are welcome to try," spoke the guardian, with just a hint of smugness.

Cope took a step back to make a run up. Lorrika couldn't be certain if it was the flicker of the lamp light or if she really saw it, but it seemed one of the hideous carved hands on the door flexed a little. Preparing to take hold of Cope and pull her in; to make her part of its grim façade, add her hands to its...

"Wait!" squeaked Pagnell and rolled to his knees.

"What?" said Cope.

The hand on the door quivered a moment, frustrated.

"If—" said Pagnell. "It said *If there are no more...*"

Lorrika looked at the door, at the terrible frozen faces staring out. *I have eyes but cannot see.* "I'd like to guess," she declared.

"You have already guessed," said the guardian.

"No. That was Lorrika. I'm Aisel from Aumeria."

"YOU SOUND VERY SIMILAR."

"We do."

"YOU'RE NOT LYING, ARE YOU?"

"I never lie," she said. She waited for a denial.

"WELL...?" said the guardian.

"Oh, okay. Um. Is it ... *flowers*?"

"NO. NOW, IF THERE ARE NO MORE—"

"There are more of us," said Pagnell, rising.

Cope looked about herself, confused. "But there's only the—"

Pagnell flapped her into silence.

"HOW MANY MORE?" asked the guardian, warily.

"Gosh. Hundreds. Possibly thousands."

Cope spun around, looking for these hundreds of people who had apparently turned up.

"Oh, Yesh shertainly indeed," said Merken in a lispy foreign burr. "For inshtance, is the ansher *water*?"

"NO."

"Is it *time*?" said Cope.

"YOU'VE ALREADY GUESSED ONCE."

"You have to do a voice," hissed Lorrika.

"Is it *time*?" Cope asked again, not so much in an accent as in the strained voice of a person who had never heard human speech before.

"NO."

"Is it *Moon*?" said Lorrika.

"NO."

"*Blood*?" said Pagnell.

"NO."

"*Boots*?" said Bez.

"No."

"*Harbour*?"

"No."

"*Hearth*?"

"No."

"*Music*?"

"No."

"*Brush*?"

"No."

"*Names*?"

"No."

She didn't know about the others but Lorrika quickly gave up on thinking of answers to the riddle and just spouted random words. Bez was simply stating objects he had on his person. Pagnell was going through Abington's book and picking words out, which was either unimaginative or clever, she couldn't say.

"*Coins*?"

"*Rum*?"

"*Jewellery*?"

"*Tunnel*?"

"*Trousers*?"

"Ooh. Is Trousers a good name?" said Lorrika. "Trousers in Trezdigar?"

"No," said Pagnell.

"How many more of you are there?"

"*Stone*?"

"*Paper*?"

"*Clouds*?"

"*Sand*?"

"*Coal*?"

"*Smoke*?"

"YES."

"*Poetry*?"

"*Knives*?"

"*Darkness*?"

"I SAID, YES," said the guardian.

"Wait. What?" said Pagnell. "Did we get it?"

The double doors swung open to the reverberation of distant and powerful machinery. Beyond, there was a simple, stone tunnel.

"Which answer was it?" said Lorrika.

"Does it matter?" said Merken.

"Told you I'd get you through," said Pagnell and offered a fist to Lorrika. She regarded it, nonplussed. "Celebratory fistbump?" he said.

"A what?"

"You don't do that round here? No?" He sighed and consulted his papers. "Beyond here begins the tomb proper. And, yes, now it's all traps and things which will try to kill us."

"Pipsqueak and Sparkles," said Merken, nodding for them to lead the way.

Lorrika considered the tunnel ahead. "Traps, huh?"

"Come now, chaps. Do you want to live forever?" grinned the old soldier.

Pagnell glanced at Lorrika. "That's a trick question, right?"

Ten yards down the corridor the floor vanished beneath them.

5

COPE THREEMEN

Eight bells, or something like it. It was hard to tell if no one was bothering to ring the bells.

Cope Threemen sat in the cell which had once held the wizard Abington and now held the highest ranking priest left in the city: a round-faced man-boy called Daedal. Cope perched on a bench, polishing her longsword with a soft leather as she watched the priest.

The taking of Ludens had been even quicker and more bloodless than General Handzame had promised. The guards at the gate had been taken utterly by surprise. Cope had smashed one in the face with a clay pot, knocked another out with the pommel of her sword and the rest had run. Then it was a race to the temple: the sounds of a thousand men and the flashes of whizzbang explosions about her. One hour to take the city, less even. If the tales were true, only the spymaster Merken had taken a city quicker, and that entirely by himself.

Cope knew she should have felt some sort of pride on a job perfectly completed, but she felt only a deep dissatisfaction it hadn't been a proper battle. She bent to polish her blade all the harder.

"You will pay for what you have done," said Daedal.

Cope paused and looked at him. "Pay?"

"The people you have hurt, killed. You will be punished."

This was news to Cope. "When? How?"

The priest blinked. "I mean ... you know, generally. I'm just saying. The wicked are always punished."

"Oh." She continued her work. "I don't think so."

"In the *Book of Truth*, Hierophant Foesen tells us after this life we are reborn, and Buqit gives us the life we deserve: the good given better lives, the wicked punished with toil and misery."

Cope thought about this a while. And then she thought about it some more. She got to her feet, walked over and delivered a backhanded slap to the priest's face.

"What did you do that for?" he warbled, a hand to his reddening cheek.

"So," she said, "I will be punished in a future life for doing that?"

"Yes!" he whined.

"And that slap was probably punishment for something *you* did in a previous life?"

"I suppose."

"Huh," she muttered thoughtfully. "So why does this place exist?"

"This place?"

She raised her hands, armour clinking. "Prison. Seems a bit redundant."

"Ah. No. Buqit wants us to show justice in this life too."

She thought about that. "So, punishment in this life reduces the misery criminals face in the next?"

"Yes."

"Because they've already paid."

"Yes," said Daedal with some uncertainty. Thinking it over, he repeated with greater conviction, "*Yes*. Yes, it does."

"Interesting." She punched him hard in the face.

Daedal clutched his bloody nose. "*Why?*" he wailed.

"I'm making sure your next life is better than this one. I'm actually helping you. I'm hurting you to pay for any bad stuff you've done. No pain, no gain."

She drew back her fist.

Daedal frantically warded her off with a raised hand. "I'b good! I'b good! Pleade, don't helb me adybore!"

"Are you sure? A couple more solid hits and you could be a king in the next life. The Hierophant even."

"No. No, I'b fide. Dhank you."

"Oh, okay." She shrugged and went back to the bench. "You have given me a lot to think about," she said.

"Good," said Daedal as he tore strips of cloth from Abington's bed sheets and shoved them up his bleeding nose.

Cope resumed polishing her sword. The weapon was already clean and polished but she polished it nonetheless. She had been taught long ago a professional soldier cleans their blade every night, and Cope didn't believe pre-existing cleanliness should get in the way of that. Cope was a follower, not a leader. She served, not commanded. She liked orders and liked following. Life was simple, clear and satisfactory when one was following orders. This made her an exemplary student.

When the militia master at Skelkin had told her she would need to practise for eight hours a day to be as good as the boys, she practised for eight hours a day. When she was as good as the boys (better even) and asked the militia captain what she should do next if she wished to join the militia, he'd given her a vexed look and said she should clear out the band of thieving grimlocks which had taken up residence in the local woods. When she had done that and brought back the webbed right hand of the biggest grimlock as evidence and asked the militia captain what she should do next, he'd given her a deeply vexed look and told her she should take up weight-lifting, and go to Master Jarden Orre and ask for a *long weight* for that very purpose. After standing outside Master Jarden Orre's door for ten hours without any sign of said long weight coming forth, Master Jarden Orre had explained the militia captain was playing a cruel joke and she should learn to *read between the lines*. That night, Cope had made herself cross-eyed trying to read between the lines of the pamphlet *It Is Every Man's Duty To Fight For What Is Right* she kept in her bed roll. When she visited Master Jarden Orre again, to enquire exactly how one should read between the lines, he gave her a vexed look not dissimilar to the one the militia captain gave her and said if she could run the fifteen miles to Dochlon and back, bringing him a demijohn of beer, he would teach her all she needed to know to become the greatest swordswoman that side of the sea. She did. And he did. And she also took up the weight-lifting, because the militia captain had told her to.

Master Jarden Orre was the finest instructor she had ever had and, since his death, she had yet to find anyone close to equalling him in skill and wisdom. But she looked nonetheless.

"Are all priests wise?" she asked Daedal.

He chuckled grimly. "I widh."

"I'm on a spiritual quest, you see," she said.

"Are you?"

She nodded. "Given to me by the High Shepherdess Gwell. After my master's death, I went to her seeking my true purpose in life, and she, in turn, asked me a question. I have to find the answer to the question in order to find my true purpose. When we have recovered the Quill of Truth, I will ask General Handzame to use it to answer my question."

Daedal had shoved as much cloth up his nose as one priest could usefully shove. Two streamers hung down from his nostrils like a rubbish moustache. "Whad id your quedion?" he asked.

Cope told him.

Daedal pondered over it for a very long time. "I'b going to day, yed," he said eventually. "Yed, dhey do."

"That's what everyone else says," said Cope.

"Aren't you habby widh dhat ander?"

She pulled a face and was about to respond when Merken walked in. Cope stood to attention.

Rantallion Merken cut a fine figure in his Amanni armour. He had the firm chin, the bold nose and the high brow of a great leader. He also had the fleshless fingers, the craggy skin and the hairy ears and nose of a village elder but, dressed as a soldier, he cut a fine figure nonetheless.

Merken looked at Daedal's bloody face and the mess he had made of the bed sheets. "Prisoner giving you trouble, Cope?"

"Not at all, sir," she said. "We were having a spirited religious discussion."

"Good girl. Does he know what happened to Abington?"

"Says he went off in search of a tavern but doesn't know which."

"Indeed." Merken fingered the velvet pouch which hung on his belt and then, conscious of the act, let it drop. "I think you and I had better go find our wizard, eh? The general wants him."

6

The invaders held the fortified temple complex and, for now, had little need to venture beyond its walls. Six men at a time were sent out each hour to patrol the major streets and remind the locals they were under occupation. For the main part, the locals were staying indoors and safely out of the way.

Cope and Merken split up in the corn market as their search for a tavern which might contain their wizard continued. Neither feared being alone in the occupied city. Both were experienced enough to recognise when an opponent was beaten and beyond constituting a threat.

A loud commanding voice was coming from the open windows of a corner tavern in a two storey stone building so ramshackle that, if wasn't for the evidence of the clay bricks and mortar, Cope would have taken it for a natural cave rather than something man made. She kicked the door open. Beaten or not, it never hurt to make an entrance.

Five dozen eyes stared at her. Abington sat at a centre table with that scrawny girl thief of his, Lorrika. He tried to hunker down in his seat and look unnoticeable. However, being considerably taller than the average man and in possession of the biggest beard for a hundred miles around, he was very noticeable indeed.

Cope scanned the crowd for signs of trouble – not that any would have lasted for long. She had her longsword; her weighty scabbard was a serviceable club; her belt, purchased from a very nice man in Yelzen, could be removed and used as an effective throwing bola. And – thanks to an educational pamphlet she had bought from an equally nice man in Yelzen (who had seen her purchase the throwing belt and knew a discerning customer when he saw one) – she knew thirty-seven different ways to disarm an opponent, four of them permanent.

To a man, the patrons were far more interested in their beer, their shoes, their fingernails and pretty much anything at all, than causing trouble for Cope. On a tiny stage, constructed from fruit packing crates, two men gawped at her. The one with the silly hat and, until now, the commanding voice, burbled something incoherently, finishing with, "—It wouldn't be Ludens without you."

It was a bloody peculiar thing to say.

Cope stepped inside properly and gestured for him to explain. "Why? What would it be?"

The two simply continued to gawp. Her arrival had clearly turned them into idiots. She sometimes had that effect. "Continue with your business," she told them.

As the mummers on stage babbled on about some story

of dragons and temples, Cope walked over to Abington. Men stumbled over themselves to get out of her way.

Abington sourly downed his drink and glowered at her. "Aren't you meant to be in the temple, Cope?"

"I am. And so are you," she replied. "The general sent me to fetch you."

"And fetch me you can," said Abington. He paused for effect and added, "After I've got a few more of these inside me."

"Only idiots drink to excess."

"I've been on enforced sobriety for over a month and am currently operating at a deficit. This is just me bringing myself back into balance."

"The general sent me," Cope said again, which should have been enough to stir him. He should at least have some respect for Handzame's position, if not her role in his release.

Abington, like a moody child, seemed entirely unmoved, decidedly unstirred.

"Hey," said the thief, Lorrika, "I'll get you both a drink. I'll even pay with actual money."

Cope managed to get her hand under her armour and reached her instruction cards. They were very helpful at uncertain moments. She unwrapped them from their waterproofed leather and looked through them until she found the one she needed.

How to Resolve an Argument with an Obstinate Person

- *Think about the obstinate person's position.*
- *Is their opinion or intention likely to cause significant problems for you?*
- *If so, restate your position clearly, offering such supporting evidence you have.*
- *If not, is there a compromise you can offer?*
- *Suggest a compromise solution and make your expected outcomes clear.*

SEE ALSO:

- *How to Present Evidence and Arguments to Others*
- *How to Identify when Someone is being Unfair*
- *How to Recognise when You are in the Wrong*

PERHAPS ONE MORE BEER WOULD BE ENOUGH to winkle Abington from his drinking stool and, Cope realised, she herself had not had anything to eat or drink all day.

"Yes," she agreed. "One drink and then we must go."

"I mean, I'll need some actual money in order to do so," the thief added.

Cope wasn't sure what the difference was between actual money and non-actual money, but she knew Lorrika had spent far too much of her childhood in the company of philosophers and was prone to bouts of nonsense.

Nonetheless, Abington begrudgingly handed a purse over and Lorrika spirited it away to the bar.

"One more and then you're coming back to the temple," Cope told the wizard to make sure her expected outcomes were clearly understood.

"I'll have as many as I bloody well please, Cope," said the wizard. "You worry too much."

Cope had to wait until the pub crowd had stopped cheering the entertainers before answering. "I don't worry at all. It's the general's orders, not mine."

"It's my plan, my maps, my knowledge!" snapped Abington.

"Her swords, her men, her gold," said Cope simply. "Be careful or she'll have Merken give you a lesson in respecting authority."

"Hmph!"

A chair scrape and there was suddenly a third person at their table, a thinly bearded northerner with an inquisitive glint in his eye.

"Go on then. Tell me how it was done," he said.

"Push off!" said Abington.

"How was what done?" said Cope.

"The sneak attack on the city," said the bearded one. "Was it magic?"

Cope considered the eager fellow. "Shall I kill him?" she asked Abington, putting a hand on her sword.

The man waved his hands in a hasty apology. They were pale soft hands, the hands of someone who had not done a day's hard work in their life. "I mean, all kudos to you guys," he said.

"I'm a pacifist myself, mostly anyway, but you've got to recognise tactical genius when you see it. A thousand soldiers – two thousand maybe? – conjured out of the featureless plains. What was it? Some sort of mass invisibility spell? Some other trick?"

"Only a fool thinks everything is a trick," said Abington.

"Ah, but we're all fools until we work out how it's done. It's purely professional curiosity on my part. I'm a wizard myself. Newport Pagnell. Pleased to make your acquaintance."

He treated them to a toothy smile – his teeth were surprisingly white and neat like they were brand new and unused – and offered a hand which neither of them took. He held it out for an uncomfortable second before withdrawing it.

"It's not my main job," he conceded. "My mead and meat is in oral hygiene and innovative dentistry."

It was all just words to Cope. This man, Newport Pagnell, talked too fast and smiled too often. She was tempted to stab him lightly just to slow him down and shut him up.

"Oral hygiene!" jeered Abington.

"And innovative dentistry," said Pagnell.

"What is den-tis-try?" asked Cope.

"Flimflammery and nonsense," said Abington, toying with his pipe. "It's teeth magic."

Cope knew teeth magic well. She had been raised on a diet of fireside stories which included those of the pale tooth fairies to whom children offered up their baby teeth in the hope of gaining fairy teeth of their own (which everyone knew were as sharp as knives and never stopped growing). However, children were warned to beware of prowling grimlocks who stole the teeth of the unwary and sold them to sorcerers and such who used the teeth in their wicked spells. It was said (by various aunts and grandmothers, gummy and toothless all) that to give a sorcerer a tooth was to give them control of your very spirit.

Cope slapped a hand across her mouth to stop the wizard stealing her teeth on the sly.

"You'll not steal my spirit with your fairy magics," she mumbled.

"Oh, I don't think that's going to happen," Pagnell assuredly her breezily. "I use a few spells in my work. *Cowell's Frictionless Unguent, Hamed's Hammer of Loosening* but dentistry is more about the application of knowledge and, occasionally, a pair of forceps of my own devising. I have them here somewhere..."

"Don't let this wizard bewitch my teeth," Cope said fiercely to Abington.

"It doesn't work like that, Cope," sighed the older wizard. "This man is no wizard."

Pagnell gave up searching for his *four seps* (though Cope kept a watchful eye on him, in case he tried to enchant her or summon grimlocks to attack her) and straightened his coat lapels with petulant self-importance.

"I am the finest wizard you'll find in a month of searching and I have letters of recommendation from the king of Yarwich and the finest merchants' guilds of Aumeria to prove it but—"

"Wizard?" scoffed Abington. "He doesn't even have a hat."

"But I was actually talking about my primary occupation," said Pagnell. "Oral hygiene and innovative dentistry. For example – Cope, was it? – by looking at just one of your teeth I could tell all manner of things about your diet, your history, your very soul which mere magic could not."

Abington was childishly indignant, as though he was made jealous simply by another wizard's presence. "Calumnious codswallop!" he spat, snatching the pipe from his mouth in anger.

"Or you, miss," said Pagnell, looking past Cope.

Lorrika has returned, with two cups of beer and one of the fool performers from the stage. The pictures man nudged Lorrika. "Oh, yes," she said. "Cope. This is Bez. He does pictures. He wanted a chat."

"About what?" said Cope.

"A request. A commission, if you will," said Bez a little beerily. He gave her the most ridiculously toadying bow. Up close, she could see the man's otherwise handsome face was covered with a fine tracery of red lines. A few more years of bad living and this drunken sot would either look like a ruddy farmer or be dead in a ditch.

Cope had come in to retrieve Abington. Now, she just wanted to get away from the tooth mage. She stood quickly, let her hand drop from her mouth but kept her lips firmly sealed. She looked at this Bez character and jerked her head towards a corner of the room where they might talk.

They stood by the stairs, the space under which was evidently used as storage for empty casks and drunkenly unconscious customers. Cope stood with her back to the wall and one eye firmly on Abington and the tooth mage, Pagnell.

"You wanted to talk?" she said, barely glancing down at the painter man.

"Yes, absolutely," said Bez, "but first let me say, wow."

"Wow?"

"Impressive or what."

"What?"

"The Amanni rising out of obscurity to reclaim their former glory and you..."

"Me?"

"You! In the vanguard as you smashed through the city gates. I've seen heroism in its time and you ... you..."

"We didn't smash through the city gates," said Cope. "They were already open."

"Well, yes, and I want to have a chat about that too."

This strange little man spoke even faster than the tooth-obsessed wizard and, as best she could tell, he'd not even got to the end of a complete sentence, let alone any kind of point. The tooth-wizard was currently staring into Lorrika's mouth and prodding her teeth while Abington watched and scraped out his pipe bowl.

"I have to say I've always been a great admirer of the Amanni," said Bez. "Decisive leadership. Great fashion sense. Strength through unity and all that. And I've always felt the city leaders of Ludens have been far too complacent of late. I've put some fairly scathing posts about them on my wall, trolled a few of the more hypocritical ones too, you know?"

She didn't know and didn't understand his babbling nonsense. She considered getting out her instruction cards. She had one entitled *How to Deal with Fools and Simpletons* somewhere. "You had some sort of request to make," she reminded him.

"Less of a request than an offer. A chance of immortality.

An opportunity to be front and centre in the annals of history. Picture it, if you will: the rebirth of the Amanni horde – horde has a good ring to it, don't you think? – marching under the standard of the great General— What's his name again?"

"*Her* name. Handzame."

"I like it. The valiant but woefully outnumbered guards of the city falling back before your might and thunder. The sun gleaming off your chainmail. Divine providence writ large on your face. I can picture it so clearly. Magnificent."

Cope might have asked what divine providence would look like on someone's face but she was already caught up in another snag.

"There was no sun gleaming off my chainmail."

"Yes, *now*. I like the plate armour. It's traditional but it's a concealer, not a revealer. Artistry is all about emotion expressed through the human form. The muscles, the sweaty sheen, the powerful and philosophical symbolism expressed by some tastefully exposed flesh. I've done a lot of work recently with Chainmail Bikini Woman. She is very popular and—"

"The sun didn't gleam at all," said Cope. "We came at nightfall."

"I know!" said Bez, as though it was the most tragic occurrence. "And we'll need to fix it in the final painting. Absolutely. Though for your information, for future reference, don't attack at night. Night attacks, no good. No one can see you. As my old fella used to say, if there's a battle in the dead of night and no one sees it, did it really happen? Now, I'm going to suggest we paint you as a heroine out of myth. Tasteful, as I say. A scrap of chainmail here, a wisp of gauze passing by on the wind here."

As he raised his hands to indicate exactly where and what chainmail scraps and wisps of gauze might be covering, Cope deliver a sharp uppercut to his jaw which knocked him clean out and sent a chunk of broken tooth pinwheeling into the air.

Instinctively, Cope caught the tooth as it fell. The idiot she let bounce off a chair and drop insensible to the floor, next to the drunk asleep under the stairs.

She needed to get Abington back to the general and she needed to speak to Merken urgently. Enough time had been wasted.

She strode over to the drinking table, put the tooth in front of Pagnell (in the hope it would pacify him and his grimlock confederates) and gave Abington her sternest glare.

"Well, I didn't mean it literally," said Pagnell, picking the tooth up.

"We're going now," said Cope.

Ignoring her instruction entirely, Abington gave a bark of discovery and pulled out a bundle of matchwood from his robes.

"At a guess – and it is a guess," said Pagnell, "I'd say this is the tooth of an idiot."

Abington ran one of the matchsticks along the tabletop, magicking a small flame at its end. "Toss a stone in this place," he said and put the flame to his pipe, "and you'd hit a dozen brainless idiots."

Cope reacted to the explosion before she even consciously registered it. The flash momentarily blinded her, the bang temporarily deafened her, and she turned away automatically. She found herself blinking away the wheels of colour in her eyes, once more facing Abington, sword already in her hand. Abington was sat exactly as before, apart from his arms which hung loosely at his sides and his head which was ... well, it was gone.

It took a second or two for her hearing to return, or maybe it took the tavern patrons a second or two to find their voices; either way, there was a moment of utter silence and then all manner of screaming, hollering and shouting.

The wizard Pagnell pushed himself back from the table, eyes wide, his face spattered with gore, sooty streaks, and a couple of minor cuts, possibly caused by flying shards of clay pipe. As he made to get up, Cope grabbed him.

"You're going nowhere!"

"What?" he said, shocked and bewildered.

Men fought to escape through the door. Others hid under their tables or behind the bar. Some, with more pragmatic and short-sighted goals, used the opportunity to drink beers which weren't theirs.

Cope had lost sight of Lorrika and wondered if the thief girl was among the press of bodies at the door. And then she saw her, on hands and knees, crawling back and forth, feverishly picking among the grue on the floor.

"What are you doing?" Cope called to Lorrika.

"Picking up bits of wizard," said Merken, suddenly at her shoulder.

Cope didn't question where the old man had come from.

"Who's this chap?" he asked, nodding at Pagnell.

"I don't know his part in this," said Cope. "He's a dentist."

"Just a dentist!" agreed the blood-soaked Pagnell, pulling ineffectually against Cope's grip.

"Is he now?" said Merken. "What happened to Abington?"

Cope shook her head, stumped. "I think he might have done something really bad in a past life," she suggested.

7

Cope was a follower, not a leader; she served, not commanded. She was content with this, but it did not mean she was blind to the theories of warfare, the need for strategy. A great military leader always had a strategy and, if that strategy failed, another to take its place. When, in the heat of battle, things went completely wrong, as they so often did, a great military leader improvised and made best use of the materials to hand.

It was for this reason that, as they waited in the temple's great audience chamber for General Handzame to officially send them on their mission into the trap-filled tomb below, Cope did not question some last minute changes. The major one was the addition of the tooth-mage Newport Pagnell and the artist Bez to their team. Pagnell was an understandable addition: a replacement for Abington. Entering the room whilst studying a scroll, he looked the very epitome of a scholarly wizard (apart from the drying blood and stuff on his face, and manacles around his wrists). The artist's presence was less explicable. Cope could not imagine he would be of much use, except as a pack animal for the bundles of wizardy books he was currently being saddled with.

General Handzame stood at a long stone table before the audience chamber balcony. Framed in the open night sky, lit by the copper glow of the open braziers in the room, Handzame should have looked like a dark conqueror, mighty and inscrutable. She'd even adopted a pose (one foot slightly forward, one hand on hip, the other held out to seize the future) which Cope was sure she'd seen on an imperial statue in Sathea. But Handzame didn't look like a Sathean emperor or a dark conqueror. Instead – Cope noted without judgement – she looked like a very ordinary woman who had, much to her own surprise, found herself to be dressed up like an Amanni warlord and in possession of a small but not insignificant city state.

"Are we all here, Merken?" Handzame demanded.

"We are, ma'am," said Merken, tying and patting a leather strap on Bez's pack.

Handzame nodded, adjusted her power stance, put a hand down to lean on the table, missed, looked down to see where the table was, put her hand on it properly, and spoke.

"It is written that over a thousand year ago," she declared portentously, "Hierophant Foesen, the high priest of Buqit, was visited by the goddess in person. She came down from the abode of the gods in the form the giant eagle Tudu and spoke with him. Her words to him formed much of the *List of Things to Be Done* which her followers attempt to complete to this day. At Buqit's command, Foesen led the faithful deeper into the plains and founded this city and this temple, to separate Buqit from the pantheon of the gods and to raise her above them. To assist Foesen in his great work, Buqit left him one of the great treasures of this world: the Quill of Truth."

"A magic feather," said Bez.

"Correct."

Pagnell laughed bitterly. "I'm sure a ton of gold and an army to command would have been just as handy."

"If you have a quill pen which writes any truth you want to know," said Lorrika, "you could just find all the buried treasure in the world, or find the words to turn any army to your cause. Least, that's what Abington said."

"Hardly the Amanni way," said Pagnell. "Is this an invasion or a burglary?"

"It can be both, boy," growled Merken.

Pagnell nodded. "It's just that the good people of Ludens are cowering in their homes waiting for you to come round and pluck out their hearts and scoop out their brains."

"This particular invasion isn't about hearts and minds," said Handzame.

"They'd probably be relieved if you just told them. Cut down on a lot of anxiety."

"I think we're happier having them cowering in their homes, Sparkles," said Merken. "Keeps them out of the way."

General Handzame held a small book in her hand. It was old, cracked, and liberally spotted with brown splodges which could conceivably have been gravy but were much more likely not. "My great and noble ancestor, Handzame of the Tall Crags – who was undeservedly given the epithet Handzame the Unlucky – had the honour of descending further into Foesen's tomb than any outsider. His diary chronicles every painful and bloody footstep, every victory and even his ultimate failure. Tonight, we will finish his great work and take the Quill of Truth for ourselves!"

"Indeed, *we* shall," said Merken. "Perhaps if we might proceed downstairs now, ma'am. Time is against us."

"Absolutely. Come!"

Handzame swept out of the room – in the manner of one who had practised sweeping at length but still hadn't quite got the knack – with her honour guard and the band of tomb-raiders behind her.

Cope found herself following the artist and the wizard down the stairs.

Pagnell made a thoughtful, digesting noise. "Thing is," he whispered to Bez, "if that's the diary of Handzame the Unlucky, and he was writing in it while at the deepest level any human had got to in the tomb, how the heck did it make its way back to the surface?"

Bez gave him a disbelieving glare. "Seriously? *That's* the most burning question on your mind? Not, *Will we ever again see the light of day?*"

"I'm sure we'll all make it through the tomb," said Pagnell. "A decent proportion of us, anyway."

"With you as our guide? Forgive me if I don't find that comforting."

Pagnell patted him on the shoulder. "I was selected for

this mission, Bez. My skills have been recognised. I'm the best wizard in town."

"You're the only wizard in town," said Cope.

"And therefore the best," said Pagnell confidently. "Come now, best foot forward."

8

Ten yards after passing the riddle door and the first threshold, the tunnel floor vanished beneath their feet.

One moment there was solid stone beneath Cope's boots, the next a sensation of the floor swinging away and a gaping nothing. In the half second before the lamps went out, Cope's flailing mind caught sight of sheer stone walls, then she hit water, feet first and plunged under the surface into cold and dark.

There were plenty of people in the world who thought overcoming the dangers of deep water by learning to swim was as mad as overcoming the dangers of lightning strikes by standing on hilltops during thunderstorms. Cope was not only a strong woman but had been fortunate enough to be raised by people who thought swimming was a valuable skill rather than a challenge to the gods to do their best to drown you. Cope Threemen could swim.

She was also an experienced warrior who could march, run and climb in plate as easily as she could without. To the inexperienced individual, plate armour was blinding, wearying and made one clumsy and slow. Not Cope. Metal plate armour was a second skin to her and Cope Threemen knew everything there was to know about swimming in plate armour. And what she knew was this:

You can't do it. You'd be an idiot to try.

She sank but she did not panic. She unbuckled her chest and back plate – left side: torso and shoulder; right side: torso and shoulder – and pushed them out and away. As her lungs started to ache, she pushed off her gauntlets and unbuckled her vambrances. Cope was now underwater wearing half-plate and a chainmail vest. Cope Threemen knew everything there was to know about swimming in half-plate and chain. And what she knew was this:

You still can't do it. You'd still be an idiot to try.

She tore the ties off her chainmail and dragged it over her head. She was still too heavy. Her lungs burned. A malicious imp in her brain told her to breathe, even though she obviously could not. Water filled her nose and the back of her throat, flooding it with the taste of rust and decay. She floundered in the dark. She found herself becoming, not afraid, but angry. The prospect of dying should, she felt, always make one angry. It was one of the few times anger was useful. However, she was mostly angry because she would no longer be able to complete the spiritual quest High Shepherdess Gwell had given her. Cope liked order and completeness; life was not a thing to be left half done.

Her foot grazed against something. She put her foot

down again. It touched upon a sloping surface: slippery, oddly knobby and unstable like a mound of rocks, but a sloping surface nonetheless. Climbing, stumbling, slipping and climbing with her feet and swimming with ever more desperate arm strokes, she ascended, inch by inch. Her arms screamed. Her heart twisted in her chest. She had to grit her teeth to stop herself taking involuntary breaths of water. The surface she was climbing became narrower and less solid the higher she climbed, but climb it she did.

When she felt her hand break the surface, she leapt. She came up, caught half a breath of air and sank again. She powered up the strange surface, almost demolishing it and broke the surface a second time.

"Oh, gods! Monster!" yelled a voice.

Cope lunged at the wall. Between balancing precariously on the material beneath her and plastering her body against the wet stone, managed to stay above the surface. She coughed, spat and heaved a rib-rattling intake of breath.

"Don't eat me, I'm too young to die!" yelled the voice again. It was Bez. The artist.

"Cope?" said another voice in the darkness. Merken.

"I'm here," she coughed.

"We thought you drowned," said Lorrika, splashing around.

"Don't be hasty. Plenty of time yet for us all to drown," said Pagnell from a short distance away.

The sounds of doggy paddles and related splashings echoed off close walls. Even with no light, Cope could picture the dimensions of the pit.

"How far did we fall?" she wondered.

"Far enough," said Pagnell.

"Smooth walls," said Lorrika. "Too wet and flat to climb."

"How far down does it go, Cope?" asked Merken, his breathing and paddling laboured.

"I don't know, sir," she said. "I'm standing on something. Not sure what..."

She felt at the slope beneath her feet. It was a mound of loose items, many of them jagged and stick-like, several smooth and round, as large a person's head—

"I think I'm standing on a pile of bones."

"People bones?" said Lorrika.

"I think so."

"How did they get here?" said Bez, a tremble of fear or cold in his voice.

"Think it through," said Pagnell. "We can wait."

After a moment, Bez wailed bitterly. "I don't want to die and become bones!"

"An admirable, if unrealistic goal," commented Pagnell.

"So," said Merken firmly as he swam about, "our situation is damnably clear. We need to think of a way out of here."

"We need to see to get out, sir," said Cope.

"Yes. Pipsqueak: can you light the lamp?"

"Everything's wet," Lorrika pointed out.

"I can make light," said Pagnell. "But you'll need to take off these manacles."

There was a pause. Somewhere in the darkness, Merken was likely pulling a range of expressions and mentally weighing up the pros and cons of freeing the wizard to cast his magic spells.

"What if he just magics himself out of here?" said Cope.

"Cope," said Pagnell reproachfully, "I assure you if I could do such a thing, I would. Sadly, I can't."

There was the click of a key in a lock.

"However, I can now do this."

There was light. A small cup of light. In its cold glow, Pagnell's wet and bedraggled face was visible.

"Excellent," said Merken. The light immediately flickered and almost vanished. "What happened there?" The light flashed on and off as he spoke.

"*Pagnell's Oral Illuminator*," said the wizard. "One of five original spells officially attributed to me. Ideal for inspecting teeth in poor lighting." He splashed. "Lorrika."

There was a second light.

"Hey, look," said Lorrika, her own light twinkling.

"Unfortunately, the nature of the spell is such that it has to be cast orally."

"What?" said Bez.

"Like this." There was a third light.

"Ngy 'outh is a yight," said Lorrika, wide-mouthed, sounding quite pleased with this turn of events.

Pagnell paddled over to Cope. She shuddered as the tooth mage's fingers touched the edge of her jaw but, spread-eagled against the wall to maintain her position, there was little she could do. She felt a faint buzzing and a bluish light shone from her open mouth.

"I must say you have a fine set of gnashers there, Miss Threemen," said Pagnell.

"Weren't you supposed to know about the damned pitfalls of this place before we blundered into them?" muttered Merken.

"Yes," agreed Pagnell, ruefully. "This is the Surprising Pit, I imagine."

"You think?"

"The notes are very clear that it would be located immediately after one of the five major doors of the tomb, and it would come as a surprise to the unwary."

"Which it did."

"Yet, logically, it shouldn't. You see, if we didn't encounter it after any of the first four doors then we'd know it was after the fifth. Of course then, it wouldn't come as a surprise, would it?"

"You are babbling like an idiot, wizard," said Bez.

"Not at all. Armed with that knowledge, if we didn't find it after the first three doors then we'd know it was behind the fourth because it couldn't be behind the fifth. And yet it would once again, not be a surprise. So, it couldn't be behind the fourth. Reason dictates the same would apply to the third and the second and indeed the first gate. Abington was convinced that, logically, this pit didn't exist."

"We're in the pit," said Cope, reasonably.

"Yes," said Pagnell. "And I'm jolly surprised, I'll have you know."

Lorrika had made a circuit of the pit. It was square, fifteen feet to a side and at least twice as deep. "Too smooth. I can't climb it."

"Some thief you are," said Cope.

"I'm an urban climber, not a thief."

"I am put in mind," said Merken, "of an ancient story about a donkey which fell into a well."

"Is this relevant?" asked Bez.

"Does the donkey get out at the end of the story?" said Pagnell.

"It does," said Merken.

"Then proceed."

Merken paddled as he collected his thoughts. "I recall the farmer had no means of rescuing his donkey but the donkey was alive at the bottom of the well and braying for all it was worth."

"We should shout for help?" said Lorrika.

"Help from whom?" asked Pagnell.

Merken ignored them. "The farmer decided it would be far kinder to kill the donkey than let it starve to death—"

"You said the donkey got out," said Pagnell.

"—*And so* he began to fill in the well with dirt, shovel by shovel."

"Burying it alive?" said Bez.

"Practical," said Cope, stretching out her fingers to each side, trying to improve her hold on the hold-free wall, feeling the water run out of her sleeves.

"The soil landed on the donkey but it shook it off and, as the farmer filled the well in further, the donkey stood on the mounting pile of soil. The farmer filled, the donkey climbed. Eventually the donkey was at the lip of the well and able to get out."

"Do you knew this farmer?" asked Cope.

"No, Cope. It's ... it's a fable, a story with a moral."

"Not true?"

"Not factually true but philosophically..."

There was a moment of quiet, contemplative splashing.

"I think I speak for us all," said Pagnell, "when I say, what kind of bloody moral is a story like that going to have? When your friend and master tries to kill you it sometimes works out for the best? It's okay to die of thirst because you've filled in your well as long as you get your donkey back?"

"I think it says something deep and true about perseverance," said Merken, hurt. "The donkey turned the situation around and didn't give up."

"I mean, it would take a day or more to fill in the well. That's two days of your farmer trying to murder a donkey."

"It's not a real story," said Cope, irritated the wizard hadn't been listening. "It's not a real donkey. It's not a real donkey, is it?"

"No. It's a metaphor," said Merken.

"Someone once told me a story about a mouse which fell in some milk," murmured Lorrika.

"It's still a donkey-murdering metaphor," said Pagnell.

"It's damned ancient wisdom," sniffed Merken.

"Which means it's not just useless but old and useless!"

"None of this is helping us get out," Bez pointed out.

Without shifting her weight, Cope felt the skull she was standing on move away a little and she dropped an inch or two into the water.

"I think the mouse swam round and round and its tail did something to the milk," said Lorrika.

"Contaminate it?" suggested Merken.

"*Hamed's Hammer of Loosening*," said Pagnell.

"The what now?"

"I could put some cracks or holes in the wall." The wizard paddled about to face Lorrika. "Could you climb it then?"

Lorrika considered the wall with new appreciation.

"You're not going to bring the whole thing down on us, are you?" said Merken.

"Oh, I doubt that very much," said Pagnell cheerfully.

"I'm remembering that thing with the tower in Aumeria."

"I'm fairly sure that won't happen here. Fairly sure."

Before anyone could raise further objections, Pagnell had raised his hands, uttered some nonsense words, and the world shook. The wall pounded and wobbled against Cope's body. In the light leaking through her gritted teeth, she saw the water shaken into choppy waves. The pile of long dead pit victims trembled and collapsed beneath her feet. She dropped below the surface.

She had a split second to prepare before going under. Time enough for a gasped breath and a mental resolve to kick and swim for her life. Cope kicked and scrabbled and, as the tremor around her calmed, her fingers found a handhold which had not been there earlier: a narrow fissure in the wall. Large enough to take four fingertips and allow her to pull herself above the surface. She coughed and spat to clear the water from her throat.

The lights of four mouths picked out the scene in flashes. The water level had dropped; the green-brown tidemark on the wall was a foot above the surface. Chunks of smooth stone had come loose here and there. Down one wall, a great crack had formed: a handspan wide. Lorrika was already testing it out, preparing to climb. In the centre of the pool, Merken was doing an ungainly backstroke and supporting Pagnell. The wizard's eyes were half closed. There was a bloody red mark on his forehead.

"Pass me a rope," said Lorrika, eager to go.

"What happened to the wizard?" asked Bez.

"Something fell and hit Sparkles here. A stone or something."

Pagnell moaned wordlessly in agreement.

"Ha!" said Cope, understanding. "He is the donkey! He is the metaphor! You should have ducked, wizard."

Pagnell moaned again, his meaning uncertain.

9

Lorrika managed to scrounge together enough dry material to make a small fire in the corridor. Once the magic lights in their mouths had faded (much to Cope's relief), the fire was their only light and heat for five recently dunked people to dry themselves by. As smoke pooled on the high ceiling, Lorrika focused on getting one of the lamps lit. Cope bandaged Pagnell's head with a strip of cloth which had the one saving grace of being merely wet and not drenched. The wizard was not making the task easier by bobbing back and forth as he laid out Abington's research notes to dry on the floor.

"You obviously did something very bad in your last life," Cope said.

"What?" muttered Pagnell.

"That's what the priest told me."

He stared at her blankly for a moment. "We're lucky the pit was filled with water: there are supposed to be some terminally surprising stakes at the bottom. It must have flooded from somewhere. The Yokigiz River isn't far away. Maybe the water found a way through."

"We encountered a hunting party of grimlocks as we came up the Yokigiz," said Cope.

"Can't imagine they caused you much trouble."

"Have you ever fought grimlocks?" she asked.

"I've met them," said the wizard. "They're stupid."

"That they are." Cope tied off the bandage and sat back to look at her handiwork. Pagnell was wearing a curious expression. "What?" she said.

"Without your black armour, you don't look much like an Amanni. And I know the famous Rantallion Merken is not an Amanni." He straightened a squidgy sheet of parchment on the floor. "I suppose most people just see that distinctive plate and think, 'Aaagh, the Amanni are coming!' That could be an advantage to a band of invaders who want to create the right impression."

"General Handzame is Amanni," said Cope.

"The only one you've got?"

Cope glared at him suspiciously and wondered if this wizard knew more than he was letting on. Not that it mattered now; there was no one he could tell.

Pagnell continued to lay out his sheets. Cope saw him come up against another carpet of papers spread around the other side of the fire. Pagnell slapped down an intricately labelled map. Bez slapped down a sodden sketch in front of it.

"You're in my way," said Pagnell.

"I need to dry these out by the fire," said Bez.

Pagnell looked at the sketch. "What is that?"

"It's a jaffled cake."

"You drew a picture of … food?"

"My muse was hungry. It was my lunch yesterday. I bought it from the vendor on the corner of Cisterngate with the stuffed wyvern head over the door."

"Why?"

"I think it's an advertising gimmick. You know: the shop with the wyvern head over—"

"I meant why draw it? I've seen cakes better jaffled than that."

Bez shrugged. "I just do sometimes. That way I can show it to people. I sometimes pop it on the wall and see if people like it."

"The w—? You think people would be interested in seeing pictures of what you had for lunch?"

"It gets a lot of likes."

Pagnell started to shake his head before stopping abruptly. He picked up the corner of a damp book and traced his finger over the drawing of a child on the open page. "You drew this?"

"Uh. Yeah."

"It's very good."

Cope could detect something in Pagnell's voice. She thought it might have been a thing called *subtext,* but she was never really sure what that was. Subtext, the late Master Jarden Orre had explained to her at length, was the things people said without actually saying them. As far as Cope could fathom, it was some sort of ventriloquism, hiding words within words but no matter how hard she listened she could never make out those hidden words. She suspected her hearing simply wasn't good enough.

She picked herself up, stepped over the warring squares of wet paper and around the fire to where Merken sat against a wall. He had removed his boots and socks, wrung out the socks and hung them over the tops of his boots to dry. His feet were calloused, cracked and bony. Cope approved. That's how old soldiers' feet should look. Those were feet which had seen the world – well, trodden on it.

Merken was fiddling with the wet drawstrings on the velvet pouch at his belt. "Damn thing," he said, struggling. "Would you mind, Cope?"

"Mind?"

He spread his hands to indicate the pouch. "My fingers aren't what they once were."

She picked at the damp knot with her fingernails until it came loose. "There you go, sir."

Merken hurriedly pulled it open and removed a small polished chestnut box. Opening it, he poked at the contents and gave a heavy sigh of relief.

"All okay, is it?" asked Cope.

Merken turned it round to show her. In a cushioned interior which had somehow stayed dry sat a complex contrivance of metal: as round as a biscuit and not much thicker. Its heart was a collection of levers, wheels and various spinning things sitting on a tightly wound coil of brass which gave the item much of its shape and bulk.

"Should it look like that?" she asked.

"It's Hary Greginax's constant force timepiece. It keeps perfect time by means of the enclosing going barrel and Greginax's eccentric cam. It also features his prototype for the adjustable carillon alarm. It's quite melodic."

"Ah," said Cope, none the wiser.

"It's a clock."

"Oh. It's very small."

Merken withdrew the box and carefully closed its lid. "Greginax envisaged a time when every gentleman would have a personal clock in his pocket."

"Do pockets need clocks?" asked Cope.

Merken smiled sadly. "Greginax of Carius was a dreamer. And a damned visionary. Handzame gave this to me as my payment."

"Is it valuable?"

"Priceless," he said, wiggling it back into its damp bag. "I suppose you got paid in good old-fashioned gold."

Cope shook her head. "I offered my services for free," she said. "On condition Handzame would use the Quill of Truth to answer a question for me."

Merken checked his socks, clearly found them lacking, but began to pull them on anyway. "What question is that?"

"It was given to me by High Shepherdess Gwell, and I must answer it if I am to complete my own personal quest in life. Now, it sounds simple, but you have to think about it. I think it's got a deeper, hidden meaning; like your donkey metaphor thing."

"Yes?"

"The question she asked me was this: 'Do b—"

"Hey!" called out Lorrika as her lamp sparked into flame. "Done it!"

"Good," said Merken. "Five minutes and then we're off again."

"I'm going to need longer to dry these out," said Pagnell, indicating his notes.

Merken's expression was grim. "So far, those bits of paper have been of little use to us. And neither have you. Five minutes."

10

The smoothly carved tunnel forked ahead. The left fork was wider than the right, but there was nothing else to pick between them.

"Well?" said Merken.

Cope held a lamp high so Pagnell could consult a still-damp book of notes. It was entirely illegible to her, and not only because some of the ink was running.

"This," said Pagnell slowly, still reading, "is *The Impenetrable Labyrinth.*"

"Good," said Merken. "And what does Abington advise?"

Pagnell tried to peel apart two sheets of paper. They ripped, refusing to part. He pulled a face before realising Cope was watching, and stopped.

"We penetrate it," he said boldly. With only a glimmer of hesitation he led the way down the right path. "Step where I step. Touch nothing unless I say it's okay to do so." As he walked, he flipped over the wet mass of pages to the next bit of accessible text. “Abington clearly did his research into mazes and labyrinths of antiquity.”

“I think that’s why he had me pack these,” said Lorrika. She was holding a ball of wool yarn a foot in diameter in one hand and a fat nub of chalk in the other.

“Excellent,” said Pagnell. “Lorrika, you’re on chalking duty. An arrow at every junction. Bez?”

“Yes?” said the artist.

“Yarn.”

“If I must.”

“Um. Can I touch the walls to put chalk on it?” asked Lorrika.

“I think you will have to...”

“But you said we should touch nothing.”

“Yes, true. Let’s play it safe and put the marks on the floor.”

“Is the floor safer?”

“Probably not.”

Pagnell continued forward. The tunnel branched every dozen yards or so. T-junctions, crossroads. Steps: up and down. At every turn there was the *skrit-skrit* of Lorrika drawing her arrows. There didn’t seem to be much actual method to Pagnell’s method. If these northern wizards didn’t have a reputation for judiciousness and wisdom, Cope would have suspected he was picking each path on a whim. A suspicion which reached a head when they came to their first dead end.

“It’s a dead end,” Bez pointed out.

“I thought you knew where you were going, Sparkles,” said Merken.

"I do," said Pagnell, flipping back through the book. "This is all ... part of the process."

"Process?"

"This is a learning experience and all experiences, equally valid and worthwhile as they are, teach us something."

"Which side of your head did the rock hit you?" asked Merken.

"This one. Why do you— Ow!" He flinched as Merken cuffed him on the other side of the head. "What was that for?"

"To teach you something." Merken turned on the spot. "We've been down here for hours and we've not made enough damned progress."

"Hitting the wizard won't help," said Lorrika.

The grizzled veteran sneered childishly. "Makes me feel better. I am wet, I am tired and I am hungry and, while these are ills I can easily bear, I don't intend to bear them at your leisure, lad. Got it?"

"We've got food," said Bez. He was munching on a whole stick of bread; his fingers sank into its damp crust and a trickle of water constantly ran from the tip.

"That's been in the watery pit of dead things," said Lorrika.

"It has a challenging authenticity about it," agreed Bez. "But it's soft. Got a certain, earthy oatiness, not unlike Rassuman's Pale Ale."

"Remind me never to order a pint of that," murmured Pagnell.

Merken shook his head. "We've had enough of your

learning process for one night. Find us the way through, Sparkles, or you will become a permanent resident of this tomb."

THERE WAS no time in the darkness of the labyrinth, only that measured by the burning of lamp oil. They walked, drying still, the tooth-mage muttering to himself, taking one turn and then another; Lorrika scoring and re-scoring arrows; Bez unwinding and re-winding his considerable ball of yarn. There were traps: tripwires and concealed spikes; pools of liquid which Pagnell declared to be flesh-burning acids; wobbly flagstones and spring-powered spears; and more than a couple of iron jaw traps set into the walls. Anyone who tried to solve the maze by putting their hand to the wall and following it would soon find themselves without a hand.

As best as Cope could gauge, it was morning when Merken called them to halt for a brief rest. Up above, the city folk of Ludens would be waking up to their first morning under Amanni rule.

Lorrika extinguished one lamp to refill its oil reservoir.

"Gods, that stuff stinks like a fishmonger's hanky," said Bez.

"It would: it's made from fish oil," said Lorrika. "It's also highly flammable: spill it near a flame and you can probably say goodbye to more than your eyebrows."

"Sounds dangerous," said Bez. "What's wrong with a good old torch?"

"Three days we might be down here. How many torches would you need? And how much would they all weigh?"

It was a good question, thought Cope. A torch, wrapped in cloth and dipped in pitch, lasted perhaps a little over half an hour. And how much did it weigh? And how many hours in three days? There were twenty-four hours in a day—

"The great wyrm, Nilfandir, lives entirely below the earth," Pagnell was saying as he consulted one of the drier books, "eating her way through hills and mountains, consuming rocks and precious metals and whatever she encounters. And as she passes, her scales ooze this ... this *ooze* which dries on the walls and floor of her tunnel and hardens to a smooth cement; shiny and hard as marble. Where she crosses her own path, she makes junctions. A man following the maze of her trails can be lost for days in a network of perfect tunnels."

"Are you saying that's what this maze is? Niffle-thingy's worm casts?" asked Bez, a question Cope would have asked if her conscious mind wasn't taken up with mathematics. Three days of twenty-four hours was seventy-two hours and at two torches, roughly, per hour, that was—

"No, not at all," said Pagnell. "This is the work of men; the invention of one man. I'm just saying it would be a neat way of constructing a labyrinth."

"We're lost. That is what he is saying," said a tired Merken.

Lorrika relit her lamp and put the flask of oil back in the pack.

"Not lost," Pagnell insisted. "Exploring."

"Well, this explorer's socks are still damp and he's not happy."

Lorrika raised the lamp and, her attention caught by something, walked a little way down the tunnel.

"Don't wander off, Pipsqueak," said Merken.

"Sure," she said and ran her hands experimentally over a wall.

"And don't touch anything!" urged Pagnell.

Lorrika tutted.

Cope, working through her torch-based calculations, wondered if she should double her figures to make two torches per party (which was sensible) or reduce the total to take into account sleep periods (which was practical). So, double the number of torches but knock off a third for sleep times. And how heavy were the torches? About half a pound each? Call it ten ounces—

"Why would anyone want to follow Niffle-thing's trail?" asked Bez.

"What?" said Pagnell.

"You said a man following her trail could get lost for days. Why?"

"Dragon dung."

"Pardon me for asking. Anyway, if I wanted to solve a maze, I'd use an army – the general's army. Come to a junction: send half one way, send half the other. Next junction, do the same. Someone would find the exit."

"Armies have died down here," said Pagnell flatly.

"Really? You'd expect there to be more bodies lying around. Skeletons; whatever."

Pagnell frowned. "Good point. Anyway, it's not about brute numbers. This maze is a trick, designed to trap the unwary for years, but to let the wise man through in a matter of minutes."

"Minutes?" grumped Merken.

"I'm not Kavda the Builder and I didn't write these notes!" snapped Pagnell. "There's a trick to this place and I've yet to see it."

"You'd better see it bloody quick, Sparkles."

"This is a door," called Lorrika.

Everyone turned to look. She was pointing at a seemingly ordinary stretch of wall. "It's a door," she repeated.

"She's gone mad," Bez whispered aside to Pagnell.

Lorrika already had her lock picks in her hand. "I can have it open in a jiffy."

"Wait!" cried Cope.

"What?" said Merken.

"Just wait!" Cope closed her eyes, muttered a final calculation and then opened them again. "A hundredweight, three cloves and one ounce!" she declared proudly.

"What?" said a baffled Merken.

"We'd need to bring six men with us just to carry the torches."

Pagnell nodded, smiling. "Thanks, Cope. Um, good work. Let's take a look at that door."

After a short inspection, the tooth-mage declared the door to be free from traps – "Definitely probably safe" – and Lorrika inserted her picks into an innocuous gap in the mortar. She wiggled and twisted until she felt the catch; a section of wall less than half an inch thick swung out.

Pagnell's hope this would be their exit from the labyrinth

was short-lived indeed. Beyond was a small room, little more than an alcove with no further doors.

"Oh, well done," said Merken icily. "Pipsqueak and Sparkles have found us a broom cupboard. Let's give them a round of applause."

"I don't see any brooms," said Cope.

The door itself was a simple metal panel, the camouflaging layer of stonework cemented to its front. An ancient parchment calendar on a loop of equally ancient string hung from the back of the door. Inside, there was a stool and a little writing shelf only big enough to hold a short stack of papers held down by a tarnished metal plate and cup. Pagnell picked up the metal cup and traced his fingers over the engraving which ran around the rim.

"What does it say?" asked Lorrika.

"'*A Vestaltide Gift from Sathea*,'" he said. "*A holiday souvenir*."

"Souvenir?" said Cope.

"You know," said Pagnell, placing the cup down again, almost reverentially, "a memento. I bet the Hierophant does it. Pops over to Qir for a spot of light pilgrimage and comes back with a box of candied apples and a piece of decorative pokerwork that says *Greetings from Qir*. Don't the Amanni go in for that kind of thing?"

"The Amanni demagogue Nirage collected the heads of the kings and chieftains he conquered, yeah?" piped up Bez.

"It's nice to have a hobby," said Lorrika.

Pagnell carefully removed the papers from under the plate. "Collecting hobbies can get out of hand though. You start off with one or two heads then, before you know it, you're proclaiming a republic which will last a thousand years."

"I had an aunt who went the same way," said Bez.

"Founded a republic of crazed fanatics?" said Cope.

Bez shook his head. "Her collection of pottery chickens. Took over the house. My uncle moved out to the shed just for a spot of peace and quiet."

"A spot of peace and quiet..." mused Pagnell, shuffling carefully through the dried and crumbling papers.

"While this is all fascinating—" Merken interrupted.

"He sat here," said Pagnell, parking himself on the stool. He scratched at a dark mark on the plate. "This was probably the remains of a cheese sandwich, or something. Never got the chance to finish it. Too busy editing his plans or designing some new, subtle embellishment."

"Who?"

Pagnell blinked. "Kavda."

"Kavda the Builder?"

The wizard nodded. "It's a big old tomb. A big labyrinth. He'd have been overseeing the construction, but would probably need somewhere quiet to do his work without having to traipse back up to the surface." He waved the parchments and a flaky corner broke off one and drifted away like an autumn leaf. "These are his notes."

"And would there be a handy map of this maze among them?" asked Merken.

"No. There's a full map of the lower levels, but not the labyrinth. Still: very encouraging. It might be reasonable to assume Kavda's cubbyhole here would be on or near the true path through the labyrinth."

"Perhaps."

"And look." He held up one sheet. There was a complex sketch of gutters and tiles in faded ink and, scribbled in the margin, a note: *Edging of acid splash pools allowing too much backwash. Remake and refit floors with these channels and run offs if we want to maintain foot-melting efficiency. Ensure all workers wear protective ceramic boots during the alterations.* "Here's a man interested in the finer details. Kavda would have been back and forth through the various levels of the tomb all the time, controlling every aspect of construction. That's a lot of legwork. Wasteful legwork."

"You think he put in some short cuts?" said Merken.

"Secret passages?" added Lorrika.

"Exactly," said Pagnell.

"Er, guys..." said Bez, his voice suddenly tight.

"You think you can find these secret passages?" Merken asked the wizard.

"Maybe," said Pagnell.

"Guys!" said Bez, louder.

"What?"

Bez held up his ball of twine. He'd been unravelling it for the mile or more they'd already walked, but was still the size of a grapefruit.

"I don't think we'll run out before we've found the way through," said Pagnell, entirely missing Bez's point. Cope had spotted it, too.

The trailing line of yarn was vibrating, twanging like a loose harp string. Cope stepped back fully into the corridor and held her lamp high. Down the long length and into darkness, the string was oscillating.

"Something's coming," she said.

The tension and frequency on the string rose. There was the soft slap-slap of wet feet against stone. Cope passed her lamp back to the wizard and drew her longsword. Lorrika took up a position to the side and slightly behind her. She held stubby knives in each hand.

Bez dropped his yarn ball, took out a pad, and started sketching.

"Is that going to help?" hissed Pagnell.

"If we die, no. If we live, you'll be glad I captured the moment. Keep the lamp steady."

The ball of yarn rolled on the floor as it was tugged. Two figures stepped into the edges of the lamp light.

Flabby yellow bellies, green webbed feet, poorly made strings of beads about their necks and equally poorly made but nonetheless lethally sharp shell-topped spears slung across their backs, they came.

Grimlocks!

The two creatures were thoroughly intent on the string they were gathering and only looked up as the light shone on their frog faces.

"*Yan tan*!" squealed one in surprise.

"*Tethera pethera*!" squeaked the other.

Pagnell pointed and shouted something. Cope swung. The two grimlocks flopped lifelessly to the floor. Cope's blade sailed harmlessly over the place where their heads had been.

Pagnell scuttled forward and held his lamp high to see if there were any more coming. Cope prodded a grimlock belly with the tip of her boot. It jiggled like jelly but the creature didn't stir.

"You killed them," said Merken.

"No," said Pagnell. "I put them to sleep."

"Put them to sleep?"

"Yes. *Pagnell's Pain-Free Insensibility*. I use it on my dental patients. It's better than having them screaming while attempting to extract a rotten molar," said Pagnell.

Cope grunted. The tooth-thieving mage's true nature was once again revealed.

Merken gave a bitter laugh. "Oh, what a wizard we have in you, Sparkles. We should have the great Abington leading us to our prize, blasting all our enemies with hellfire and lightning. But, no, we have a damned tooth-puller who sings vicious grimlocks to sleep with lullabies."

"If I may add," said Bez, waving his sketch about, "a drawing of *Pagnell sends the Savage Grimlocks to Beddy-Byes* isn't exactly newsworthy."

"If I may add something of my own," said Pagnell tartly, "these vicious and savage grimlocks weren't about to kill us. This one was gathering string and this one, we observe—" he crouched and picked up a pathetic mess of sticks and string. "—was knitting it. We weren't being stalked. We were being harvested."

He was right. The creature had turned several hundred yards of string into a mostly shapeless sheet of ugly knitting. Was it supposed to be a scarf, Cope wondered. No, too wide. A shawl perhaps? In truth, it would probably serve best as a fishing net.

"Now," said Pagnell. "Unless I have failed to identify knitting as one of the deadly martial arts..."

"Ah, Sparkles was being merciful," said Merken. "No wonder this damned world is going to ruin."

"Are there more of them?" asked Lorrika.

"Where there's one grimlock, there's hundreds," said Merken.

"You said you ran into some on the river," said Pagnell. "And water has clearly managed to seep in here from somewhere. And that could be why we've found this tomb to be remarkably ... tidy."

"Grimlocks famous for tidying up after themselves?" asked Lorrika.

"They're scavengers and thieves," Bez replied. "They'll take anything not nailed down – actually they'll take things that *are* nailed down, along with the nails – and use it or sell it."

"Like the journal of Handzame the Unlucky?" Pagnell murmured to himself.

"So there's a horde of the damned things down here," muttered Merken. "Planning on putting them all to sleep, Sparkles?"

"No." He poked a grimlock in the belly. It gurgled but did not wake.

"You shouldn't touch them," said Lorrika. "Abington said their slime was poisonous to eat, gives crazy visions and such."

"I wasn't planning on licking it," said Pagnell. "However, we could wake one of them and encourage him – her? Possibly it – to show us the way through the labyrinth. One of the side-effects of the spell is that upon waking the patient is a mite compliant."

"Oh, and you speak grimlock, do you?" sneered Merken.

"*Yan tan figger covada tan*," said Pagnell.

"Ah. *Pimper seth a yanerik tan*?" smiled Bez.

"*Bumfit*," replied Pagnell.

"Wonderful," sighed Merken,

Although to Cope the plan seemed a moderately decent one, she suspected when Merken had said "Wonderful" he actually meant something else.

After a spot of rummaging, Pagnell produced a sealed jar of pink crystals. He uncorked the jar and wafted it under what passed for a grimlock's nose.

The stinking creature sat up with a jolt and a wide-mouthed "*Gah*!" of disgust. Cope readied her sword to kebab it if necessary.

The grimlock's protruding yellow eyes rolled drunkenly. Pagnell gripped its slimy, stick-thin arm and muttered intently to it. The grimlock replied sluggishly.

"Yep," said Pagnell, standing up and dragging the creature with him. "Our friend, Clive, is going to lead us to the exit."

"Clive?" said Merken.

"An approximation of his actual name."

"*Bumfera*!" agreed the grimlock woozily and padded off.

Cope looked at the other grimlock which was snoring gently on the floor. "Are we leaving this one here?"

"No," said Merken and gestured for her to bring it.

Cope stared at the damp ugly thing, consider her options and then rolled it up in the pathetic and jumbled net of its knitting (belatedly realising its knitting needles were a pair of long bones whittled down for the purpose) and slung it over her shoulder. The grimlock stank like something dredged up from the bottom of a stagnant pond. Undoubtedly what it was.

Cope walked at the rear, unwilling to subject anyone to the wake of the dripping horribleness she carried on her back. Up ahead, the other grimlock, Clive, led the way through the tunnels: left turns, right turns, down steps, all the while jabbering away in its own incomprehensible language. Despite her travels, Cope was not a natural linguist. She had enough trouble grasping the subtleties of one language, never mind subjecting her poor mind to others.

While the tooth-mage conversed with Clive, Merken found a ready audience in Bez in a heartfelt discussion on the general lack of greatness in the world today.

"We live in a world of tiny, petty men," complained Merken. "Our leaders are faceless and forgettable. No sooner is someone raised up as an exemplar of virtue than they are revealed to be a mountebank, damned degenerate or cad."

"We are pampered fools compared to those genuine, authentic giants of old," agreed Bez.

"Where are the giants of today?" huffed the old soldier. "Gone! The wizard Abington was a great man and what do we have now? A damned dentist."

"I can hear you," called Pagnell.

"Good! What have you ever done of note, eh, Sparkles? Abington saved the city of Dalarra from plague. What was it, Pipsqueak?"

"Marsh fever," said Lorrika.

"There," said Merken. "A city on its knees. Death stalking the very streets. Pauper and noble alike struck down by a disease brought in by – Yarwish traders, wasn't it, Pipsqueak?"

"That's what they said."

"And if not for Abington's magic and wisdom, who knows what might have happened."

"Perhaps it might make a suitable subject for one of my paintings," suggested Bez. "The great Abington stood on the steps of the ... of the— What grand building do they have in Dalarra?"

"The Great Meethouse," said Merken.

"That's the one. The steps of the Great Meethouse with the sick and the dying, all artfully arranged in the streets, with arms raised in supplication. And Abington with a vial of the cure – what was it—?"

"Drapim," said Lorrika.

"A common weed," said Pagnell.

"—A vial of the magical elixir held aloft in Abington's hand. A ray of sunlight catches the glass and it gleams like a diamond, casting benevolent rays over the grateful populace."

"Was it like that?" Pagnell asked Lorrika. "The sun's benevolent rays and all that."

"Not quite," said the thief.

Grimlock Clive guide burbled something and led Pagnell down a turning.

"But of course, if we're talking of great men, we have one of the finest here," said Bez and slapped Merken on the shoulder.

"Don't touch me, bard," snapped the soldier.

"Let us muse on the glory of your victory over Abrelia," said Bez unabashed. "There's a story worth commemorating in oils, no?"

"All words," said Merken. "Nothing but words."

"You conquered the island with – what? – five words."

"Fifteen."

"Fifteen? Wow. That's ... astonishing. Fifteen words. Such bravery. Such cunning!"

Down a side tunnel, by what reflected lamp light there was, Cope saw a stone arch: two huge uprights and a lintel, very much like the first threshold they had passed through.

"Should we not be going that way?" she asked, but Pagnell and their little guide were trundling on. The wizard acted like he knew what he was doing. Maybe the archway was just an archway. She hurried to catch up with the others. The grimlock on Cope's back shuffled in its sleep and made a rude noise. Cope tried not to think about which end of the creature the noise might have come from.

"... island of Abrelia stands little more than twenty miles off the coast of Carius," Merken was saying. "Abrelia was a vassal state to Carius although it was a wholly amicable arrangement. Abrelia's harbour was large enough to hold almost the entire Carian fleet. Its high cliffs were a challenge to any invader, and when topped with fortified walls, entirely unassailable. When the Satheans planned their attack of Carius, they knew they had to take Abrelia first or be caught far from home at the mercy of the Carian navy."

Cope's feet splashed on the floor. The stone was wet, covered with a slow but constant trickle from ahead.

"And the Satheans hired you to help them?" Bez asked Merken.

"That they did," said the old soldier. "I presented them with a strategy and travelled to Abrelia to implement it. I greased a few palms and managed to acquire a number of accounts and letters from the treasury. One of them – oh, a dull piece of paper it was – detailed how Abrelia was paying Carius the equivalent of twenty gold for every man, woman and child every year. Twenty gold."

"That's a lot."

Merken laughed. "Yes. And if you paint that on the side of a wagon and have a man drive it around the island, soon everyone gets the idea they'll each be twenty gold a year richer if the Carians were given their marching orders."

The tunnel was widening, slick and uneven with mineral deposits. The ceiling rose away, beyond the light of their lamps. Cope's boot slipped on the floor and she trod carefully. This didn't look right.

"Within the month, the Carian satrap was expelled from Abrelia by the ruling council," Merken continued. "Carius' ships were told to leave and all future tribute cancelled. You see—" Merken paused to pontificate, "—twenty gold a year – even the thought of it – is enough to blind the average man to certain truths."

"What truths?" said Lorrika.

Further ahead, Pagnell called to his grimlock guide. "Uh, Clive. Where are you taking us?"

"*Yan a figgotik*!"

"Ah," said Bez.

"Ah?" said Lorrika.

"An error in translation, that's all," Pagnell assured them.

"What's the problem?" Merken demanded.

"We need to turn back," said Bez. "Now!"

Something glinted darkly in the heights.

"I asked Clive here to take us to the exit," said Pagnell, starting to back away. "Unfortunately, I didn't specify which one."

"Gods. We're not back at the beginning, are we?" said Merken.

"No. Not that."

There were other glints in the dark. Sharp edges. Bulging eyes. Cope dropped the grimlock she carried, it landed with an unhappy '*Umf!*', and she raised her sword. A hundred throats hissed in the darkness. Above them, in front of them, and behind them.

"Those grimlocks you met on the river," said Pagnell, whispering even though there was no longer much no point. "I think we've found their home."

11

RANTALLION MERKEN

Evening was falling on Ludens. It would be six bells soon enough, and the Amanni invasion could begin.

Rantallion Merken found himself reflecting, not on the imminent attack, but the grimlocks they had slaughtered yesterday. The stink of grimlock slime clinging to his cloak was a constant and unwanted reminder. Of course, grimlocks had been bigger in his youth. Much bigger. The raiding party they had blundered into at the Yokigiz River yesterday had been squat things, barely more than upright frogs with pointy sticks for weapons. The grimlocks Merken had fought in decades past had been twice the height, built of solid muscle and possessed of animal guile, with weapons which would disembowel the unwary in the blink of an eye. As always, the young had no idea how easy they had it these days.

Despite the grimlock stench, Merken wrapped the cloak

tighter about him. The long cloak was scratchy and unpleasant as well as smelly, but it was the only protection against the hot wind which blew in across the plain, sucking the moisture and very life from his lips. Merken hunkered down against a cart wheel and cursed the hard ground, the hot wind, his cloak, grimlocks and anything else which sprang to mind.

General Handzame and a dozen warriors sat along the weed-choked outer wall of the city. In their cloaks, they were indistinguishable, their leader invisible. A fitting metaphor. Handzame was nothing. This was Merken's battle, his stratagem, perhaps his final sally into the fray.

When the sun had gone, Merken stood, old knees clicking, tired back straining. He turned to the cart and gestured for the driver to pass him one of the clay pots. The rear of the cart was filled with such pots, each stoppered and sealed with wax; each protected from its neighbours by packing straw. Merken hefted the pot, surprised as always by how light the contents felt. Then again, he wasn't sure how heavy they were supposed to be.

Still, they were going to be even more of a surprise to the Ludens city guards.

Merken liked the look of surprise on people's faces. It was the physical embodiment of the fact he was cleverer than them. He liked his intelligence to be acknowledged.

Would the Ludensians be as surprised as the Abrelians were when he had handed their island home to the Satheans? They were surprised to discover declaring their independence from Carius did not bring instant wealth and fortune. The stupid islanders had neglected to consider

Carius had provided Abrelia with all of its military defences; that Carius had for years given Abrelia preferential trade deals; that Carius had made use of Abrelian store houses and mercantile services when they could have easily used those elsewhere. When the Sathean navy sailed into the harbour, come winter (oh, what fresh surprises on the Abrelians' faces!) they found a former jewel of trade and enterprise reduced to a poxy island of goat-herders and olive-farmers, all of them disappointed to realise their promised twenty gold a year each had magically vanished with the Carians.

Merken put his fingers to his mouth, licked his dry lips and gave a sharp whistle. The dozen warriors by the city wall stood and approached. Standing up, it was obvious which was Cope Threemen. She was a good head taller than any of the others. Gods, the woman was simple in the head but she could have made a fine warrior with the right training. He passed the first pot to her.

General Handzame pulled down the hood of her cloak. She, unlike Cope, was an unremarkable woman. Merken had known great leaders in his youth, but all the great men were dead now. Handzame wasn't even fit to stand beside what passed for today's "great" men. She had a famous family name but nothing more. Without it, she was truly anonymous.

"It is time," said Handzame.

Merken wasn't sure if that was a question or a statement. Either way it made no sense. It was clearly time. Merken's plan had been precise. They had rehearsed it until their bones were sore and they could have executed it in their sleep.

"Remember," Merken said to the soldiers. "It's all about speed."

"All about speed, men!" declared Handzame, pulling on her helmet with the ridiculous horse hair crest.

"Speed and fear," said Merken.

"It's all about speed and fear, my fine soldiers!" announced Handzame.

Merken stopped and looked at Handzame. "Perhaps you wish to give the orders, ma'am?"

Handzame gave him a benevolent nod of the head. "I've delegated that to you, Merken. It's what you're here for."

"Indeed. Cloaks off."

"Cloaks off!" ordered Handzame.

Merken held back a sigh. He was proficient at holding back sighs. He had a lifetime's worth of sighs pent-up in his breast – the cost of enduring forty years of marriage. He was sure they'd be the death of him one day. One pent up sigh too many and he'd pop.

He drew his sword, silently waved for the others to follow and headed towards the gate. They walked at first, broke into a speedy jog and then – Merken's knees creaking like ship's sails as they neared the gate – charged.

The guard's expression of dumbfounded surprise, a split second before Cope Threemen smashed her clay pot into his face nearly made Merken laugh. That alone made the whole venture worthwhile. With a half-grin, half-grimace on his face, he led the assault on Ludens to the bloodthirsty roar of a thousand Amanni warriors.

12

Merken put two men on the temple complex walls, another two on the gate itself and sent out four on the first patrol of the city. Ludens would need a constant reminder it was a city under occupation. Happy with the positioning of the troops, he went into the temple to give Handzame his report.

She was in the great audience chamber of the eighth floor. It said a lot about a person who immediately sought out a throne room as her command headquarters, with no regard for the isolated position of those headquarters or the aching knees of her most senior officer.

Merken rubbed some life back into his left leg before entering. Handzame was pacing the floor with a passionate will. Merken had seen military leaders pace the floor. It was, as best as he could fathom, a substitute for actual thinking, which was what intelligent people did. Nonetheless, there was still an art to pacing. A man with the intellect of a pickle but the art of the pace, could give a jolly good impression of a great leader deep in profound thought. Handzame paced like someone in desperate need of the bathroom.

"General?" said Merken.

She looked up sharply. The flames from the open braziers either side of the Hierophant's throne accentuated the panicked fury on her face. "He's gone!"

"Has he?" said Merken smoothly.

"Do you know who I'm talking about?"

"The wizard?" said Merken.

She stopped her pacing and stumbled. "You know?"

Merken allowed himself a thin smile. "I do. And I expected it too."

This did little to alleviate her temper. There was a very real prospect she might start pacing again. "Doesn't he know we enter Foesen's tomb in a matter of hours?"

"I should think he does."

"And you aren't at all put out by this turn of events?"

"People are predictable," he said. "They like to think they are free agents, like the gods. But they are simple creatures of habit and patterns. Simple, like dogs. Predictable, like clocks," he said, pointedly.

Handzame had calmed sufficiently to be able to think straight. She read Merken's meaning. "We are not done here yet."

"The city is taken," he replied. "We agreed."

Handzame took a dark velvet bag from an arm of the throne and passed it to Merken. He luxuriated in its weight for a while before opening it. Inside was a polished wooden box with a clasp. He opened this too, looking at the clockwork marvel within. One of only two surviving timepieces by the great Hary Greginax. There was nothing in this modern fallen age to compare with it.

"Happy?" said Handzame.

"Very much so," sighed Merken and snapped the case shut. "Some dogs can never be let off the leash. You beat them when they bite, you reward them when they follow commands; but you can never let them off the leash, or else they turn on each other. Or indeed you. Other dogs can be trained, sent off to round up herds or find game, and they will respond to a single word. And then there are other dogs, little more than damnable wolves, who will hang around the campfire, guard the tribe from enemies and join in with the hunt. They might go off into the wild for a time and pretend to be wolves again, but will always return because the camp is where the fire and the meat can be found." Merken secured the drawstring of the velvet bag and tied it to his belt. "Abington has gone off to be a wolf for a few hours. We will find him." He turned to leave.

"And what kind of dog are you?" Handzame asked. There was a sudden attempt at bonhomie in her tone, a sort of *We're both experienced soldiers, leaders of men. Only we can understand the burden of command* kind of thing. "You see yourself as a wolf, I bet," she said.

Merken held her gaze, eye to eye. He hid his utter contempt. Forty years of marriage made him good at it. "A dog which thinks it's a wolf is a damned fool. And will only realise it when it meets a real wolf."

13

Merken slipped into the tavern on the corner of Mercer Row and Kidgate and, through force of habit, stepped from nook to shadow to cranny until he had placed himself, entirely unnoticed, in a corner with an excellent view of the tavern crowd.

He watched Abington in conversation with Cope. He watched the smart chap with the ready smile and trimmed beard dismiss the blonde-haired girl he was with and go join their conversation. He watched Lorrika return from the bar with some sort of bard, possibly drunk, in tow. He watched Cope get up to speak to the bard. He watched the smart chap peer inside Lorrika's mouth and the increasingly heated conversation between Abington and the smart chap. He watched Abington reach for one of the many pouches at his belt and stuff his pipe. He watched Cope abruptly fell the bard with a single punch. He watched Abington put a lit match to his pipe and blow his own head off.

Merken was pushing through the crowd before most people realised what had just happened. The smart chap got up to run and Cope took him firmly in hand. Lorrika was crawling around on the filthy floor, trying to gather together bits of Abington that had been blasted around and about. It was mad, but Merken had seen men attempt madder things in the shock of combat.

"What are you doing?" Cope was asking Lorrika.

"Picking up bits of wizard," explained Merken. He glanced at the smart chap firmly held by Cope. "Who's he?"

Cope shrugged. "I don't know his part in this. He's a dentist."

"Just a dentist!" whimpered the man.

"Is he now? What happened to Abington?" asked Merken.

"I think he might have done something really bad in a past life," said Cope grimly. She looked at Merken and then pointed towards the stairs. "The artist. I knocked him out cold. We need to take him with us or kill him."

"Why?"

"Because he knows too much."

14

Knees aching more than ever, Merken entered the great audience chamber on the eighth floor. Handzame was still pacing the floor. It was a large and imposing room and ideal for those who wished for a large area in which to pace. On a broad table beneath a wall mosaic of the divine eagle Tudu, piles of books, papers, scrolls and charts had been set out. Unrolled charts were held in place by candlesticks and bowls of fruit.

The Mad Empress Kalladia owned a library which, it was claimed, was one of the largest in the world. Kalladia had commissioned its construction but had never read a single book from it. Inspired by some new-fangled philosophical notion called *rude particulates*, Kalladia took daily walks along its aisles and alleyways in the belief she would simply soak up knowledge by her proximity to so many written words. The pretence of learning without any of the effort.

Handzame might have Abington's research on Foesen's

tomb in front of her but Merken suspected she had spent more time arranging it than reading it. Handzame tried really hard to create the right appearance of things. Merken would have felt sorry for her if he didn't despise her for it.

"Well?" she demanded.

"The wizard is dead," said Merken. There was no point in pouring honey on a cow pat. "His head exploded."

Handzame's mouth actually fell open a little. "Is that— Is that something wizard's heads do?"

"In my limited experience, ma'am, no. We arrested two men: a bard and one who claims to be a dentist and a wizard."

"What's a dentist?"

"It's something to do with teeth, I believe."

"Did they kill Abington?"

"I do not think so. They're guilty of something, although I'm not sure what. I've given the order for them to be beheaded."

"And you expect us to now enter the tomb without Abington to guide us?" said Handzame.

"There's certainly little point taking him with us, ma'am."

"But how are we to succeed? It was Abington's research which was going to get us through the labyrinth, the traps…"

Merken had been afforded plenty of time to contemplate this as he had climbed the steps to the eighth floor, cursing his limbs, his burning lungs and the inventor of stairs all the way. "We take his books. We can read, ma'am. We navigate as best we can. We may take a day or so longer, but we will succeed."

Handzame grabbed a book from the table, seemingly at

random but, Merken could tell, it had been specifically chosen, specifically placed. She thrust it towards him. Merken looked at diagrams of some sort of vice-like device: all turning screws and pulley weights. He looked at the text written underneath and in the borders. It was meaningless squiggles to him, like no writing he knew.

"Oh, hell," swore Merken.

"That's what I said," said Handzame. "I'm glad we agree."

Merken hurried to the balcony and shouted down to the people in the courtyard below, hoping the beheadings had not yet taken place – one headless wizard was as little use as another — but it was eight storeys down and no amount of shouting or waving in the dark was going to draw their attention.

Merken cast about for something to throw.

15

The address was a small house on the corner of Cisterngate with a wyvern's head (clearly a papier-mâché forgery) mounted above the door. The sight of a half-drawn sword was enough to buy the silence and compliance of the woman at the door. Merken sent Lorrika climbing the outside wall to the window, he taking the stairs to the first floor. The door to the guest room was unlocked. Merken entered, expecting to find a darkened room, maybe the lump of small sleeping body in the bed. Instead, he saw a young girl with white-blonde hair and skin as pale as spider silk sitting at a table, swinging her legs as she scratched at the table top with a small knife; all by the barely sufficient light of a candle. Merken recognised her from the tavern earlier that evening: it was the wizard Pagnell's girl. The soldier quickly took in the rest of the room. There were some odd-looking implements laid out on another table. They looked somewhat familiar to Merken, who had seen many a well-equipped dungeon. Drills, a variety of sharp probes and a rather sinister crescent-shaped bowl with a handle. However, rather than being encrusted with dried blood from the last victim, these looked shiny and clean and were arranged neatly on a white linen cloth.

The girl looked round at Merken and then at Lorrika climbing through the window. She should have screamed. Merken had sons and daughters (a vaguely indeterminate number; he could count them if he chose but rarely bothered) and also grandsons and granddaughters (a decidedly indeterminate number; he'd dangled a fair few on his knees but never bothered to keep count). He knew children, after a fashion, and the girl should have screamed. But she didn't.

"Are you ghosts?" she said.

"No, little girl," said Merken. "Do we look like ghosts?"

"I don't know," she said. "I've never seen one."

"Then why...?"

"She—" the girl pointed her knife at Lorrika "—came in through the window. People don't come in through the window. That's what doors are for."

"Do ghosts come through windows?" asked Merken.

"I don't know. I've never seen one. I *did* say," the girl added very seriously.

"Yes, you did. Your name is Spirry, yes?"

"Windows are stupid," said Spirry.

"Are they? Well, you are to come with—"

"People decided they wanted to live indoors and then as soon as they did they put holes in the walls so they could see outside."

"I suppose that's because—"

"And when they started having fires indoors, they put holes in the ceiling—"

"Chimneys."

"I *do* know what they're called, mister man. To let the smoke outside. And don't get me started on balconies."

"I don't plan to."

"It's almost as if people didn't want to live indoors in the first place."

"Shall I bag her?" asked Lorrika, holding up a sack she had with her.

Merken held up a liver-spotted hand, a command to be patient. "We have your father prisoner," he said.

Spirry appeared to give this some thought. "I was told my mother was the earth and my father was the rain, and that I was found in the cup of an acorn."

Merken wasn't sure what to do with that damned statement. "Newport Pagnell," he said.

"Oh, him," said Spirry. "Sure. Got it."

Again, Merken would have expected some sort of emotional response. Screams, tears, confusion or stunned silence but, no. Maybe the girl was simple in the head.

"And you need to come with us," said Merken.

Spirry put the knife down. "I don't think I want to."

"I'm not giving you a choice, young lady."

"I still don't think I want to."

Merken gave the nod to Lorrika. The thief pounced on Spirry with the sack. It should have been straightforward. The girl was a little dot of a thing and now unarmed. But she had sharp teeth. Maybe that's what you got for having a dentist for a father.

And finally there was screaming. Not Spirry's but Lorrika's. And there was blood. Again, not Spirry's but Lorrika's. Lorrika yelled and kicked as the girl clung to her, teeth buried in the fleshy part of Lorrika's hand.

They eventually got the girl into the sack, but it was a messy and undignified success which, on honest reflection, was more difficult than invading the city.

16

In the ante-room to the great audience chamber, Merken watched Pagnell pore over the papers the soldier had brought him. Pagnell read them with what looked like genuine scholarly curiosity. The wizard's hands were still bound with manacles to prevent him casting spells. Merken wasn't yet convinced this man was a genuine spellcaster – he'd known a fair few mages, even a wizard or two, and this youngster hardly looked like he was cut from the right cloth – but Merken wasn't going to take any chances.

"Newport Pagnell," he said.

The man glanced up. He still had smears of exploded wizard on his face.

"I've heard of a wizard called Newport Pagnell," said Merken. "A student of Tibshelf, I recall. Only heard of him because of that damned business with the tower in Aumeria.

Last I heard, he went off into the wilderness to consort with fairies and the like."

Pagnell shook his head. "In my defence, the tower was going to collapse anyway. Shoddy foundations. If anything, I gave it nothing more than the magical equivalent of a nudge. I was wholly exonerated by the guild. And, as for the thing with fairies – seriously? Fairies? Grimlocks, trolls and even a sea serpent or two, yes; but fairies? Magical elfin creatures with gossamer wings? Please, sir. Do not joke."

Merken pulled a tired face. "Every morning, my wife has the serving girl cook me three eggs, a thick slab of gammon and maybe a slice of blood sausage. I don't have to ask her. She just does it. In my study, she will gather my letters and papers and sort them and ensure they are carefully stored on the correct shelf. If my shirt or trews are so stiff with sweat and muck they could walk out by themselves if they chose, she has them cleaned and returned overnight, as if it was the work of fairies."

"She sounds delightful."

"Mmm. Doesn't she?" Merken stepped closer. "I can't stand her."

"Oh?

"I think I would go so far as to say I hate her."

"I see," said Pagnell, who clearly didn't.

"I like clocks. I like clockwork things. I went to the court of the Mad Empress Kalladia – an entirely unjust epithet I should point out. In this world of pretend kings and child rulers, she is the closest thing to greatness I've seen. I went to her court to see the clockwork city she had commissioned and installed in the palace ballroom. It is truly beautiful. I love clockwork things. They are honest."

Merken could see the wizard Pagnell frowning, determinedly trying to work out where Merken was going with this line of conversation. Merken enjoyed the look on Pagnell's face. He liked to keep the young confused; it gave him a mental head start.

"People – like clocks, like clockwork – are predictable things. But they are dishonest and like to pretend to themselves they are otherwise. A clever man can read people, understand what makes them tick – ha! – and predict their every action."

"And your wife can predict your wants and needs?"

"She presumes to!" said Merken with a sudden passion. "She presumes to know what I want for my breakfast, what needs doing in my study. She thinks she knows what I want as well as I do! Better even! She thinks she can read me! Unacceptable! I rather think if it wasn't for her presumptuous ways, I'd never have come on this fool mission."

"You don't like eggs and ham and blood sausage, huh?"

"I love them!" said Merken furiously. "That's what makes it worse!" The soldier coughed and calmed himself. His fingers drifted to the comforting presence of the velvet bag at his belt.

Pagnell sniffed and considered his manacles. "I would say it's been delightful talking to you and I've really got things to be getting on with," he said, "but that would be a lie."

"You think you're clever, Sparkles," said Merken.

"I don't think I'm clever," said Pagnell with just a fraction of emphasis on the word *think*.

"I loathe people who say what they think I want to hear or do what they think I want them to do. It implies they possess a certain mental superiority, and I despise people who think they're cleverer than me. It's damned insulting. You understand?"

"I think so."

"Good, because in a minute, we are going to go through that door and you are going to inform General Handzame you can follow Abington's notes sufficiently to lead us through Foesen's tomb. And then you will do just that. And if at any point in time, you think you can betray us, trick us or abandon us, remember I am cleverer than you."

"Understood," nodded Pagnell.

"And remember also that in the Hierophant's cells of justice, locked up and all alone, is a little girl."

For the first time in all their conversations, there was a truly honest turn in the wizard's expression, a dropping of his charming façade and a glimpse of real human doubt underneath. The real Newport Pagnell: just a man. "Now, wait—" he began to say.

"Her name is Spirry," said Merken. "She's safe, for now."

"If you dare hurt her—"

"I dare. I really do." Merken wrung his hands. "I don't want to hurt her, naturally. I'm a man, not a monster, and I have enough terrible deeds on my soul. But if we do not make it back with the Quill of Truth then ... well, I'm sure you get my drift."

The colour had gone from Pagnell's face. He was almost as pale as his little girl.

"Very good," said Merken and gestured to the door. "Let's go in. And pray you do not lead us astray, eh?"

17

Merken rattled his chains in the dark hole of the cell the grimlocks had thrown them in and said, not for the first time, "See where you've led us, you damned conjurer! Did you actually want to kill us?"

"A small miscommunication. Clive did lead us out of the labyrinth, just not to the exit we wanted," replied Pagnell. "I did say."

"He did say," agreed Cope.

"I wasn't asking you," said Merken. "Can't you magic us out of here?"

"Iron bonds," said the useless wizard, which was damnably bad luck given that the grimlocks, being too backward to work metal properly, had only what metal they could scavenge. And what they had apparently scavenged in abundance was chains.

"You can pick them, Pipsqueak," said Merken.

"They took my lock picks," said the rat-faced thief girl. "And my beard. And my nectarine stone."

Merken held back a sigh. Beards?! Nectarine stones!? Being in the company of wizards had destroyed what little wits she'd had. The grimlocks, pressed in on all sides of them, had ransacked their packs and belongings and robbed them of nearly everything. Weapons, tools, lamps, books and – Merken swallowed hard! – the velvet pouch containing the priceless Greginax timepiece. All gone into slimy grimlock hands before the five of them were bundled off into a cold pit of a cell: little more than a hollowed-out recess in a dank corner of the grimlock lair.

"Improvise," Merken suggested to Lorrika. "If we don't free ourselves, none of us are getting out of here alive."

"I'm confident we'll think of something," said Bez, in a tone more desperate than optimistic.

"It would be damnably easier to think if someone could please *stop that infernal singing*!"

Outside the cell, a choir of tone-deaf grimlocks sang, and had been singing for the last half hour.

Yan tan tanera tether
Tethera yan a bumfit sether!
Hovad pimperik
Tanot yanarik
Yanatik tanada pether!

. . .

"I THINK IT'S QUITE CATCHY," said Lorrika and then exclaimed "Ah!" as she pulled free part of her boot buckle and experimentally wiggled it inside the lock on her chains.

"What have that lot got to sing about anyway?" said Merken.

"Probably best not to enquire," said Pagnell.

"I *am* enquiring," said Merken coldly.

"He is," agreed Cope.

"They're delighted to have captured us," said Bez. "And are describing what they plan to do with us."

"Which is?"

"Well, there's a lot of *slap* and *cracks* and various *yo ho, me lads*," said Pagnell. "It's quite a jolly song."

"And lots of *welcome to grimlock town* type stuff," said Bez.

"And then references to squishing and crushing and the making of jam."

"Jam?" said Merken.

"Yes," said Pagnell.

"From our lungs," said Bez.

"Our spleens too."

"And our wobbly kidneys in their goo."

"Did they mention kidneys?" said Pagnell.

"Fairly certain they did," said Bez. "That bit about *hovata cova* a few verses back."

"That means *finely chopped vegetables*," argued the wizard.

"No, no. That's *hovata cova. Hovata cova* means kidneys."

"I don't know who taught you grimlock, but that's completely the wrong way round. If you're going to mistake *hovata cova* for *hovata cova* then you're just going to look a right fool."

"*Hovata cova*?" scoffed the shifty bard. "No one mentioned *hovata cova*. We're talking about the distinction between *hovata cova* and *hovata cova*. *Hovata cova* doesn't even come into the conversation."

Merken, who was used to being surrounded by idiots, although not normally in such enforced close proximity, considered today might well be the day he truly lost his temper. Since he was likely to lose his life as well, it seemed to be a last opportunity. He bit down on a scream and said, "Could you please both stop saying *hovata cova*!"

The wizard and the bard looked at each other and then at him.

"Who said *hovata cova*?" said Bez.

"*A fine and delicious wine*?" said Pagnell. "Not me."

"I'm going to go mad," Merken muttered to the ceiling.

"The language of the grimlocks is notionally simple but devilish to master," explained Pagnell under the misapprehension Merken was remotely interested.

"It only has nineteen syllable sounds," said Bez. "Which means much of the meaning comes from tone, and from rising and falling inflections."

"And the use of the phlegmatic gutterals."

"Indeed. So the difference between *hovata cova* and *hovata cova* is in the extra phlegm on the second syllable. A sort of *huuurgh* sound, yes?"

"I think it's more of a *hurrrgh*," suggested Pagnell.

"Not a *huurrgh*?"

"Nearly. But definitely *hurrrgh*."

"*Huurrgh*?"

"*Hurrrgh*."

"*Huuurgh.*"

"*Hurrrgh.*"

"*Hurrrgh*?" said Cope.

"Oh, that's very good," said Pagnell.

"*Huurrgh*," said Bez.

"*Hruuugh*?" said Lorrika.

"No. *Hurrrgh.*"

"*Huurrgh.*"

"*Hurrrgh.*"

"*Hruugh.*"

"*Hurrrgh.*"

"*Huurgh.*"

Merken wasn't certain whether he was going to drown in spittle, throttle them all to death with their own chains, or even succumb to the madness and join in. He never got to find out because, at that moment, the cell was opened and a band of grimlocks, armed with clamshell knives, came in to cart them off to certain death. He was almost relieved.

"*Tanita yaner figg*?" demanded the lead grimlock.

"They want to know which of us is the leader," said Pagnell.

Merken stood. "That would be me."

"*Tethada setherik yan.*"

"You are to be presented to the queen."

"Queen?"

"Apparently."

The grimlocks came forward and uncoupled Merken's chains from the others'.

"I will need a translator," said the soldier.

"*Tan*?"

"That one," said Merken, pointing at Bez. "Bring him."

"Picked for my superior linguistic skills," said Bez.

"No. Because I want to keep you where I can see you, bard. Lorrika, sort out the wizard's chains while we're gone."

Horribly clammy hands grabbed Merken's elbows and steered him and Bez out of the cell.

18

The grimlock queen's throne room was a cavern. It was not particularly wide, and a shallow, sluggish stream wound through much of its width, but it was deep and it was tall. The grey walls came up at an angle and met, high above them, around a ragged circle of dusky yellow light.

"The gods smile on us," said Bez as they were marched forward.

"What?" said Merken.

"That's daylight up there."

"It is," said Merken. "Evening. We've been down here nearly a day. Two more days and the Hierophant's army will be back and the damned jig'll be up."

"Reckon we could get out up there," said Bez.

Merken tried to gauge distance and size. "The opening's too narrow."

"For a big guy like you, maybe. If you'd known about this

way in, you wouldn't have needed all that rigmarole pretending to take the city."

"Pretend? We *took* the city, bard."

"You know what I mean."

Grimlocks lined the cavern, standing in ragged rows, peering down from high ledges, clinging to walls with their sticky mitts. Merken was automatically assessing their strength. There were near to a hundred of them visible in this room alone. The most prominent and well-armed had feathers threaded through the skin of their scalps. The grimlocks' weapons were primitive and followed the general theme of sharp-thing tied to stick-thing. Flints, bones, shells, even sharpened coins and repurposed pots and pans were used in their construction.

Merken had seen grimlocks use manmade weapons but not often, and rarely for the purpose intended. They were the kind of creature to use swords as ploughshares and attempt to use ploughshares as swords. Or, more likely, fail to comprehend the function of either and attempt to use both swords and ploughshares as cutlery.

Oh, look, thought Merken, and there's a grimlock with a swinging morningstar-flail-hybrid composed mostly of forks and spoons. Cutlery as weaponry.

The grimlocks' weapons were, in short, tat; but there were genuine treasures among the junk. One grimlock was wearing a jewel-encrusted plate as chest armour. Another was using a spiky crown as a fire stand to cook on and – what was that? – a polished statue of the goddess Buqit as a toasting fork. It was ingenious. Moronically ingenious, but nonetheless... Whether the grimlocks had brought these treasures with them or had raided Foesen's tomb was unclear. It would be ironic to discover the grimlocks had found the Quill of Truth and were now using it as ... as...

"Why have they stuck feathers in their heads?"

"They want to fly?" shrugged Bez. "I understand their language. I don't pretend to understand them."

A large fire pit dominated the centre of the cavern. Its red flames burned low and weak, fuelled by piles of rags and rubbish which gave off a foetid reek as they smouldered. Merken was forced to paddle through the cavern stream as he was prodded round the pit toward the throne.

The grimlocks' undifferentiated booty, the scrap, the garbage and the valuable were piled highest beneath the queen's throne: a lopsided raft of a chair made from bleached sticks and reeds bound with twine. On top of it sat an enormous grimlock with a bloated head into which a whole coxcomb of feathers had been inserted. It was remarkably similar to the horsehair crest General Handzame wore and, frankly, no more or less ridiculous.

Beside the throne stood the yellow-bellied grimlock, Clive, now dressed in a poncho-cum-robe of knitted string.

"*Yanaik bumfer letha*!" declared Clive grandly.

"Ah," said Bez. "Clive here – who it would appear is a shaman or vizier or what have you – invites us to kneel before the almighty Queen Susan of the Clodhopper tribe."

"Invites?" said Merken.

Bez waggled a hand. "Commands."

Merken regarded the hideous thing on the ramshackle throne. "Susan?"

"*Dikata hovera*," said Clive.

"*Queen* Susan," said Bez.

"I'm not kneeling for some damned dirty frog," spat Merken. "And you can tell her as much."

"Um. Really?"

"Yes."

Bez grimaced. "Er. *A peth figger tana—*"

Queen Susan silenced him with a wave of a flipper-like hand and spoke with a throaty rattle. "*Yanera bumfa yan.*"

Clive nodded eagerly. "*Yanad pimper hov.*"

"Queen Susan," Bez translated, "would like to thank us for the gifts we have brought."

Merken felt his gorge rising, perceiving full well what this meant. "Gifts!"

Clive bowed and waved a hand theatrically over the pile of backpacks, weapons and other items they had confiscated. Merken saw his velvet pouch resting on the top.

"That's mine," he said. "Give it back."

"*Figgot*?" said Clive.

Queen Susan ripped a bunch of papers from the top of a pack and leafed through them. She held a sketch of a girl and Merken recognised it as Bez's drawing of Pagnell's girl, whatsername. Susan gave a coy and altogether repugnant smile. "*Ik pimpota*?"

"They're mine, your Majesty," said Bez. "I'm an artist and News broadcaster."

"Broadcaster?" sneered Merken.

"Indeed!" Bez made a sweeping gesture as though scattering seeds. "Broadcaster. But for News."

Queen Susan simpered. "*Lethad taner*?"

"No, not a bard as such, your Majesty. I'm much more

into serious reportage. I dabble with oils too, if you'll allow me to demonstrate."

"*Lethad tanit?*"

"Again, not a bard, your Majesty. The distinction is—"

"You're a damn bard," said Merken. "Quit complaining and get my pouch back."

"*Lethad teth pimp,*" said the grimlock queen.

"*Yanada yaner tethotik,*" added Clive.

"I'm sure you do need a new bard but, as I said, I'm not the— Oh!" Bez followed the direction of Clive's pointed claw. A bell-shaped cage hung from an outcropping of rock. Perhaps pilfered from a menagerie somewhere, it might originally have contained a pet songbird or similar, but its current occupant was a rotting corpse which was decidedly human and evidently lacking a number of limbs.

"*Teth ik yanada.*"

"Your last bard?" said Bez, his voice trembling. "Yes. Ah. I notice he appears to be lacking one arm and, yes, both of his legs. Is there a...?"

"*Tanot dik a tan,*" explained Clive.

"He knew hundreds of songs, yes."

"*Yan yanad lether.*"

"Had a voice like a trickling brook. How poetic."

"*Pethera dika a.*"

"And could recount the entire true history of the grimlock nation. Yes, but that doesn't explain the missing appendages."

"*Bumfad diker seth.*"

"I see," wheezed Bez, his face bloodless and horrified.

"What is it?" said Merken.

Bez gave a hoarse squeak before finding his voice. "He says: a bard that good, you don't eat him all at once."

Merken, despite the grimness of the situation, barked with laughter. Bez threw him a hateful look.

"*Tanit yanera*," said Clive.

"You might need a new bard," said Bez, "but not me. Now, if you like the pictures, I could paint you a fine portrait. Portrait? *Bumfada*?"

Queen Susan gave this some thought. "*Yanadik tanatik*?" she said and pointed at Merken.

"Rantallion Merken. A great warrior." Bez made a pantomime of flexing his muscles. "He's leading us on a quest into the Foesen's tomb. *Pimpota cov*."

There was a sudden and prolonged flurry of mutterings between Susan and her advisor.

"*Lethota dik*?" said Clive. There was angry hissing from the amassed grimlock warriors.

"Ah, yes." Bez turned to Merken. "He points out a raiding party was slaughtered by men such as yourself by the banks of the river above."

"What of it?"

"*Dik a sethera*."

"The queen's two brothers, including the king, were among those killed."

"Oh, I see," said Merken. "Well, do tell her we had absolutely nothing to do with that and we're offended by the very suggestion—"

"*Hov a dik bumfera*."

"And the queen would like to thank the man who cleared her path to the throne," said Bez.

"Oh." Merken did his best to offer a gallant smile to the vile grimlock queen, which wasn't easy. It was as improper as shaking hands with a beggar, or stealing a kiss from a princess. Gears of social custom ground against each other as he forced his mouth into a vaguely amicable rictus. "Then that would be me."

"*Teth a dik*?" said Queen Susan.

"*Teth a dik*!" Clive assured her.

"Now, I'm sure the queen is grateful," said Merken, "and will let us on our way with our belongings – starting with that." He clicked his fingers and held out his hand to be given the velvet pouch.

Queen Susan, misunderstanding the gesture, reached out and took Merken's hand in hers. Merken shuddered at the touch.

"*Dikada yan taner*," she said.

"Oh, yes," agreed Bez. "A great man indeed. Scourge of the plains. This is the man who single-handedly conquered the island of Abrelia, yeah?"

"*Ik*?"

"Yes, just him, with nothing but words – a battle cry – and some waggling of his sword, I'm sure."

"*Cov tana*?"

"I know. You wouldn't think it to look at him, would you? He may look like a gin-soaked granddad and, yes, I'm surprised he's still got all his own teeth—"

"Oi," Merken growled.

"—but he's as strong and as virile as any man. You won't find better."

"You're not lining me up to go in their cooking pot, are

you?" muttered Merken.

"Not exactly," whispered Bez with a crooked smile.

Queen Susan shuffled aside on her throne and patted the seat next to her. Merken stared at it.

Queen Susan's eyes jiggled in a most alarming fashion, as though they were trying somehow to escape her face. Merken feared this was the grimlock equivalent of seductively fluttering one's eyelashes. He found this doubly alarming given that the closest he'd come to any woman – any female – making advances at him in recent years was his infuriatingly pleasant and tolerant wife giving him an extra sausage for breakfast and a peck on the cheek.

"*Yanada hovera dik dik*," said Clive.

"The last bard recounted a tale of a princess and a frog," translated Bez. "A familiar tale involving a kiss and a magical transformation."

Merken grimaced. "If she thinks she's going to get a damned kiss from me and magic her into something less hideous, she's got another think coming."

"No, you misunderstand," said Bez. "In this situation, she's the princess."

"What?"

Merken saw the cruel smile on Bez's face.

"What are you grinning about?"

"I just think it's refreshing to meet a woman who's happy with her looks. Totally confident in her own skin."

19

Merken had spent less than a quarter of an hour on the throne, squashed up next to the leathery baggage which was the grimlock queen, but it felt as if it had been so much longer. There was scarcely enough room for the two of them and each time he shuffled to make some distance between them, the wooden chair creaked warningly. The prospect of it breaking at the seams and spilling them both on the floor was very real. Merken found it increasingly appealing.

Bez was down by the fire pit, struggling with the simultaneous tasks of translating Queen Susan's utterances, painting a portrait of the monarch and fending off the various grimlocks who were showing a distinctly hands-on interest in his art.

"*Hov ik pimper*," said Queen Susan.

Bez pushed away an overly curious grimlock and righted

his makeshift easel. "Her majesty says the occasion is to be celebrated with a feast."

"The occasion?" said Merken.

"Your, er, coming nuptials."

It was almost enough to make Merken leap from his seat, but he was master of his damned emotions, not the other way round. There was no point getting oneself killed over pride. With any luck, Lorrika would have the wizard freed by now and – assuming the damned man had any concern for his daughter – they would be coming in at any moment: spells blazing, Cope ready to crack the skulls of any grimlocks who got in her way. Failing that he would think of something soon enough. He had brought down chieftains, satraps and revolutionaries. A filthy tribe of grimlocks shouldn't be anything more than a minor inconvenience.

A line of grimlocks marched in bearing more fuel for the fire on which the feast was clearly to be prepared. Damp logs, mulchy bundles of grass, rags and bones of those long dead, all went into the fire pit, sending up billowing clouds of steam and smoke, and a marshy funk which caught in the back of the throat.

Bez coughed at the stink. A pair of enterprising grimlocks took advantage of his helpless hacking to pilfer some of his parchments and paints and, splodging their fingers in the jars of paint, began creating their own pictures.

Recovered, Bez, who was treating his artwork with far more seriousness than it warranted, put a thoughtful thumb to his lips.

"Your Majesty," he called, "do you perhaps have a sceptre

or similar which you could hold? You know, something to convey your supreme regalness?"

"*Cov diker*?" said Queen Susan.

"*Peth a diker*," suggested Clive.

"Yes, very much," said Bez.

Clive rootled through the pile of confiscated objects. Clive passed over Lorrika's filthy little knives, gave a lump of chalk an experimental lick, briefly suggested Queen Susan try one of the lamps as a hat, and was about to toss Merken's velvet bag aside when the soldier lashed out and snatched it from him.

"Mine! You hear me?"

Instantly, there were a dozen spear tips pressed up against Merken's chest.

"Nice work guards! That looks very good," enthused Bez. "*The bold guards gathered round*. Do you think we could get more of them in the picture? *Dikad tan*?"

Grimlocks shuffled in and stood to attention.

"That's right," said Bez. "Let's make a great scene of it."

Queen Susan had only eyes for Merken. She swung the velvet bag by one of its ties enticingly. "*Hoverik seth*?" she teased.

"Yes. I would like it," Merken replied.

She leaned in closer. "*A yanota*?"

"Can I have it?"

Queen Susan puckered up. Merken understood.

"No, I don't think so," he said.

"*Dikera*?"

"I don't even kiss my own damned wife."

Susan held the bag over his hand. Mere inches from his grasp.

Merken shot Bez a look. "This doesn't make it into your painting, you hear me?"

"What doesn't?" said Bez innocently.

Merken had once crawled through half a mile of clogged sewers to infiltrate the city of Qir. He had climbed up Lord Protector Shallandar's guarderobe to deliver a rather pointed message to the petty despot. He had dressed as a buxom kitchen wench in order to get into the king's castle in Yarwich and suffered many slaps on the behind in the process. He had certainly made sacrifices in his life. This, he told himself, was just another.

He closed his eyes and presented his lips for a chaste kiss. Queen Susan grabbed his head in both hands and smushed her fat lips across his entire jaw. The gross creature had a powerful sucking slurp, like the grip of a monstrous eel. For an instant, Merken thought she was going to suck his moustache clean off his face.

Merken wrestled himself free and came up panting and spitting. He wiped slime from his whiskers and coughed.

"*Dikera*," said Queen Susan happily and plonked the pouch in his lap.

"You!" said Bez, pointing at an idling grimlock. "Yes, you with the kettle on your head. Come in a bit. And look fierce."

Some damned grimlock spit had gone in Merken's mouth. He spat and spat but there was no shifting the rotten taste. He felt violated and damned queasy.

Clive, struggling under the weight, tried to hoist Cope's sword onto Queen Susan's lap. He half succeeded and managed to prop it up between her legs, so the filthy monarch could grip its hilt like a staff.

"*Figga*?"

"No, it's a good look," said Bez. "*The warrior queen on her troubled throne*. I like it. And let's get more of you up there. Everyone crowd in behind. Hey—!"

One of the amateur painters beside him had knocked over a metal pot of paint, spilling a puddle of brilliant blue on the floor. Bez snatched the paint away and grabbed up the others they had taken.

"You can't waste this stuff, you know! You think cerulean is easy to get hold of?"

The grimlock waggled its tongue angrily and snarled. "*Teth a letha*!" it snarled and pointed contemptuously at Bez's work.

"They're meant to be bigger than the ones behind," snapped Bez. "It's what we call perspective. Now: shove off!"

The grimlock huffed and daubed what little paint it still had on its hands onto the page. The other grimlock, bereft of painting materials, looked around for fresh paint and, failing to find any, bit the end of its finger and splashed its own blood onto the paper. It seemed very pleased with the artistic results.

"Pollok!"

At least, that was how it seemed to Merken, but he was having trouble concentrating. The nausea he felt after tasting grimlock lips was growing and his eyesight blurring. Everything looked as if it was being viewed through several feet of water. The submerged feeling extended to his ears; everything was muffled and distant.

"Ask them about the feathers!" Merken shouted down to Bez. He wasn't sure why he asked. The words had bubbled up from within him on a whim.

Bez didn't hear. The two would-be grimlock artists had decided their chosen painting material was going to be each other's innards and Bez was trying to keep their violent scuffle away from his easel.

Merken turned to Queen Susan. Her fat face swam in and out of focus. What was it Lorrika had said about grimlock slime being poisonous, possibly even hallucinogenic?

He pointed at the feathers inserted in her scalp. "Your feathers!" shouted Merken as loud as he could: his voice was coming from so far away. "Why? What are they for?"

Clive, who was still investigating the confiscated items and currently sniffing at a large flask of lamp oil, looked at Merken. "*Yaner yanad figga cov.*"

"It's protection from death in battle," said Bez. (Merken assumed it was the voice of Bez; concentrating on what was and what wasn't was proving increasingly difficult). It must be Bez, he thought, or else my mind has learned how to translate grimlock very quickly.

"The grimlocks scavenge battlefields," translated Bez (possibly). "Rich pickings on a battlefield. They noticed those without armour were more numerous among the dead than those with. And so the grimlocks decided wearing armour was clearly beneficial."

"Astute of them to notice."

"Ah, but then King Colin – Susan's predecessor and brother – noticed among the dead there were no individuals with feathers in their heads. It seemed only logical feathers were a better protection than any armour."

That sounded damned stupid. Merken knew it was damned stupid. But he couldn't for the life of him work out why. The pink blotches wobbling across his vision distracted him and prevented him from thinking clearly. He tried to wave them away, but his fingers had turned into spindly sticks and wouldn't do what he told them.

"I think I poisoned be might," he said, frowned, thought about it and declared with confidence, "I poisoned might I think be."

"I didn't say you should kiss her," said Bez. "Although we should all recognise lust is a powerful motivator."

"I wanna didn't kiss her," Merken retorted. He patted Susan amiably. "I wanna didn't kiss you."

"*Bumfera dik a seth*," said Clive.

"Ah. Here comes the feast," said Bez.

Merken could well imagine what might pass for a feast among these creatures. Rotten funguses, skittering critters, the entrails of unfortunate rodents, all served up in a soup of pond scum. He fervently hoped the wizard, the thief and the warrior woman were moments away from rescuing them all.

"Hello!" called Pagnell as he was carried in, strapped securely to a long roasting spit. "We got lonely so we thought we'd join you."

A gaggle of grimlocks carried in Lorrika and Cope on similar spits, the pole and the grimlocks straining beneath the warrior woman's weight.

"This'nt good," slurred Merken. His tongue was taking on a life of its own.

"You think?" said Lorrika. "We're going to be eaten!"

"Always about you, isn't it!" said Bez. "*We're* the ones who are going to have to eat you!"

Queen Susan nudged Merken and passed him a flask, encouraging him to drink. Merken took it automatically. Any drink, however rank, would be preferable to the foul aftertaste of grimlock snogging which filled his mouth. However, the concentrated fishy pong from the flask was utterly repellent. Merken squinted at the vessel. It was the damned lamp oil!

"This disn't rink," he muttered. Flashes of dreamy colour raced across his eyes. In amongst them was a thought, a half-formed plan which refused to settle or make itself known to his delirious mind. He tried to focus on it but the wizard, who was being positioned over the fire, made focussing increasingly difficult: shouting about not wanting to be cooked.

"I am a great and powerful wizard!" he shouted at the grimlocks. "You do not want to harm me!"

Advisor Clive danced and clapped his hands. "*Tethota taner peth*!"

"Eating wizard flesh does *not* give you their powers!" yelled Pagnell. "That's unsubstantiated rumour!"

Pagnell, Merken decided, was a very annoying wizard. He would be quite pleased when the wizard had been cooked. That would silence the damned smug fool. Then Merken would be able to focus on some sort of plan...

He presented the flask genially to Queen Susan.

"Must some try, Majesty. S'lovely. It's..." He screwed his

eyes up, searching for the words in the mess of his increasingly jellified brain. "*Hovata cova*?"

"*Hovata cova*?" she said.

"A fine and delicious wine. Drink up, darlin'."

The grimlock queen upended the flask and drank. Grimlocks probably had cast iron guts, what with the filth they usually consumed. Merken was nonetheless surprised to see her chug down more than a pint or two of highly flammable oil.

"Yes, let's have you all gather round," Bez was instructing the grimlocks. "All press in close. Let's make it a busy scene. We want this painting to say: *Here is the queen. Look at her surrounded by her loyal subjects in all their finery.* Yes, get on his shoulders if you like. You too, grandma. *Pimpa! Pimpa!*"

Queen Susan put down the half-emptied flask and nodded reflectively like a true connoisseur. The fool Pagnell was blathering on about being painfully hot or something but Merken only had eyes and ears for the monarch.

"*Bumfad dikota*," she said.

"'Tis. Yes," agreed Merken.

Her eyes bulged suddenly, and not as eyelashes all aflutter. The fish oil was plainly too much for even a grimlock's constitution. Queen Susan hiccupped, mumbled something unhappy and threw up more than a pint or two of oil, all down herself, the throne, the pile of booty, and the floor.

"*Bumfot figg*!" she exclaimed. Merken had no idea if it was horror, joy or indignation in her voice. His damned judgement, like his vision and co-ordination, was all but gone. He would have asked her but then the trickle of vomited oil reached the edge of the fire pit.

The fire leapt up and out.

Merken leapt too: dragging Cope's longsword from between his betrothed's legs as he bounded from the throne.

Bez screamed.

The fire exploded upwards along the trail of oil, billowing in sun-bright clouds of flame.

Merken hit the floor hard. He twisted, ankle clicking as he landed; the pain would come soon enough, but not yet. As he turned, he saw Queen Susan, the half-full flask in her hand, her vomit-stained mouth open as she stared agog at the racing flames.

She really shouldn't have her mouth open, Merken thought.

There was, figuratively and literally, an explosion of grimlocks. Jumping away from the conflagration or thrown by the exploding oil. Grimlocks went in every direction. A couple even flew straight up, making noises like surprised fireworks.

Merken wasn't looking; he was racing to free the others. Which wasn't easy. Looking down through a treacle-blur, he was sure he was currently in possession of the wrong number of legs, and none of them would do what he wanted. But he had a sword, which was something.

The grimlocks who had held Cope on her roasting spit dropped her in fright and she lay, trussed, on the ground. All Merken had to do was cut her free. He raised the sword.

"Sir?" squeaked Cope in alarm.

"There's no need for alarm, Cope," said Merken. Or that

was what he attempted to say; something more along the lines of "No nee'fr'arm, Cups," dribbled from his mouth.

He swung with force and precision, neatly slicing through the pole and ropes just above her chest. Cope rolled away and ripped at her other bonds.

"Now me! Now me!" yelled the damned wizard from his position over a fire which was burning all the fiercer with the addition of the oil. Fire raged throughout the cavern. The grimlocks yelled and yammered, jibbered and jabbered, and screamed like a bag of cats on a bonfire. They ran and flung themselves about without purpose, but it wouldn't be long before they used five humans to vent their anger and energy upon.

Merken raised the long sword to meet the grimlock savages. Cope snatched it out of his hands.

"I'll take that, sir," she grunted. Rapidly, she hauled Pagnell from the fire, his heels dragging through the hot coals for an instant, before slicing through his bonds. Pagnell still wore manacles and chains, but he was now free to move; at least in an awkward and ungainly shuffle.

A grimlock, the feathers in its head aflame, came barrelling towards them through the confusion. Merken turned aside the creature's flint spear by instinct rather than design, and used the shaft to catapult the unhappy warrior against the cavern wall. Another figure stumbled their way. Merken swung the spear round to impale it.

"It's me!" squeaked Bez, stumbling and ducking with a bundle of papers and reacquired belongings clutched in his arms.

Merken was half-tempted to run the man through

anyway. Damned bard was as much the architect of their current predicament as anyone. Wasn't like the world would mourn the loss of a bloody street artist.

A cry went up among the grimlocks: not of panic, but a determined and angry tone.

A spinning axe whirled across the cavern, cutting curlicues in the rising smoke. It smashed against the cavern wall a foot or two from Merken's head.

"Time to go," said Lorrika, ripping off the last of her bonds and snatching her leather roll of lock picks from of the heap of items Bez held. A flurry of arrows clattered around them.

Cope pushed the others ahead of her towards the nearest tunnel exit. "You too, sir," she said, and gave Merken a shove.

Cope picked up the broken remains of a door for a shield as a trio of spears were flung across the burning cavern floor. Merken didn't see where they landed. He stumbled after the thief and the wizard on uncooperative legs.

They ran, down dark unlit passages, with the yells of the grimlock cavern growing fainter behind them. There was a click, a "Thanks", a mutter of arcane syllables and a pale blue light was now leading them on.

"Which way?" said Lorrika, the light spell the wizard had cast on her mouth flickering as she spoke.

The light bobbed left and Merken staggered after it, like a drunkard following ghost lights into a marsh. Merken felt a sudden dread he was being led to his doom and hesitated. Bez stumbled into the back of him, chains clinking.

"Don't stop now, granddad. They're coming!"

Merken himself bumped into the back of someone.

"A dead end!" shouted the wizard. Someone pushed Merken back the way they'd come.

He had not tottered more than dozen steps when they ran right straight into a grimlock war party in hot pursuit. Lorrika's mouth light picked them out in flickering snatches. The grimlocks had brought their own light too: one of their feathery headpieces was fully ablaze.

Grimlock warriors hissed. Merken gave his best battle cry and reached for a blade which was not there. Pagnell raised his arms and, in a puff of light, two of the grimlocks dropped to the ground. Spears were rattled and primitive bows loosed. Lorrika raised a knife, grunted and dropped it. Then Cope Threemen stepped into the fray with a yell loud enough to start an avalanche, her longsword whirling around her head so fast it was a blur of silver light. The blade flashed down and grimlocks scattered like skittle pins. The blade swung up and the ceiling was splashed red.

"This way!" cried Pagnell. "Quick!"

Merken thought moving quickly was a capital idea, but was surprised to realise his body hadn't received the memo. He started swearing at his legs, when a hand gripped his elbow and hauled him down a fresh tunnel.

They heard grimlock noises far behind in the passages they had left. It encouraged them on faster than ever. Merken felt the floor rush invisibly beneath him, yet could no longer feel his feet at all. He wondered if he still had feet, or if had perhaps mastered the art of effortless flight.

And then there was darkness and silence and a soft but insistent slapping sound.

"Are we all here?" whispered a voice.

"M'all here," said Merken.

"What's he doing?" said a voice.

"Jogging on the spot," grunted another.

"N'm'not," said Merken. "M'flying."

"What's wrong with him?" said a voice.

"He kissed a grimlock," explained another. "I think he liked it."

"Din't. Dun't'ven kiss m'wife. Wifey wife wife." The word floated around Merken's mouth, in and out. He tried to swat it away.

"I've got something for that," said a voice.

There was the pop of cork and something cold was pressed against Merken's lips. He drank. It tasted bitter but, more importantly, it struck his senses and gave his conscious mind a good slap, sending it from gibbering drunkenness to stark sobriety with just a split second of stunning hangover in between.

"*Gnnh!*" gasped Merken.

"Back with us?" said the wizard.

"Yes. What was that?"

"Liquid bezoar," said Pagnell. "Felt like getting a bucket of water thrown in your face, yes?"

"Along with the bucket!"

With a cloth and a dab of oil, a fire was lit. It cast light on a sorry state of affairs. They had come to a stop in a short cul-de-sac, by a turn in the tunnel. Lorrika slumped against a wall, her face ashen and slick with sweat, a grimlock arrow embedded in her wrist, just above where the bandage around her hand ended. Cope stood beside her, an arm held tightly across her midriff, her jerkin stained with blood. Bez crouched over the pile of belongings he had managed to steal back from the grimlock trove: papers, scraps of food, a blade or two. No lamps, no weapons of note apart from Cope's sword.

Merken scanned the pile, panic rising in him for a second, before realising he was holding the velvet pouch already and had been all this time. He tied it to his belt and felt all the better for it.

"What's in there?" said Bez.

"Never you mind, bard," said Merken. "How's Pipsqueak?"

"She'll live," said Pagnell, who was inspecting the thief's injury. Gently, he touched the arrow. Lorrika screamed.

Cope glanced down the tunnel. "You must keep quiet," she muttered. "If the grimlocks hear us I do not know if we can fight them off."

Merken nodded at Cope's wound. "They get you too?"

The look Pagnell gave him was cold and hateful.

"You did it, sir," said Cope. "When you cut me free from my bonds."

Merken tried to remember. The poison-addled escape was naught but a damned dream now. "I thought I only cut through the wood and the ropes."

"You thought, huh?" said Pagnell and returned his attention to Lorrika's wound. "If we can pull out the arrow, I can stitch this. If we had something to stitch or bind it with."

Moving with difficulty, Cope brought a hand up to her jerkin pocket. Her fingers fumbled inside and, as she pulled out a purse, a fat wad of dog-eared cards spilled onto the floor. She passed the purse to Pagnell. Merken bent to pick up the cards. What he had assumed were simply playing cards were actually rectangles of thick yellow card, each marked with a title such as *How to Ask for Directions, How to Buy Goods in a Shop* or *How to Greet a Person of Importance.* He read one:

HOW TO RECEIVE a Compliment

LISTEN to the compliment

- *Is the person being sarcastic or ironic? (see: How to Detect Sarcasm)*
- *If not, how does the compliment make you feel?*
- *Say "Thank you" to the person who gave you the compliment.*
- *Smile (no more than two seconds)*
- *Determine if you should say something nice back.*

SEE ALSO:

- *How to Handle Drunkards*
- *How to Fend off Predatory Men*
- *How to Deal with Salesmen*

"WHAT ARE THESE?" said Merken.

"My instruction cards," said Cope. "May I have them back, sir?"

Pagnell pulled a needle and bobbin of black thread from the purse. "This is ideal," he said. "Right, Lorrika. I'm going to tend to your wound but I'm going to need to pull the arrow out. It's going to hurt."

"Pain is an illusion," said Lorrika and, as Pagnell's fingers brushed the arrow flights, she gave a yell.

"Can't you damn well knock her out like you did the grimlocks?" said Merken.

"I'd have no way of waking her up. I've lost my smelling crystals." Pagnell looked around and picked up a short, corked bottle. He emptied the silvery liquid within and muttered an incantation before putting the bottle in Lorrika's good hand. "Scream into this."

"Into this?"

Pagnell nodded and gestured to her to put it to her mouth. "Ready?"

"To scream?"

"For all you're worth. Three, two, one—"

In one swift action, Pagnell snapped off the arrow flight with one hand and yanked the arrowhead through her arm with the other. Lorrika did indeed scream: screamed fit to burst. He mouth contorted, her face went red and the sound went ... nowhere. Merken could hear a tight, whispering wind from the neck of the bottle, like a draughty door in a storm. As Lorrika panted in silent agony, Pagnell cast the arrow aside, pulled her torn sleeves away and readied the needle and thread.

"Hold her still!" he told Merken.

"Why not him?" said the soldier, scowling at Bez. The damned artist had found parchment and charcoal and was sat cross-legged, indulging in some pointless scribbling and sketching.

"I want you to hold her because I need to keep her still," said Pagnell tersely. "And I trust you to do it." He quickly cast a spell.

"What's that?" said Merken.

"*Nolan's Magic Thread*," said Pagnell as the needle magically set to work stitching Lorrika's wound with abnormal speed. Lorrika bucked and kicked, silent screams magically soaked up in the bottle. Merken kept the arm rock steady.

"So, what now?" asked Bez as he doodled.

"We find the next gateway," said Pagnell.

"I saw something which could have been it," said Cope. "A tall arch made of three stones?"

"Why didn't you say?" said Merken.

"I assumed the people in charge knew where they were going," she said.

If Merken didn't know Cope was incapable of conversational subtleties, he would have taken that for insubordinate sarcasm.

"And then it's onto the *Pathways of the Righteous*," said Pagnell.

"Sounds easy enough," said Merken.

"It's a vast tiled hall. Each stone is linked to a different deadly trap and, if you step on any of them in the wrong order, then—" Pagnell made a strangled throat-slitting noise.

"—A duck appears?" said Cope.

"I *meant* 'What now?' as in we're injured, depleted and lost and shouldn't we turn back?" snapped Bez.

Merken glowered at him. "What did you expect? A gentle jaunt? Hot meals and a warm welcome at every turn? Damned fool. Any more talk of turning back and I'll put a knife in you."

"Got any knives left?" sneered Bez.

He had a point. "You'll never know," said Merken.

"We're done," said Pagnell.

"What?" said Merken.

Pagnell took the bottle from Lorrika's lips and stood. Lorrika's voice returned in ragged, weary gasps. Merken released her arm; his grip had left a row of tiny bruises.

"Right, Cope," said Pagnell. "You're next. Let's get you sewn up."

Cope unbuttoned the lower half of her jerkin and gingerly raised the bloodied tunic underneath. There was a long, shallow cut across the bottom of Cope's ribs.

"I barely nicked you," muttered Merken.

"Indeed, sir," said Cope.

Pagnell held out the bottle to her. "Scream if you need to."

"I won't," said Cope.

"This will hurt."

"I was told never to cry out unless I wanted to draw attention," said Cope. "And I don't. So, I won't."

Pagnell corked the bottle and stuffed it in his coat. It made a muffled cry as he did.

Cope was true to her word and stood, lips pressed so

tightly together the blood went from them entirely, but was otherwise silent. *Nolan's Magic Thread* worked rapidly and neatly along the wound with the speed of a master seamstress. When it was done, Cope inspected the work and nodded in approval.

There were no clean bandages or cloths among the remains of their belongings, so Pagnell unwound the bandage from around his own head and used it to cover Cope's midriff as best he could. Cope pulled her tunic down and buttoned her jerkin tightly.

"This *Pathways of the Righteous*," said Merken. "Do you know how to cross it safely?"

"There's a formula, a series of steps to remember," said Pagnell. "High Priests of Buqit of the Sixth Order of Lamentation are taught it by rote. Only High Priests of the Seventh Order are actually allowed to cross the hall: they're expected to have remembered it from their previous life."

Bez laughed. Cope shushed him and looked down the tunnel.

"Most priests of my acquaintance," Bez whispered, "can't remember what they had for dinner yesterday. I've got more chance of sprouting wings than they've got of remembering past life events."

"But do *you* know?" Merken insisted.

"The wizard Abington made notes on it somewhere," replied Pagnell. "There's a bunch of charts and diagrams."

"That's the *If the tile has three sides and you've stepped on it with your left foot then consult Table F* one," said Lorrika. "I remember Abington working all of it out with an abacus. It made him quite cross."

Merken knew Abington, and could imagine what *quite cross* looked like. He suspected the wizard had gone through several smashed abacuses before the task was done.

"Here," said Lorrika and pulled Abington's much battered, soaked and recently scorched journal from the pile. "It's in here."

Pagnell thumbed through it.

"So, to repeat, Sparkles," said Merken. "You can get us across this hall of traps?"

"Absolutely," said the wizard with a confidence Merken did not trust one jot. "When have I ever let you down?"

20

With a makeshift torch made from a grimlock spear, a bundle of rags and the last of their oil, Cope led the way back along the tunnel. Pagnell followed close behind her, muttering to himself as he studied the contents of Abington's journal. Almost all of the dead wizard's papers were lost: drowned in a waterlogged pit, scattered in the labyrinth or turned to ash in the grimlock cavern. A man's work brought to naught.

Though he wouldn't tell them as much, Merken didn't hold out much damned hope for this mission now. With a wounded thief, an unarmoured warrior, a tu'penny-ha'penny wizard and a damned bard who was – even now! – sketching little caricatures when he could at least be acting as lookout, they were hardly a crack team of tomb raiders. *If* they could find the next threshold, *if* they could avoid wandering back into the labyrinth, *if* they could stay clear of a tribe of vengeful grimlocks, *if* they could cross the *Pathways of the*

Righteous then they still had several levels of traps, guardians and barriers to pass through and not enough time in which to do it.

"Down there," said Cope turning right.

She was, to Merken's surprise, correct. The turning brought them to a stone archway, beneath which stood a great door of age-blackened wood.

"Another riddle door?" said Merken.

Pagnell inspected it at length. "Ah, no. I think..."

He prodded it with his fingertips and it swung open on improbably well-oiled hinges. The space beyond was as black as the door. Blacker.

Pagnell took the torch from Cope and stepped warily through. Spots of light flickered overhead and grew until the hall before them was illuminated by six orbs of blue-white light, like giant hovering fireflies. The orbs hissed softly like insects in long grass.

"The work of the gods!" breathed Cope, impressed.

"Or a contained construction of permanent enchantment," suggested Pagnell. "But, yes, it's all very pretty."

The hall was as big as any of the chambers in the temple above, as big as any banqueting hall Merken had been in. Large enough to hold jousting tournaments, and have room for spectator seating and a pie and ale stand on the side. Fluted columns lined both sides and between there was, as Pagnell had promised, a floor of coloured tiles. Marble, granite, quartz and other slabs of polished stone – which Merken could not identify – had been used to create a perfectly interlocking patchwork of squares, triangles, kites, arbelos, lozenges and shapes without names. Or at least, not names Merken knew.

The door on the far side of the hall looked very distant.

"These traps...?" queried Bez, looking on with trepidation.

Pagnell consulted his book. "Kavda the Builder was fond of, er, metaphorical descriptions. *The Traitor's Sting, The Touch of Purification*, et cetera. Does it matter?"

"I was just wondering how severe they were."

"Let's assume they're pretty severe," said Lorrika. "I doubt any of the traps in here result in a strong verbal reprimand or unwarranted tickling."

"Certainly not," agreed Cope. "Unwarranted tickling would not be much of a deterrent, and it would be difficult to administer."

"Fine, fine," said the artist peevishly. "But I'm not going first. I'm not."

Merken was tempted to throw the untrustworthy coward into the hall, just to see what would happen, when he was struck by a memory. "When we finally cornered Lothwar the bandit king, he had holed himself up in a hill fort and had laid pits, wolf traps and razor-sharp snares all across the surrounding land. We could have made a slow approach, checking the ground, but his longbowmen would have picked us off with ease. Instead, we herded together all the mud hogs from the highlands and drove them ahead of us as we charged: let them fall into the traps so we could just run over them with ease."

"Yes," mused Pagnell. "Beside the fact we don't have any,

um, mud hogs, I doubt very much any of these traps would be so easily fooled."

He produced a coin and flicked it out into the hall. It struck one tile – huge blades shot up from artfully concealed holes around its base – bounced onto another – a gout of blue flame burst forth – and rolled onto a third. There was the tiny *phut! phut! phut*! of darts flying out from unseen openings in one of the wall columns.

"These traps reset themselves to strike again and again and again," said the wizard.

"Very well," said Merken. "Then we'd best not put a foot wrong."

"I'll go first if you wish," said Pagnell, opening the journal.

Merken put a restraining hand on Pagnell's arm. "Not so fast, Sparkles. I'm not going to let the only one who knows the way across put himself out of my reach. Cope."

"Sir."

"You're first."

"Very well," sighed Pagnell and consulted Abington's journal. He stuck his tongue out slightly as he read and re-read a page. Merken was firmly of the opinion people who had to stick their tongues out to think were probably not the world's greatest thinkers. It was as bad as people who had to use their fingers to read.

Pagnell ran his finger down the page and muttered to himself.

"Damn it, man!" snapped Merken. "Can you do it or not?"

"Yes. Yes. Any tile with an even number of sides if you would, Cope, and tell me what colour it is."

Cope stepped. She did not die. "Green," she said.

"Green. Good. Consult section D…"

"What should I do?" said the warrior behemoth.

"Nothing, just—" Pagnell flipped a page, skimmed down. "Any tile with a curved edge."

Cope took a giant stride onto a red semi-circle.

"Good, good," said Pagnell. "Green square and red semi-circle. Five straight edges. Table three brackets five— Star! Are there any star tiles you can reach?"

"There's this pink one," said Cope and swung out her leg.

"*Not the pink!*" shouted Pagnell. Cope's leg froze. "Go for that blue one! Never tread on a pink tile!" He turned to the others, repeating, "*Never* tread on a pink tile."

"Never pink," nodded Lorrika. "Why? What do they do?"

"Let's try not to find out."

Cope continued across the hall, step by step managing to not be impaled, shot, fried or otherwise killed as she followed Pagnell's instructions. Merken watched the wizard closely, trying to glean some understanding of the squiggles, ledgers and charts he was following.

"What's that?" said Merken, tapping a page.

"It's a decision tree," said Pagnell.

"Ah, I thought it looked like a tree."

"Don't the Yarwish pray to sacred trees for guidance?" said Bez. "Something like that, yes?"

Pagnell ignored him and called out to Cope. "You need to find a regular nonagon next."

"A what?" shouted back Cope.

"Nonagon!"

"*What?*"

"She's too far away," muttered Pagnell. "A nine-sided shape!" he yelled.

"Five?"

"Nine!"

Cope shouted something back but she was halfway across the hall. The space and distance simply sucked the sound away.

"She can't hear us over the hissing of those damned lights," said Merken.

"I'm going out to her," said Pagnell.

"Don't try anything funny," warned Merken.

"Oh, funny just bounces off you, Rantallion," said Pagnell. He cupped his hands to his mouth. "Just stay there!"

"What?" shouted Cope.

"Stay! There!" yelled Bez.

Book in hand, talking to himself as he read, Pagnell walked out into the hall, a grown man doing a ridiculous and ungainly hopscotch. Over long minutes, he made his way to a point where Cope could hear him again. He called further instructions to her and then turned back.

"Who's next?"

"You're up, Pipsqueak," said Merken.

"Step on a triangle," called Pagnell.

Pipsqueak found one and began her slow journey across. Bez scribbled in one of his pads as they watched her.

"Do you never give it a rest?" said Merken.

"It's called suffering for your art," said Bez. "Suffering is the fuel of great art, and right now I'm totally on fire."

"That might be arranged."

"You could just leave me here."

Merken held back a sigh. "Pretty sure I threatened to kill you if you suggested turning back again."

"Not suggesting turning back. You could just leave me, collect me on the way out. I'm sure I'm just holding you up."

"I'll let you know when you're holding us up," said Merken. With a hard shove, he propelled the bard into the hall.

Bez teetered and stopped on an oval tile. He whirled around, animal fear in his eyes. Nothing happened. Nothing continued to happen. No slicing, stabbing, crushing death. Nothing.

"Lucky first step," said Merken, grinning.

The bard swore, a stream of curses and general insults regarding Merken, his mother, the circumstances of his birth, his daily habits and bodily functions. Merken let it wash over him. Swearing was the last resort of the impotent.

"The bard and I are coming next!" he shouted to Pagnell.

Pagnell waved and began to call back instructions.

Like climbers, moving from precarious handhold to precarious handhold, the five of them moved across the deadly mosaic in a chain, none too far ahead, none left behind, all guided by a dentist with a dead man's notes. Black square, silver triangle, blue crescent, plum-coloured circle...

"What colour was that?" asked Pagnell.

"Plum," said Merken.

"Plum?"

"Plum."

"As in...?"

"As in the colour of a plum. A bit red, a bit blue. Like a dark wine."

Pagnell, balancing on a grey trapezoid, twelve yards ahead, gestured violently at his book.

"So, red then," he suggested.

"No," said Merken patiently. "It's not red. If it was red, I would have said it was red. But it's not. It's half red, half blue. Or, as one might say, plum."

"Where do I step next?" asked Lorrika. The wizard was too intent on the colour problem.

"There is no plum colour in the notes," said Pagnell.

Merken shrugged. "Is that somehow my fault?"

"I'm just saying."

"You are welcome to come over here and inspect the damned tile."

Pagnell looked at the range of tiles between them. "Bez, Can you see it any better?"

"I'm not blind!" snapped Merken.

The bard, who was scant feet from Merken, made a pretence at peering over. "It's plum. Or perhaps more of a pale damson. Frankly, I don't give two hoots what colour his bloody tile is. Call it turquoise for all I care."

"*Is* it turquoise?"

"No!" said Merken. "It's plum! A blue-red. Dark violet. Beetroot. Plum!"

Pagnell threw his hand in the air. "Maybe they didn't have the colour plum in Kavda's day."

Merken was near speechless. "Didn't have the colour—! What?"

"Maybe it didn't exist."

"Where do I step next?" repeated Lorrika.

"How could a colour not exist?" demanded Merken.

Pagnell's frown was deep and troubled. "It's like ... what if in this part of the world, in the time of Kavda the Builder, there were no plums and nothing was plum-coloured? There would be no need for the colour to have a name. And, do you ever wonder, is the colour plum named after the fruit or the fruit after the colour?"

"I've never wondered," said Merken firmly. "Particularly at moments *like this—!"* he bellowed, "—when I am standing on what I imagine is some sort of spring-loaded mincing machine!"

"It's just an interesting question with philosophical and cognitive consequences. Maybe there are other colours or concepts we don't yet comprehend. They surround us but we simply don't see them as distinct and separate. Maybe Kavda the Builder looked at that tile and simply saw it as a shade of blue."

"Yeah, it's blue," said Bez indifferently. "Just pretend it's blue."

"It's like," continued Pagnell, "I sometimes look at the sunset, and that moment when it turns from yellow to red."

"When it's a light red colour?" said Bez.

"Exactly. But it's also a bit yellow. And I think to myself, maybe there should be a colour to describe it."

"Light red!" snapped Merken. "It's light red!"

"But with a hint of yellow too," said Pagnell. "Maybe somewhere in the world there's a fruit like a plum – or not like a plum – and we'll start calling things which are a mixture of red and yellow by the name of *that* fruit."

"By all the gods, I am going to kill you if you do not help me off this tile," growled Merken.

"Can you move me on a bit before you do?" said Bez. "I'd like a little distance before this wrinkled plum steps to his death. Don't want to be in the splatter zone."

"I'm ready to go," insisted Lorrika. "I've been waiting a while. Tell me where to step next."

"I'm very near the end," added Cope. "I could probably jump it if I had a little run up."

Pagnell snapped his book shut. "Everyone be quiet! We cannot do this if you all behave like needy school children! Cope, you are not to jump it and you are definitely not to do 'a little run up'. Think about it. Merken?"

"Yes."

"There is no mention of plum or violet or beetroot in Abington's notes. I cannot help you if you are on a 'plum' tile."

"Ha!" laughed Bez.

"So, look at it very very hard and decide what other colour you think it looks most like."

"But..."

"As if your life depended on it." Pagnell turned away. "Lorrika, what are you standing on?"

"Um, that shape like a wonky rectangle with two of the lines leaning inwards."

"Trapezium?" said Pagnell.

"Yeah. Trapezium. Ooh, Trapezium in Trezdigar. Is that a good name?"

"Bit of a mouthful really. What colour is it?"

"Well, it's a sort of reddish-yellow. It's like you said, when the sun's setting and—"

"Light red then," said Pagnell and reopened the book.

"Hey!" said Merken. "How come you know what her colour means?"

"Because everyone calls it red, even though, perhaps, just perhaps, there's a better name for it. Step to a five-sided shape, Lorrika. A decision, Merken?"

Merken felt queasy. On such a decision, he might go to his death. There were stupid deaths – arguably all deaths were stupid – but to die because of a colour...

"I'm going to go for red also."

"It's your life."

The queasiness in Merken's stomach hardened into a bitter stone. "Not only my life. Have you forgotten your little girl already? Think what will happen to her if I don't return safe and sound."

"Oh, hell," whispered Pagnell.

Merken smiled. It took him a good few seconds to realise Pagnell was not staring at him, but past him. The soldier looked back.

Scores of grimlocks tumbled and scampered through the entrance to the hall.

"The grimlocks have found us," said Cope.

"I can see that!"

Bouncing off each other like drunkards at a barn dance, several grimlocks tripped, ran or leapt onto the mosaic of tiles. One vanished in a blast of white steam. Another twisted as metal bolts impaled it from below. A third was hoisted high on invisible wires and then came down again in an unhealthy number of pieces.

"They cannot reach us," said Cope.

"They don't have to," said Pagnell. As if to prove his point, a shell axe came spinning out, rebounded off a tile and skittered across a dozen more, setting traps off in its wake. A silver caltrop thrown out by a death trap tinkled to a stop less than a stride from Merken's feet.

"Red, damn it!" he said.

"Step to a green shape," said Pagnell.

Merken avoided the lime green trapezium directly in front (he didn't want to get into a green-yellow debate) and took a difficult stride to a leaf green rectangle. He waited a full five seconds before congratulating himself on a choice well made.

"Now me!" cried Bez who was furthest back and therefore nearest to the chaos the grimlocks were generating. "I'm on a white hexagon."

"Hexagon." Pagnell read. "Oh—"

"Oh?"

"It says you should never step off a hexagon. Ever."

"Well, I've stepped on it now!"

"Yes. But you should never step *off* one."

"Why?"

"It just says. Did it make a sort of click when you stepped on it?"

"Yes..." Bez's voice was a warble of fear.

"Ah," said Pagnell. "Let me have a think."

"That's clever," said Lorrika, nodding past them.

Back along the hall, some grimlocks had by luck found themselves on safe tiles. Others were now passing over blocks and rough cut lengths of wood to make a bridge from one safe space to another.

Other grimlocks were scaling the walls and jamming

what looked like bone pitons into gaps in the stonework to hold their soggy twine ropes.

“Surprisingly inventive,” said Pagnell.

“We’re out of time here, Sparkles,” said Merken.

“Yes.” The wizard coughed uncomfortably. “Cope. Go to the blue squircle.”

“The what?”

“The squircle – the square with round corners – and you’re across. Lorrika, that pentagon’s black. Go to a triangle – yes, the red one, the plum red one – and then the diamond. That’s it. Bez!”

“Yes?”

“I’m coming to you.”

Merken gawped as Pagnell took a step back, retreating down the hall towards Bez.

“Do not waste your time with him. If he was fool enough to step on a hexagon then that’s his damned problem.”

Pagnell seemed not to hear him and stepped by.

“Attend to me!” barked Merken. He would have grabbed the wizard if he could have reached.

There was a crash further down the hall. At least one grimlock had been caught up in a spring-powered vice trap larger than a double bed. Glass flew out across the hall from places unknown and, on a cushion of fire, something catapulted out towards Merken, set off a blade-filled trap over to his left, rolling to a halt close enough for Merken to see it was a grimlock head with an (understandably) frustrated look on its face.

“Sparkles!”

Pagnell waved at him without looking. “Grey ellipse and

then any shape with more than four corners. You'll be fine."

One part curiosity and three parts indignation kept Merken where he was.

The rickety mess of makeshift bridges the grimlocks were building had progressed at startling speed, overtaking the climbing group who were swinging from ceiling to pillar to wall. The bridges were littered (and intermittently charred) with evidence of their trial and error tactics, but the vicious creatures were definitely closing in.

Pagnell crouched down beside Bez and scratched his beard thoughtfully.

"What if I just leap off it really quickly?" said Bez.

"You're not that quick," said Pagnell.

Overhead, a grimlock launched itself from a ceiling hold. It swung out on a rope, only to collide with one of the great glowing orbs. The critter was wreathed in white lightning fire as all along the chain of ropes, grimlocks jerked, spasmed and fell. One landed hard on a square which folded up into a set of chisel-like steel teeth, mincing and dragging the body under the floor in moments. A second grimlock fell onto the same square. It lay there untouched while Merken made a silent count of three. The metal mouth sprang to life and consumed it.

Pagnell felt around the edges of Bez's tile. "If it's pressure activated, maybe we can weigh it down."

"Maybe?"

"Put your pack down."

Bez stuffed papers inside his shirt for safekeeping, leaving what was left at his feet.

"It's not enough," said Pagnell. "Lose the jacket."

Bez fingered the finely embroidered garment sadly. "But this was a gift..."

There was squeal, an enormous elastic *boing,* and Bez's complaint was cut short by a rain of shrapnel which, on inspection, appeared to be mostly grimlock fingers. Bez quickly shucked off the jacket and placed it under his feet.

"And the boots," said Pagnell. "No – still not enough. Cope!"

"What is it?" shouted back the warrior.

"Chuck us your leg things."

"Leg things?"

"The armour."

"My greaves?"

"Yes! Them. Throw them to me. Carefully!"

A spear, thrown by design rather than collateral damage from a detonating trap, flew past Merken. It was considerably off target but the grimlocks had them in range now.

"Leave him, wizard. Your life is worth more than his," said Merken. He took the two long strides to take him to the safety of the far side.

Pagnell caught the first of the pieces of plate armour thrown by Cope, then overbalanced trying to catch the second. Bez grabbed his coat to stop him tumbling.

"There," said Pagnell, placing both greaves on Bez's tile.

"Why are you doing this?" asked the bard.

"Well – the principle is the weight should hold the mechanism in place even when—"

"No, I mean why? Why put yourself to all this trouble?"

Pagnell gave a helpless gesture. "Same reason I became a dentist."

"You weren't clever enough to become a surgeon?"

Pagnell laughed. "Okay. Now, here's the crazy part of the plan."

"This was the sensible part?"

"Everyone! Step back!"

Merken was only too happy to move away from the mosaic of death. A grimlock axe landed close by. Cope picked it up and hurled it back with force and accuracy.

Pagnell produced a purse.

"Magic beans," said Lorrika knowledgeably.

"Coins actually," Pagnell replied. "Right, Bez, the traps take at least a second or two to reconfigure themselves after being triggered. We're going to run for it."

"What?" said the bard. "But the traps..."

"We're going to set them all off."

"But... You said..."

Twenty feet behind them, a grimlock possessed of greater bloodlust than sense, jumped from the nearest bridge and charged. He didn't make it to Bez and Pagnell, but bits of him came very close.

"It's going to work," said Pagnell and tossed a fistful of coins in the air. "Probably."

Merken shielded his eyes as the coins rained down on the nearest squares. A wall of light, flame and wicked sharp things erupted like an explosion in a blacksmith's workshop. Shapes barrelled through the chaos. The blizzard of death mushroomed out in a second wave and then subsided with the *tink tink* of cooling metal and the ratcheting of invisible cogs.

There was no sign of the wizard or the bard, except for

the pile of clothes and armour they left on the white hexagon.

"Fools," said Merken.

Something coughed on the steps beside him. A tangled lump of cloth and limbs rolled apart. There was a large sooty mark on Bez's face, and the sleeve of his shirt was a blood-stained mess. The bottom of Pagnell's outer coat was now more ribbon than cloth and it looked like something had taken a bite out of the heel of his boot. The pair of them were laughing.

"Damned fools," muttered Merken.

Back along the hall, the grimlock tribe hissed and spat and renewed their efforts on their bridge.

"Time to go," said Merken. "Pipsqueak, lead the way. Check for traps. Up on your feet, Pagnell. We need you telling us where to go."

Cope pushed open the door leading out of the hall and Lorrika stepped through. Out on the floor, devices whirred and crunched and burned, a musical accompaniment to the stupidity of the grimlocks, bashing their heads against the machinations of wiser men of old. Merken shook his head. The world was full of idiots but did there have to be so many of them?

He turned to go and there was a sudden cold sensation as a blade entered his chest.

He stepped back involuntarily, felt a tugging at his belt, looked down and saw he was standing on a tile. The tile was pink.

Merken began to sigh. He had a lot of sigh within him and there just wasn't enough damned time.

21

"PICTURES" BEZ

Bez spent most of the day sitting in the belfry of the calendarists' tower, sketching views of the temple of Buqit.

Shortly before two bells, he commented, "You know, I know you're there." When he received no reply, took out his string-bound pad of Instant Pictures and drew a study of the cold jaffled cake he had saved for lunch. It was a good picture. Artistry was in the details and he had, with certain lines – here and here – given the cake an air of wistful sorrow. It was quite something, he told himself, and ate the cake.

Shortly before three bells, he said, "You know, I know you're there." When he got no reply, artfully added a swig of Gawk's Old Pentacular Ale to his bulging belly and a red dragon to his temple picture. He was quite pleased with both and wondered what real dragons looked like.

Shortly before four bells, he said, "You know, I know you're there." and, when he received no reply, flicked through his Book of Faces and, using a polished circle of bronze as a mirror, dashed off yet another self-portrait. This time he put a smouldering look in his eyes and a sort of handsomely intense pout to his lips. When it was done, he concluded he had simply made himself look confused and constipated, and didn't like it. There was more humanity in the picture of his lunch than in his own face. Bez understood how it had happened. The only real question was when it had happened. A trawl through the ages of Bez in his collection of self-portraits would probably have given him some clue.

Shortly before five bells, he said, "You know, I know you're there." When he received no reply, added his regular muse Chainmail Bikini Woman to his temple picture, her burnished red hair blown by an imaginary breeze. People liked Chainmail Bikini Woman. Men liked Chainmail Bikini Woman. He liked Chainmail Bikini Woman – through from a purely artistic stance naturally.

Shortly before six bells, he said, ""You *do* know I know you're there."

"No, you don't," Lorrika replied.

"You've been there for quite some time."

"Prove it."

He looked round. "That's you, there."

Lorrika dropped to the floor. She was silent, like a cat. Or, as Stentor would probably describe it: *Silent, like the sound of approaching fog taking great care not to wake a colicky baby.*

Bez looked her up and down, appraising her. Some girls would have a problem with men looking at them as directly, but Lorrika seemed entirely unselfconscious. He had added her likeness to his Book of Faces several times. He'd also created a number of purely speculative impressions of what she might look like if she ever did agree to model for him. Chainmail Bikini Woman was getting kind of old now. Maybe it was time for a rooftop prowler character to make a debut in his News pictures. Lithe, agile and appropriately re-dressed in something which both captured the edgy, morally ambiguous nature of the character, whilst showing an aesthetically pleasing amount of young flesh... Ripped Leather Bikini Woman? Cat girl?

He'd certainly have to clean her up a bit for the public taste. Lorrika had muck on her face and munched gracelessly on a nectarine she swore she hadn't stolen.

Bez showed her today's picture. She made what Bez chose to believe were complimentary noises although she seemed to have some problems with the basic concept of Chainmail Bikini Woman.

"I mean it must chafe," she said. "The chainmail. Cos it's chain, isn't it?"

The world was full of critics. "I've always considering chafing a matter of personal taste. Besides, I'm pretty sure they don't make woolmail." Bez was beginning to regret showing her the painting. The young, what did they know?

She continued with her critical remarks, adding, "Everyone says you have a problem with perspective."

"Everyone can go to hell," he snapped. He took an angry swig of his Old Pentacular and found it to be empty but for some hoppy foam. "I do not have a problem with— Look, if you don't mind, it's been a slow News day, but I've got to get this finished if I want to eat."

"You want news?" she said.

"I could be persuaded to listen if it means I get to eat."

With fingers covered in sticky nectarine juice, she turned him round and prodded him towards the other side of the belfry. "Not listen, look. In that direction," she said, pointing towards the north gate and the plains beyond.

The sun had fully set in the west. The world was composed mostly of shadows. But Bez had sharp eyes. He stared at the gate. "I'm not exactly unfamiliar with the view, so if that's all..."

The bell began to toll six bells.

"Just watch," Lorrika shouted over the fifth bong and, with that, she was gone.

Bez untied his cloak from the clapper of the great bell, spread it out on the floor and sat. He stared at the gate. To most people, the fading light would have made a dark blur of the distant gate or started to play tricks on the eye. But Bez's eyesight was indeed superb.

Several minutes later, when the first Amanni soldiers burst through the gateway, he swore to himself and picked up the charcoal. But he didn't put the charcoal to the board. He watched, with increasing confusion and interest.

22

A few hours later, in the tavern on the corner of Mercer Row and Kidgate, as Bez was in the middle of his third bottle of Old Pentacular and the beginning of explaining his artistic vision to the gigantic warrior woman, Cope, things got inexplicably out of hand and very very hazy.

"The sun didn't gleam at all. We came at nightfall," said Cope.

"I know!" said Bez. "And we'll need to fix it in the final painting, absolutely. Though for your information, for future reference, don't attack at night. Night attacks, no good. No one can see you. As my old fella used to say, if there's a battle in the dead of night and no one sees it, did it really happen?"

And then, just as he was just getting into the details of how, by creatively tweaking Cope's attire, they could present an altogether more meaningful and *truer* version of the events of the Amanni invasion, something whacked him in the jaw and knocked him dead to the world.

He woke in groggy pain, moaning as he rolled on the straw-strewn floor. There were voices and then there were hands and he was being hauled up and outside into the night air.

Bez had been thrown out of taverns on several, nay, many occasions but somehow this didn't feel like the usual bum's rush. For a start, it had never actually taken so long before. Although he wasn't happy about this turn of events, there didn't seem to be much his body was able to do about it. Besides, he'd heard unhappiness was just a state of mind. So was pain apparently, but Bez's mind clearly hated him and the pain stayed with him as he was dragged through the city streets.

He saw a gate, a great big gopherwood gate, and he saw guards in Amanni uniform. His recovering brain gave him a bit of a nudge and a general *Uh-oh, you're in deep trouble now* kind of look. By the time all the pieces of his punch-jumbled mind had been slotted back into their rightful places, Bez saw, recognised and understood he was in one of the Hierophant's cells of justice.

That was what they were called. Cells of justice. Bez had, years before, stopped believing in justice (the evening's events had only confirmed this) but, he supposed, *cells of political expedience* or *cells of maintaining the status quo and creating an illusion of civil safety and stability* just didn't have the same ring. That said, even Stentor would have said *cells of justice* was a euphemistic metaphor too far.

They left him in his own private justice cell, giving him

just enough time to conclude incarceration didn't suit him, before a grey-headed soldier, who looked as if he had become an old soldier through something other than luck, entered the cell.

The soldier stood stock still and looked down at him. Stock still but for his hand which stroked mindlessly at the fabric of a velvet pouch at his belt. "I hate bards," said the old soldier.

"Then we're bonding already," said Bez. "I hate bards too."

"You hate yourself?"

Bez attempted a laugh to show he appreciated the joke. The old soldier wasn't in joking mood. "Got any beer?" asked Bez and when he was met with stony silence said, "I'm not a bard."

"Do you tell stories?" said the soldier.

"Yes."

"Do you make your living entertaining people."

"Is it entertainment or is it information? Can we not do both?"

"You're a bard. I hate bards. But, fortunately, most of them are harmless idiots. You have exactly one minute to prove to me you too are a harmless idiot."

"Uh...?"

"A good start. But you'll have to do better. Do you know who I am?"

"No," said Bez.

"Rantallion Merken. Heard of me?"

"No, sir," lied Bez. Of course he'd heard of Rantallion Merken, the conqueror of Abrelia, the scourge of – actually pretty much everywhere, really. But surely that was years and years ago...

"Tell me what you know," said the old man.

The words, "I had nothing to do with the fireball which took the wizard's head off," just sort of rushed out.

"I never thought you did. Until now."

"Oh." Bez continued. "I saw him fiddling with his pouches. All pouches look the same really. Probably went for the wrong one. Pipe weed. Firework powder. Easy to get confused. A pinch of this, a dab of that. You smoke the wrong one and ... you know."

"Your head explodes?"

"Probably."

"I see," said Merken. "What do you know about the assault on the city?"

"Who can really know anything? Like I said, it was dark and— Oh."

Merken picked up one of Bez's picture boards which had been brought along with the creator to the temple. Through blacks and murky greys, it was still clear to the perceptive eye it was either a painting of an invasion or, possibly, a dangerously exuberant street party.

"Like I said," said Bez. "Dark."

"And yet – unless I'm reading too much into these skilfully dropped splodges, here and here – you were able to capture much of the visceral drama."

"A lot of flashes and bangs and shouts is all," said Bez. "If I didn't know better I'd say you were using some sort of magical fire?"

Merken gave him an open and unreadable gaze and said nothing.

"I know nothing. I swear," said Bez. "I was merely chatting to your woman, I mean the soldier, the one twice as tall as me and cut from solid oak. Offering my humble services, to paint a historically pleasing interpretation of your mighty victory."

"Historically pleasing?"

"Totally," he said, warming to the sales pitch. "Real life rarely gives thought to lighting conditions, or framing and composition. It certainly doesn't give any consideration to the motifs and symbolism and juxtaposition which true art demands."

"I'm sure it doesn't," said Merken, losing interest and turning to the door.

"In exchange for my freedom and a reasonable fee – I'm talking practically cost – I could immortalise this night's work in oils with you at the forefront of this celebrated triumph."

"I don't wish to be at the forefront of anything, young man," Merken said tiredly. "And immortality has very little appeal."

"Picture this!" said Bez, seeing his potential patron about to leave. "You – a paragon of knightly virtue: wisdom, nobility, righteous judgement – striding through the shattered remnants of the city gate, a great warrior unbowed by the years, a little leavening of the some of the greyer hair to black should easily achieve that..."

"What grey hair?"

"Er... The rising sun appearing over your shoulder like a

benediction from the gods themselves. At your back, a thousand Amanni warriors, a true reflection of your military might in the face of—"

"True reflection?" said Merken.

"Of your military might," said Bez firmly.

"So you will paint us a picture of a thousand Amanni warriors?"

Bez could see a yawning chasm open up in front of him. The conversation was a galloping horse and he could think of nothing to do but grip the reins all the tighter. "Two thousand?"

"Instead of...?"

"Call it three?"

Merken clicked his fingers. "And you almost had me convinced."

Bez blinked some more. The horse was gone, tumbling end over end. All Bez could hope for was to avoid a metaphorical hoof in the face before they hit rock bottom.

"Did you know, the mud hog tribes believe it's good luck to be executed on the same chopping block as a wizard."

Bez wrinkled his nose. "That doesn't sound like an actual thing."

"No. But you're welcome to believe it if it offers you comfort."

23

The execution escort came for Bez some time after midnight.

He had spent much of the intervening hours wondering what his last words would be. Stentor was his words man but the fellow wasn't around to provide any assistance when you actually needed him. When the soldiers came, Bez hadn't progressed much beyond, *I'm really not happy about this at all.*

Bez resisted as they dragged him out; not in any sincere effort to escape, but just to let them know he was ruddy well displeased.

In the lesser courtyard, a barrel had been placed as an impromptu chopping block. Had he not been about to lose his head, he might have smiled at the irony: it was a barrel of his favourite, Gawk's Old Pentacular.

Beside the barrel stood the wizard Newport Pagnell and the armour-clad warrior, Cope Threemen. Neither looked overly pleased to be there, although Pagnell's displeasure was the more understandable.

Torch-bearing soldiers stood in a loose circle about the execution spot. In the flames' flickering light, there was a savage, bleak beauty to the scene. If he'd had his materials and free use of his hands, Bez would have compulsively recorded the moment in oils. If he'd had the free use of his hands and feet and a five second head start, he'd have made a run for it – to hell with the savage, bleak beauty.

"Right. Let's get this over with," said Cope.

Pagnell turned to look at her. "*Let's get this over with*? Is that what they teach you at executioner's school? No sense of occasion? No appreciation of the solemnity of the moment? I'm about to die and I'm really not happy about this at all."

Bez found himself wondering if mind-reading was included in a wizard's bag of sorcerous tricks, along with plagiarism.

Cope made a noise which was only a few vocal grumblings away from a growl. "I am a warrior, not an executioner. There's no honour in butchering the defenceless."

"So, you'd be far happier if I was coming at you with a sword in my hand?" spat Pagnell sarcastically.

Cope nodded slowly. "Could we do that?"

"What?"

"I would really feel a lot better about it." She reached behind her and pulled out a long knife from a sheath on the small of her back. "Here."

Pagnell stared at the knife. "This is your idea of fair?

You've got a really big sword and that – it's a kitchen knife at best."

"More like a fruit knife, I'd say," ventured Bez

Cope made a small head jiggle of agreement. She drew her longsword, spun it in a circle, rolling it over the back of her hand, and offered it to the wizard. Pagnell looked like he'd been given a poisonous snake for his birthday. He took the blade in his manacled hands. The tip of the blade clanged heavily on the ground and he clutched at his bent wrist.

"Are you all right?" asked Cope.

"Apart from being barely able to lift it?"

"Yes. Apart from that."

"No."

"Swap?"

Pagnell spluttered. "Why am I trying to make this easier for you? It's my head on the block. Literally. And, if you're going to take my head, that's where you can damn well do it."

"Very well. Let's get this over with." She held out her hand to receive the sword.

Bez could see a battle waging on Pagnell's face, a tension in his hands as he contemplated trying to give Cope the sword pointy end first (Bez's inner voice screamed, *Do it! Do it!*). Reports from Pagnell's arm muscles about the general heftiness of the big blade reached his face and the battle died quickly.

"Fine!" said the wizard and, with effort, pivoted the sword back over into Cope's hand. "But I warn you, the death curse of a wizard is a terrible thing."

"I've not heard of such a thing," said Cope.

"Oh, it's real all right," affirmed the wizard.

"Absolutely. And it applies to friends of wizards too," said Bez, placing himself next to the wizard. Pagnell sneered down at him for muscling in on his last ditch gambit, but what could he do?

"I think I will risk it," said Cope. "On your knees."

Pagnell hesitated. Cope took hold of his shoulder and forced him down.

"Right. Wait. Listen," said Pagnell. "This really shouldn't be happening..."

"Head on the barrel, wizard."

"This is a bad idea. You're making a terrible mistake!"

She bounced his nose forcibly off the roughly coppered container and stepped back to take her swing.

"A curse on you!" yelled the wizard. "Gods' vengeance from on high! Fire! Lightning! Plague!"

A lemon bounced off the ground barely a foot from the wizard's head.

"And fruit!" Bez added.

A pair of plums smacked into the earth and exploded on impact. A bronze candlestick rebounded off nearby stonework with a *ba-doing* and landed at Cope's feet. A mango struck Bez a glancing blow off the forehead, sliming him with juice.

Cope looked up. In the darkness above, someone was shouting. "Is this your doing?" she asked the wizard.

"No," he said turning over to look up. "Or possibly yes. Who can say?"

Bez's keen eyesight saw a figure high up, waving from a window and shouting.

"Who is that?" said Cope.

The thief Lorrika dropped from the shadows, slid down a wall and rolled to the ground. "It's Merken. He wants you to stop."

"Are you sure?"

"The fruit has spoken," said Pagnell, a little giddily. "Trust the fruit. Here." He held out a white tablecloth to Bez.

"Where did you get this?" asked Bez, as he wiped mango pulp off his face.

Pagnell shrugged. "It was just lying on the floor."

Five minutes later, with the dread of imminent death still hanging over them (maybe Merken just wanted to pop down and give them a good kicking before putting them to the sword) the old soldier emerged in the lesser courtyard with red cheeks and a piece of parchment clutched in his hand. He uncrumpled the paper and shoved it in Pagnell's face.

"What does this say?"

Bez looked at the page and saw only arcane squiggles.

"*Kavda's Vice of the Infidels*," read Pagnell. "*Only a true shepherd can guide the faithful through. Maximum capacity sixteen persons.*"

Merken looked simultaneously relieved and deflated.

"You need a wizard, don't you?" said Pagnell.

Merken nodded wearily. "You're coming into the tomb with us."

"I'm what?" squeaked Pagnell. "I don't think so! That place is a death-trap!"

"Come now, boy. Don't exaggerate."

"I'm not exaggerating. Foesen's tomb is the very definition

of death-trap. It is several death-traps. Whatever the collective noun is for death-traps, Foesen's tomb is it!"

"You'd rather lose your head?"

Pagnell looked from Merken's face to Cope's sword and back. "It amounts to the same thing, doesn't it?"

"Have him brought inside," Merken instructed a soldier.

"And this one?" Cope said, with a prod of her sword at Bez.

Bez could have wept at the disinterested look Merken gave him.

"Kill him," said the old soldier.

"Wait!" Bez shouted as the wizard was taken away, leaving him to face execution alone. "You need me too! It's bad luck to take the sorcerer without his apprentice."

"Apprentice? I don't think so, bard," said Merken.

"But I have vital information critical to the success of your mission. *Vital* information, yeah?"

"And what is that?"

Bez glanced momentarily at Pagnell before beckoning Merken over. The soldier wavered. The gods smiled: he approached.

"What is it?"

Bez leaned in close and whispered a single word.

24

"Right," said Merken to Bez, "you've got one damned minute to prove to me you're not a useless idiot and actually have something of worth for me."

"Seems to me you have an unhealthy obsession with things only taking one minute, sire."

"What is Spirry?"

Bez dug around inside his embroidered jacket for the right sketching pad. "It's not a what, it's a *who.*" He pulled out two pads of paper. Casting aside the pad of Instant Pictures he began flicking through the other.

"What's that?" said Merken.

"My little Book of Faces."

"You do portraits."

Bez pulled a face and made a *not quite but nearly* noise. "Just faces. I mean, faces rendered with some considerable expertise, obviously. A lot of selfies but also sketches of whoever I'm with, people I see. I sometimes do a little impromptu show in the Ramsgate tavern, pop 'em up on the wall and see if people like them."

Merken was still listening, which meant Bez was still alive, so he continued.

"You'd be surprised how much people want to just look at pictures of themselves, even doing the most tedious or ridiculous of things. Course, if people have irritated me, then maybe I'll give the picture a tweak. Give them trolls ears or—"

"There is a particular picture you wish to show me?" said Merken impatiently.

"Right, yes." Bez had his finger in the page. "One of my best. Really captured the authentic innocence; the wide-eyed wonder."

Merken peered down at the sketch. "Spirry? I've seen that girl before."

"She travels with Pagnell. Arrived in Ludens only a couple of days ago. Generally kept themselves to themselves, but the comings and goings of the city are my business, so..."

"So?"

"So," said Bez, "you require a wizard to see you through Foesen's tomb, someone who is wholly committed to the job in hand. And such commitment requires leverage."

Merken ran his tongue around the inside of his cheek thoughtfully. "You are a piece of work, bard."

"Self-made, And still, not a bard."

"But all you've told me is the wizard has loved ones. Hardly enough to save your neck."

Bez closed the Book of Faces. "What about the name of the place where they are staying? Would that be enough?"

"Is it nearby?" said Merken.

"Five minutes' walk from here."

Merken nodded and looked down at the velvet bag on his belt as though the answers might be found in there. "Very well. You will tell me the name of the place. And you will be coming into the tomb with us."

"What? Why?"

Merken smiled. "As our official artist. To immortalise the night's work in oils."

"But ... you said you had no interest in being immortalized!"

"What can I say...?"

Bez felt fury, a wild and impotent fury rise within him. "No. You can't do that. It's not what we agreed!"

"We agreed nothing," said Merken. "You'll do what I say, at sword point if need be. And I want to keep you close in case I need to kill you."

In an instant of fury, Bez resolved if there was to be a death, it would be Merken's.

25

In the small dark hours, they passed into the tomb, through the arch shaped like an eagle's head. Bez could not help but feel they were entering the belly of a dry, dusty beast and towards their doom. His guts roiled with fear and lack of ale; automatically, his hands went to his sketching pad. He dashed off a sketch of the group as they moved through the crypts lined with the bodies of priests of old. Artistry was in the details and, with just a certain line here and a shaded portion there, he transformed the figure of Rantallion Merken into something twisted and ancient and sinister as though he was one of the desiccated priests who'd just got up for a moment to have a bit of a wander.

When they reached the first threshold, Bez held back, sitting down to draw a picture of the genuinely horrible carvings and arcane symbols before it on the floor. He realised the carvings – the hands and the faces – were not entirely still. They twitched, they yearned. Bez suspected what they wanted, but said nothing. If that idiot thug Cope – his jaw still ached from where she'd clocked him – or that vile Merken wanted to feed themselves to the door then so be it. Bez kept his thoughts to himself and made a note of all their suggested answers to the riddle, throwing in a handful of random phrases himself to show willing.

WITHIN THE HOUR, Bez was sitting beside a pitiful fire, feeling wretchedly sorry for himself; a state of being both unnatural and unwelcome. The fall into the Surprising Pit had soaked and ruined most of his work. His pad of Instant Pictures and his Book of Faces had come wetly apart and he attempted to salvage what he could by drying individual leaves by the side of the fire.

The wizard Pagnell looked scornfully at Bez's sketch of jaffled cake. "You drew a picture of ... food?"

"My muse was hungry," said Bez and explained. The wizard failed to appreciate genuine art and couldn't see the wistful sorrow suffusing the picture, nor, hopefully, the faint map of their progress through the tomb Bez had hidden within it.

Pagnell put it aside and touched the soggy Book of Faces. It was open to the picture of Pagnell's girl, Spirry. Bez's throat constricted. Why had he left it open at that page? Idiot! Bez hoped his panic didn't show. Pagnell couldn't know Bez had told Merken about the girl, that he had provided the means of blackmailing the wizard. It was just a picture; an image of a child seen in the corn market, the day before yesterday.

"You drew this?" asked Pagnell.

"Uh. Yeah."

"It's very good."

And Bez knew. He knew the wizard knew.

Bez had hoped for Pagnell as an ally, an accomplice if they needed to make a bid for freedom. Now, that seemed increasingly unlikely.

THE ROAD of trials through the tomb continued. The darkness compounded the oppressive horror in Bez's breast, the feeling this was an unending hell, that time and reality had lost all meaning, that he was doomed to spend forever in this horrid dark, that his blessed, sun-kissed existence before Foesen's tomb was only a dream, and one to which he would never return. Bez cursed himself for hanging around with Stentor for too long; *blessed sun-kissed existence*? *doomed to spend forever*? There may have been a sun-kissed existence once, long ago, but his memory of it had faded with every embellishment he had been required to make to his works in order to ensnare the paying populace.

In the grimlock cavern, Bez stood painting with a makeshift easel, while gibbering muppets capered around, waving their weapons in his face and mocking his work. Yeah, this was a hell, one he had visited in his nightmares before. Next to him, two upstart grimlocks were attempting to ape his style on picture boards of their own. Their chosen medium had shifted from paint to blood. Bez might have found some amusement in that metaphor, but he didn't have the time for reflection. Bez had a commission to execute: Queen Susan upon her majestic throne, with her consort and soon-to-be prince at her side. As Bez worked on the image, he could not stop the truth coming through in his brushstrokes: that of the two of them, Rantallion Merken was the more disgustingly repugnant and worthy of death. The horrible old soldier was fretting and fussing over the velvet purse sitting on the top of the grimlock's treasure pile which he had not let far from his sight or touch all the time they had been down here.

Interesting though that was, Bez's eye was drawn time and again to the high walls of the cavern and the small chimney-like fissure at the top, leading to the open air. He sucked his belly and thought. Yeah, a nimble fellow could squeeze through there; maybe, probably, it only looked too narrow because it was so far away.

On the floor next to him, the two grimlock artists were taking shell-knives to each other's bellies, apparently in search of new painting materials. It seemed all creative types had to suffer for their art.

Bez studied Lorrika as she crossed the tiled floor of death traps.

Despite the arrow injury to her arm along with her other scrapes and knocks, she still moved with the easy grace of a cat. Bez sketched, primarily intent on noting down the shapes and colours of the tiles she trod, but he also had time enough to dash off a couple of cartoons of Lorrika herself, poised, reaching, stepping. Yeah, he was becoming more and more convinced Chainmail Bikini Woman would soon be retired from the city's evening News reports and replaced by Ripped Leather Bikini Woman (or Cat Girl; he still hadn't decided).

"Do you never give it a rest?" said Merken, disdainfully.

"It's called suffering for your art," said Bez, "Suffering is the fuel of great art and right now I'm totally on fire."

"That might be arranged."

"You could just leave me here."

"Pretty sure I threatened to kill you if you suggested turning back again."

"Not suggesting turning back. You could just leave me, collect me on the way out. I'm sure I'm just holding you up."

The old fart said something Bez didn't quite catch and then, without warning, shoved him out onto the tiled floor.

Bez tried to stop himself but not before coming down on a green oval tile. He felt it give slightly beneath his feet. Bez froze upon that moment, waiting for the click or the crunch which would precede his death. Nothing occurred.

"Lucky first step," laughed Merken, laughing all the harder as Bez swore and wept. "The bard and I are coming next!"

As the ale ebbed from his system over the hours, Bez filled up the space with passionate hatred for Merken. Now he had nothing else and was awash with a reckless rage. It spilled over and onto others. Bez hated the giant swordswoman, Cope: she was a mindless lackey of the bloody invaders and the first one to bring him to Merken's attention. Bez hated Pagnell: he should have been a confederate and confidant to Bez. Together they could have dispatched Merken before escaping this well of tortures; but he'd turned out to be nothing of the sort. And Bez hated Lorrika: she was a proper stooge like Cope, with nothing to gain from serving the Amanni now her master Abington was dead. If she didn't make it out of this place alive then it was no-one's fault but her own. It seemed Ripped Leather Bikini Woman would outlive her inspiration. It would be a posthumous tribute to a girl Bez had once had a soft spot for. *Ripped Leather Bikini Woman, the Ghost Who Walks*. Oh, that was actually rather good. Bez warmed to the idea and felt a keen, sweet grief for the poor girl already.

When finally, after heart-pounding terror and dangers unnumbered, Bez found himself lying on the steps on the far side of the hall, the side of his face aching keenly from a burn, his belly growling, and a numbness in his hand where something had savagely raked him, the rage had not subsided.

Merken towered over him and scoffed. "Damned fools. Time to go. Pipsqueak, lead the way."

The soldier looked away, oblivious to the torment he had inflicted on others, giving instructions for them to all move on. The damned old goat didn't even care.

Cope and Lorrika led the way out. Pagnell in his freshly ripped coat followed closely behind. Merken paused to look back at the frenetic efforts of the grimlock tribe to close the gap on them. Why was he looking? What did he care?

Bez slipped out the knife he had hidden in his trousers when fleeing the grimlock cavern. As Merken turned to leave, Bez held it out. There was no effort needed. The man practically impaled himself. The old bugger blinked in incomprehension. Bez pulled at the strings on the velvet purse and tugged it away as Merken staggered back, looking down at the tile he had trodden on.

Merken sighed. The damned man just sighed as if this was a petty inconvenience, nothing more. And then the trap took him. In that final instant, Bez caught the briefest expression of world weary regret and bitter disappointment in Merken's face. An ordinary person would have missed it, but the gaze of the artist was all-encompassing. Bez saw that bitterness and regret, committing it to memory. He'd revive it for a little portrait he'd hang on the tavern wall once he was out. He'd share it with the world and make sure everyone saw Rantallion Merken for what he was.

Bez shoved the velvet purse out of sight and hurried to catch up with the others. Cope appeared in the doorway, waving for him to hurry.

"Where's Merken?" she asked.

"What...?" Bez made a big pretence of looking back. "He was just behind me. He..."

Cope scoured the hall but there was nothing to see. A field of tiles, scattered with debris, wreaths of smoke drifting across it. Who could tell whether that piece of limb was Merken's; which shreds of clothing had once belonged to the wicked man?

"He's gone," said Cope.

"He totally has!" breathed Bez in his best shocked voice.

"*Lether yanera*!" screamed one of the nearest grimlocks shaking his axe furiously.

Bloody snitch, thought Bez. He flicked the treacherous creature a few gestures which required no translation.

"He's gone," said Cope. She pulled Bez through the door and closed it behind them.

26

There was nothing to barricade the door with in case the grimlocks managed to cross the floor. Nonetheless, Cope grabbed a chuck of trap-flung stone and wedged it under the door for what good it would do.

"He's gone," she said for the third time.

"Great," said Lorrika. When Cope gave her a sharp look, explained, "I was being sarcastic. This is not good."

"He *was* a great man," said Cope.

Bez bit back a bitter, sarcastic response.

"Let's leave history to be the judge," said Pagnell diplomatically, considering the way before them. "We'll just have to manage without him. Things are going to get tougher ahead, not easier."

"Ahead?" said Bez. "I'm sorry. I thought for a moment there you said, *ahead*."

Pagnell pointed at a simple stone archway. "That's the third of five thresholds. We're over halfway."

"Are you insane?" said Bez. "The man who brought us here under duress is dead. We're not prisoners anymore."

"Okay," said Lorrika, frowning. "What are the alternatives, Bez?"

"We go back," said Bez. "We leave, depart, withdraw, get the hell out of here. We grab our things, shrug and head back to the surface."

Pagnell knocked on the door. "Um. Grimlocks, anyone?"

"We deal with them."

"Make a deal with them?" said Cope.

"No, you simpleton. *Deal* with them."

"Maybe we can pretend they don't exist," suggested Lorrika.

It took Bez a second to realise Lorrika wasn't being facetious.

"Perception is everything," she said. "At least, that's what Rabo Poon believed. When we close our eyes, can we be certain the world is still there?"

"I'm going to risk saying yes," said Pagnell.

"Defeatist," she muttered. "If we concentrate hard enough, maybe we can remake the world beyond that door as we wish it."

"Oh, come on people," said Bez. He gave Cope's arm an appraising squeeze – gods, the woman's muscles were hard as stone! "We have the greatest swordswoman in the world here and she's got a sword. I bet nearly all of those grimlocks are dead. A bit of the old snicker-snack and that's the rest sorted."

"*Snicker-snack*?" queried Lorrika.

"I am under instructions," said Cope. "If the tooth-mage tries to run before we get to the Quill of Truth, I'm to *damn well kill him*."

"Instructions from a dead man. All bets are off."

Cope seemed uncertain. Bez could work with uncertainty. The warrior pulled out the pack of instruction cards from her jerkin pocket and searched through them.

Bez took advantage of her confusion. "We know the route back. We've walked it once. I've made a few notes of my own. We could actually survive this thing, yeah?"

Neither Pagnell nor Lorrika jumped to agree with him. It was perplexing.

"I mean, Lorrika, why are you even down here? You want to steal some stuff? Fine, let's go back up top and rob the great and good of Ludens blind."

"I'm not a thief," she said.

"Right. Course you're bloody not. So, what is it then?"

She shrugged. "It's the technical challenge, isn't it?"

"Is it? You want to put yourself through all this, stand in front of a great big magic feather, so you can tick it off your list? Didn't put you down as a follower of Buqit."

"I'm not. But the key to a happy life is the setting and completion of goals."

"It would be something, wouldn't it?" agreed Pagnell. He saw the disbelief on Bez's face. "Oh, come now. Have a little professional curiosity. A wizard, a news-bard-person and a … a recreational treasure seeker. Down there lies magic, wealth and the greatest news story to hit this town since the invention of the falafel."

Cope held up a card. "What's a *tontine*?"

Pagnell frowned. "I think it's a kind of musical instrument."

"Probably not relevant then," said Cope and put the cards away.

"Well?" said Bez.

Cope nodded. "Yes, apart from the cut to my chest, I'm fine, thank you."

Bez swore a silent curse on the literal-minded. "What do you think about our situation?"

"Oh," said Cope. "We're going on. We have to."

"But do we?"

"I want to. The Quill of Truth is the only way I'm going to find the answer to my question."

"Maybe we can answer it for you," said Bez. "Save you the trouble."

"Oh, I don't think so. It's a very deep question. Lots of layers. You really, really have to think about it."

Something thumped against the door. The wedge beneath it held, but Bez couldn't see it lasting long.

"Onward," cried Pagnell.

They moved down the tunnel as the thumps continued, through the third threshold, and towards another door.

"What do we face next?" asked Cope.

Pagnell had few notes left to consult. "The, um, Vice of the Infidels. *Only a true shepherd can guide the faithful through.* Doesn't have a friendly ring, does it?"

The doorway in front of them was no wider than a common townhouse's, although it was a good ten feet high. The open door was several inches thick and either made entirely of riveted metal or plated with it. Pagnell swung the door experimentally.

"So?" said Bez.

Pagnell shrugged and looked inside. The tunnel extended beyond the light of the torch. "There are regularly placed holes in the floor," he noted.

"Maybe something shoots up through them," said Lorrika. "Noxious gas?"

"Vicious spikes," said Bez.

"Sausages," said Cope.

Bez could have slapped the woman, but held back. Not because she was a woman but because she would have certainly slapped him back. "Sausages?"

"Would fit through those holes."

"This is meant to be a deadly trap."

"Poisoned sausages," said Cope, undeterred.

"If we ever enter a trap called the Barbecue of Doom, I'll look out for poisoned sausages. But this is the Vice of the— What was it, Pagnell?"

"Stay here," said the wizard, taking the torch from Cope. He ventured down the corridor.

"We'll just wait here, yeah?" Bez shouted after him. "Scream if you need anything."

As the torchlight faded, darkness closed around them. From behind the hall door came the sounds of continuous bashing and thumping.

"Cope: tell Bez about your great quest," Bez heard Lorrika say.

"I'm sure he's not interested," said Cope.

"I think he will find it ... enlightening." There was an

amused tone in Lorrika's voice.

"Very well," said Cope's voice. "My quest is in the form of a question, given to me by High Shepherdess Gwell. Once I have understood the answer, I will know my true purpose and understand what I must do with my life. In all honesty, it is a vulgar question, but I understand truth can come from the basest sources."

"The question," prompted Lorrika.

"Yes," said Cope. "In search of a true answer, I have tracked beasts from the Aklan Plateau to the sea, and observed their ways. I have consulted the mage academics of Aumeria. I have studied philosophy with the wisest men of Carius. I have learned the Finoreans believe the great black is the spirit of their forefathers. I have heard the Ainuma legend of the demon grizzly. I fought with one in the Yarwish forests while trying to inspect its leavings and I kept one of its teeth as a keepsake but I—"

"The question!" snapped Lorrika.

"Of course—"

The hammering on the wedged door through which they'd recently passed changed abruptly in tone. One hard thump and there was a scraping and twisting sound: of wood coming apart, of something being forced open.

"Gods!" yelled Lorrika. "Inside!"

Blindly, they moved forward in the dark, through the thick door to the hole-lined tunnel. Bez reached out for the door; felt hands bigger than his reach over and ram it shut behind them. There was the solid unarguable sound of several bolts sliding into place.

"Did you do that, Cope?" said Bez.

"Do what?" said Cope.

"Anyone?"

"I didn't touch anything," said Lorrika. "Cope?"

"What?"

"Did you do that?"

"What?"

The yellow light of the torch grew: bobbing and weaving along the tunnel towards them.

"Okay, okay," said Pagnell, a little out of breath. "Some of the flagstones wobble. Not sure why. There's a door down the other end, locked in some way. I don't think the trap is set off until both doors are—" He stared at the closed door.

"Cope did it," said Bez without hesitation.

"Can't leave you alone for a minute!"

"Because Lorrika told me to!" said Cope.

"I never!" Lorrika protested.

"Oh, and I suppose you always do what people tell you do, do you?"

Cope appeared to give this some thought. Whatever that thought might have been was interrupted by a clunk and a grind from above.

"I have a bad feeling about this," said Bez.

Spikes of black iron, two feet long, emerged from holes in the roof even as the ceiling slowly began to descend. Lorrika, quicker thinking than the others, shifted her feet away from the holes in the floor. Bez leapt in alarm but no spikes came up.

"Top and bottom match," said Pagnell, forefinger pointing down. "Pegs in holes."

"We're going to get squashed?" squeaked Bez. "The Vice of the Infidels. Why is it never a metaphor?"

"We have to get out," said Lorrika reasonably, pushing past Pagnell.

She had not gone far when the ceiling, which had been descending at a sluggish crawl, gave a *thunk* and dropped an inch all at once.

"Whatever you just did – don't!" said Bez.

Lorrika looked down at her feet. She shifted her balance and the paving stone she stood on rocked. The ceiling dropped another inch. "Look."

"What?" said Cope.

Lorrika rocked the stone again and the ceiling dropped again.

"Which part of *don't* is confusing you?" squeaked Bez.

"The more we move, the sooner we die," said Pagnell.

"Grand!" muttered Bez. "We just stand here and wait to die. That's some plan!"

"We would have had more time to think about it if someone hadn't shut the door!"

Bez glared furiously at Cope. "So what do we do?"

"We find a way out, right?" said Lorrika, already exploring along the floor, testing stones and feeling at the seams. She had the nub of chalk in her hands and was marking each stone in turn. "Don't tread on the crosses."

A thumping noise began on the door behind them. It sounded distant, muffled.

"They'll not get through that so easily," said Cope.

"And we'll have the same problem at the far door," said

Pagnell. "Neither will release until the trap has gone through its full cycle."

"Cycle?" said Bez. "You mean...?" Speared by spikes or crushed by the descending ceiling. It wasn't much a choice of deaths. Bez was unhelpfully put in mind of the grimlocks' song, of jam composed of lungs and spleens and wobbly kidneys in their goo. "What kind of depraved sadist would come up with a contraption like this?" he demanded of no one in particular.

"Kavda the Builder," answered Pagnell. "Although I don't think he was either depraved or a sadist."

"You don't think? You *don't* think? A huge mechanical mouth designed to mush us up into paste! *Not* depraved? You have to give me sadistic at least!"

"A lot of this does seem a bit excessive, true. But, it's like Lorrika said, it's the technical challenge. I believe Kavda the Builder was more interested in whether something like this could be done, not if it should be done."

The tips of the descending spikes were now at eye level. Bez shifted his head so it wasn't in any danger of getting poked by one. Cope took two of the spikes in hand and, for no visible reason, tried to bend them away from each other. It was pointless activity, but Bez guessed if you spent your life hitting, squashing and bending things then why change your ways right at the end.

"Well, marvellous," he said. "We're all about to die the most horrible deaths imaginable—"

"Do you spend a lot of time imagining deaths?" asked Cope.

Bez ignored her. "—but, it's okay, because the guy who

made this didn't really mean any harm. Let's spend the last few minutes of our lives in silent admiration the craftsmanship of this bloody inescapable magic trap."

Cope grunted. She had bent the spikes maybe an inch out of true. They were no less spiky and no less deadly, but there was an odd sense of achievement on her imbecilic face. She moved forward, avoiding a flagstone marked with a cross and set to work on two more spikes.

"It's not inescapable," said Pagnell, quietly, to himself.

"What?" said Bez.

"An inescapable trap would be dangerous."

"What? Yes. Obviously totally dangerous! You do know it's going to kill us?" The fact he was having to explain this while stooping to avoid the ceiling was beyond stupid.

"Kavda was very safety conscious," said Pagnell. "That note of his. He made sure his builders wore protective boots while filling the acid pools. He was a details man. He was down here every day, overseeing the construction. He must have considered the possibility someone, himself even, could have accidentally triggered this trap. There has to be a reset switch, or a secret passage to get out."

"There are no secret passages in this place," said Lorrika, coming back up the tunnel, at a crouch.

"Okay, no secret passages." Pagnell scuttled around in frantic thought. Bez hoped the wizard could produce evidence he had a remarkable brain before the descending stones did the job for him.

"Vice of the Infidels," Pagnell murmured.

"Yes?" said Bez.

"Only a true shepherd can guide the faithful through."

"Yes?"

"A true shepherd."

"Yes."

"A shepherd."

"Not sure repetition is the answer."

"What's special about a shepherd?"

"Not a lot," said Lorrika. She took a nasty sharp thing from her belt and shoved it in the narrow gap between wall and descending ceiling. It instantly snapped under the pressure.

"They have sheep," called Cope as she bent spikes.

"Yes," said Pagnell. "What else?"

"Rams."

"Yes."

"Lambs."

"*Apart* from the animals," Pagnell groaned.

Cope grunted loudly. The spikes in her grip were now gently curved, like the fangs of a serpent. She moved off in search of others, the giant woman almost bent double under the falling ceiling.

"A crook," she said. "You know, their staff."

"Is this helpful?" said Bez. "Because I'm struggling to see the benefit..."

Pagnell considered the grimlock spear-turned-torch in his hand. He stabbed it into one of the holes in the floor. It sank a distance.

"You're not going to be able to prop the ceiling up with that," said Bez.

Pagnell shook his head.

"You think there's a catch or lever down one of the holes," said Lorrika. "A release switch—"

"—That would be pressed by the descending spikes—"

"—Or could be activated by a man with a stick—"

"—And Kavda and the high priests of Buqit would have known which hole."

A quiver of excitement and dread fluttered through Bez's innards; excitement there might be a way out and dread he might die with the hope of release so close. "What are you waiting for?" he said.

Pagnell bent the spear in the hole, snapped it in half, and passed one half to Lorrika. "Start down the far end," he said. She scurried away.

Pagnell waggled his half a spear in hole after hole, bent-backed as he worked along. "Got anything long and thin?" he asked Bez.

Bez was about to make a glib comment when he remembered he still had a paintbrush on him. He whipped it out and began to jam it in holes.

"Jiggle it a bit," said Pagnell.

"Take it from me," said Bez, "I'm jiggling for all I'm worth."

The space between floor and ceiling had shrunk to the point Bez was crawling on hands and knees. Ahead, Cope was forced to scuttle like a crab, still yanking on spikes whose tips were scant inches off the floor.

"They're not magic either, you know," said Pagnell.

"What?" said Bez.

"These traps. You said it was a magical trap. It's not. Kavda was an engineer, a scholar of natural philosophy. This trap, I'm sure there's a cunning pulley mechanism or such to raise the stones again but, at the moment, this is just falling stones trying to kill us."

"I don't see the difference," said Bez, crawling to the next set of holes. "Magic. Natural philosophy. What makes rocks fall to the ground if not some form of magic?"

"It is the earth breathing in," said Cope, speaking in grunts as she struggled through the forest of spikes.

"The earth is doing what?" said Pagnell.

There was a loud and piercing crunch from several points along the tunnel. Bez turned awkwardly in the rapidly shrinking space to look back. Spikes which had been pulled out of their vertical alignment by Cope no longer matched up to the corresponding holes. They pressed against the floor and, for the time being at least, stopped the stones' descent.

"Oh, gods, you're a genius," said Pagnell.

"I didn't know if it would work," said Cope.

The bracing spikes creaked and groaned in a way no metal should.

Pagnell attacked the holes with his half spear with renewed intensity. Bez did the same. "We can do this," he whispered to himself.

Cope, who had nothing to jab into the holes (the ceiling was too low for her to use her sword) worked herself backwards to get out of their way. "Bon Jowen, the Carian philosopher, told me the world, which is a living goddess, breathed out life in one long breath and is now breathing in again," she explained. "It is the breath of the earth which sucks all objects downwards."

A trapped spike screamed and buckled. Another three

followed in quick succession. The ceiling dropped a hand's span, pushing Bez flat in a crawlspace no higher than that under the house he grew up in. He had to turn his head sideways to stop his chin being crushed.

"Oh, this world sucks all right," he said, somewhere between a gasp and a sob. He rammed his paintbrush down the point of a spike and into a hole and wiggled frantically.

"Can't breathe," grunted Cope.

Pagnell flailed. Bez couldn't see but something very much like a boot slapped into his side.

"Keep ... keep..."

The paintbrush wouldn't come out of the hole; there wasn't enough room. Bez would have screamed but there was no room in his lungs either. "I'm really not happy about this at all," he whispered.

There was click in the floor beneath his pinned ear. Slowly, but decidedly, the ceiling lifted. Bez didn't say anything, didn't dare hex things with shouts of relief or disbelief. He lay there until Pagnell put a hand under his arm.

"We did it."

"We did?"

"One of us did."

"Yeah," said Bez, dazed.

There was room for them to manage a stooped walk. Bez let himself be guided forward, stepping over the wobble stones to the far end where Lorrika was already at the now open door.

"Found it," she said, pointing to a hole in which the half a grimlock spear was firmly wedged.

"That was close," said Cope, flexing her shoulders.

"Well done on the trick with the bent spikes. Kudos," said Pagnell. He held out a fist to her. She looked at it.

"I don't know what you expect me to do with that," she said.

"Does no one do fistbumps round here?" said Pagnell and shrugged. "Look, there's the fourth threshold!"

Back down the corridor, there was torchlight.

"Grimlocks. Oh, grand," said Bez.

They closed the door behind them. Bolts thunked into place and the machinery of the trap began to lower the ceiling again. It was a glorious sound to Bez's ears, if short-lived. There was a click, the grinding ceased, and the door unbolted itself. Lorrika pushed the door closed again, firmly. *Thunk, clunk, grind, click.* The door unlocked again.

"I'd wager we've permanently disabled the Vice of Infidels," said Pagnell.

"Which means?" said Bez.

"We run. We run quickly."

Bez found himself being dragged along the tunnel. With every stride, he felt the growing wrongness of it all. Treasure and professional curiosity be damned. He would trade it all for a tankard of Old Pentacular.

27

In the gloom, Bez stumbled on the bottom step. He hadn't been counting but they had descended for what felt like a long way. The dying torch Pagnell carried was illuminating nothing now but itself. The hollow echo of their footsteps told him they were in a large open area, but even Bez's keen vision could make out little of the dark space around them. Apart from a flat stone floor and some long lumpy shapes lying on the ground ahead.

"What is this place?" asked Lorrika.

Pagnell had slowed to a walk and was pointlessly attempting to look through his remaining sheets and notes. "I genuinely have no idea. We've lost the diary of Handzame the Unlucky, along with half of Abington's journal."

Cope dropped to her knee beside one of the shapes on the floor. It was four feet long and a lumpy lozenge shape.

"Careful now," said Bez. "That might be one of them poisoned sausages you warned us about."

"It is clearly too large to be a sausage," said Cope. She dug her hands into its bobbly surface and ripped it apart. "Besides it appears to be made mostly of hair and fur and bone."

"You've obviously never ordered the market-day special in the Kidgate Tavern," remarked Lorrika.

Bez crouched beside Cope. It was indeed made from pieces of fur and fibres, wrapped around fragments of bone and other hard materials. It was as if the contents of a town ditch had been scooped out and left to dry in the sun. There were dozens of them, in various stages of dusty decomposition.

"I got nothing," said Bez.

Cope pulled out a long piece of bone. Bez was no anatomist, but guessed it might be a human thigh bone. Cope wrapped a bundle of matted fur, straw and thick cobwebby stuff around the end of it before lighting it from Pagnell's torch. It burned brightly.

She nodded in approval, then put her torch to one of the nearest lumps. It caught in an instant.

There was now light enough to properly see the square hall. Walls, ceiling and floor were of blocks of cleanly cut stone. There were – Bez was pleased to see – no spikes, pits, suspicious holes or obvious traps. He was less pleased to see (and he spun round three times to be certain) there was no other exit from the room. There were the dozens of strange dusty lumps on the floor. There were a number of huge pots or urns along the walls to either side. There was, on top of the steps at the far end, a large lump of stone, which may once have been a carved statue, eroded by centuries of wind or rain.

What wind? What rain? thought Bez. "I have a bad feeling about this," he said aloud.

"That's just your inner pessimist talking," said Pagnell, standing on tiptoes to peer into one of the stone urns.

Cope dismembered another dry husk with some gusto. She removed a short blade and a helmet and chucked them onto the floor. The helmet bounced with a dull clang.

"We need to equip ourselves," she said.

"We need to get out of here," Bez pointed out.

"Working on it," said Pagnell, exploring the hall.

Lorrika pulled apart one of the lumps and retrieved a short-handled axe and a handful of coins. "Score!" she said, pocketing the money.

"Definitely not a thief," commented Bez.

"It's unlucky to leave coins lying around," she replied. "Well known fact." She spared the mound another glance. "Don't spiders wrap their prey up in cocoons like this?"

Bez jumped back, his eyes scouring the ceiling for monstrous spiders. When it was clear there were none, he pretended he had done no such thing.

"This isn't the work of spiders," said Cope.

"And you're the expert, are you?" said Bez.

"There's no flesh in these. No meat. No digestible materials."

"Enough with the sausage theory."

"It's just twigs and bone and metal." She took out a curved section of worked metal armour and brushed it off. Sorcerous runes were worked into the material. She pulled out a larger piece, a black chest plate, also covered in arcane symbols. "Is that—?"

"—Amanni armour," said Lorrika.

"Maybe you've found the final resting place of Handzame the Unlucky," called Pagnell from where he stood at the base of the eroded carving.

"Don't spiders suck all the juicy goodness out, leaving a dry husk?" said Lorrika.

"This isn't just one body. This is all mixed up, like it's been eaten, digested and spat out," said Cope.

"Ancient dried out poop?" said Bez. "Call me old-fashioned, but not my idea of treasure."

"It's like owl pellets," said Lorrika. "They throw up whatever they can't digest."

"Either way, that's totally horrid."

Cope shushed him.

"What?" he muttered.

She shushed him again and tapped a finger to her ear. They listened. They all heard it. The approach of gibbering creatures, the flap of feet, the ringing out of weapons.

"Poop indeed," said Bez.

"You'd think they'd give up," said Lorrika.

"Possibly too stupid to give up," said Pagnell. "We need to mount a defence."

Cope scanned the room. "At the foot of that rock thing. Everyone arm yourself."

"I'm a painter, not a fighter," said Bez.

"They're going to kill us if we don't fight them," reasoned Cope.

"I have built my reputation as an objective observer. I've got to maintain some impartiality."

"Then you're going to be an impartial corpse." Cope rammed a dust-covered short sword into his hand and propelled him towards the eroded carving. As she ran, she put the torch to as many of the dried lumps as she could, creating an obstacle course of bonfires.

The rock they gathered around was shaped like a crab's pincer: a high, round-backed central piece curving down at each side, more notably to the left. As the grimlocks bounded into the room, Bez prudently sheltered in the crook of the left hand curve.

"Gods, why are there still so many of them?" he whimpered. "Are they breeding as they go?"

"Rabo Poon had a philosophical theory about that," said Lorrika, drawing the axe back to throw.

"I really don't care," said Bez.

He clutched the sword he'd been given but no real intention of using it. He had his own philosophical theory, this one about weapons and fighting. The brainless grimlocks of the Clodhopper tribe wore feathers in their heads on the basis feather-wearers were rarely found among the battlefield dead. Bez *knew* what kinds of people ended up dead in battles: the ones carrying weapons. Especially the ones who thought carrying weapons would save them. Bez might as well throw the sword aside, pull out his charcoal and paper and just draw what would undoubtedly be his final masterpiece.

The grimlocks yowled in fury as they saw their enemies. Lorrika let the axe fly. Bez didn't see where it went but he heard a hearty thunk and splat. Cope gave a roar and ran at the grimlocks, sword swinging. Pagnell took up a position on the arm of rock just in front of Bez and let loose with his soporific spells. Bez captioned the scene in his mind. *The battle of the idiot warrior, the delusional thief and the bloody dentist.*

Bez turned away, closed his mind to it all, and looked at the stone formed around him instead. It wasn't a natural formation, he could see that much. There was deliberation in its contours; an almost, well, shape – as though it was ready to burst into some recognisable form. Like the sculptor's block, if one could just chisel away that which wasn't right, a pre-existing form would be revealed beneath.

Cope yelled. Grimlocks screamed.

Bez put his hand to the rock. It yielded to his touch. The filth of centuries fell away and revealed the dusty reality beneath. A series of branch-like rods with finer rods running off from them in tight rows like the needles of a fir tree or—

"Feathers?"

Pagnell looked down at him from the top of the dusty pile. "Stop hiding! Do something!"

"Um..."

Bez gently levered himself away from his safe spot and looked carefully. Yes, from the angle of the feathers, *that* would be the neck, *that* dirt-covered block could conceivably be a curled up talon and – he followed the shape round – therefore *that* protuberance Pagnell stood on would have to be the head. And the beak. Tiny puffs of air appeared just to the side of Pagnell's feet. *It's breathing!* his mind yelled. How come no one saw it was breathing?

"Oh, crap," said Bez softly.

"Do something, man!" shouted Pagnell.

"I am doing something. I'm being quiet and so should you. Move away. Quietly."

An arrow flew past Bez and embedded itself in the mound; the body. "Please don't," he squeaked. In a moment of terrified madness he found himself trying to shush the arrow.

At the centre of the melee, two grimlocks threw themselves at Cope. She eviscerated one with a sword swipe and tossed the other away. It collided with the bird's head, just below Pagnell's feet.

An eye opened: black in a circle of gold.

"*And Buqit came down from the abode of the gods in the form of the giant eagle Tudu*," Bez whispered.

"What?" said Pagnell. It was all he had time to say.

The enormous eagle reared, flinging Pagnell backwards. It shook itself out, driving who knew how many years of rock dust and muck from its body, creating a choking cloud which obscured everything for a long and dreadful moment.

As the dust settled, the silhouette of Tudu loomed, larger than a house, wings wider than ships' sails. Humans and grimlocks alike had seconds in which to re-evaluate who they were fighting and whether fighting was going to do any good. Bez had already come to a solid conclusion on that point.

He ran.

A beak descended out of the dust and swept his legs from under him. He stumbled and rolled over one of the eagle pellets on the floor: the remains of one of the beast's ancient meals. Tudu stepped forward and shrieked. The god-eagle's cry was the screech of a thousand battle horns. Bez could see himself reflected in the black pools of its eyes. He was a tiny, miserable dot, and he knew he was about to die.

A grimlock spear rebounded off the bird's flank.

Tudu screeched, turned and snatched up the offending grimlock in its sharp beak. Grimlock weapons were thrown, Tudu rounded on the throwers. From the floor, Bez could see Lorrika caught in the middle. She tried to get clear, sidestepped the swipe of a grimlock knife and, her back turned, was knocked to the ground by a savage blow from the eagle's beak. A talon came forward to rake her like a worm teased from the ground. Cope ran in and chopped at the raised claw. Her blade slid off the gnarled yellow hide, but it was distraction enough for Lorrika to roll away. The two of them were still beneath the creature's breast, surrounded by a confusion of battle-ready grimlocks.

The great stone hall, the billowing clouds of dust, the low and filthy grimlocks, the mighty monstrous Tudu, the two women, bloodied and about to die. It was a magnificent scene, and it was a crying shame Bez couldn't record it while fresh, so to speak. Unfortunately, he was almost entirely out of sketching paper and he couldn't remember where he'd put his charcoal. He'd just have to remember it as best he could and paint it later.

Bez kept low. He was prepared to pretend to be a corpse if anyone so much as looked his way. He was a short sprint from the entrance and he doubted Tudu could squeeze through there. No – there *was* another exit from the room: a similar doorway, in the far wall. The bloody bird had been curled up asleep in front of it. Was it luck? Chance? Or a bloody smart feeding strategy? It didn't matter; Bez had no thoughts of heading that way.

"Here! Over here!" Pagnell had stripped off his outer coat and was waving it around to attract Tudu's attention. The mammoth eagle turned to charge him, its tail swinging like the stern of a racing ship: sweeping aside any in its path.

Cope helped Lorrika up and shouted to Pagnell. "What's the plan?"

"Plan?" said Pagnell. "Well, I do have this pouch and—"

Tudu lunged at the wizard. He barely jumped back in time.

"Birds of prey," he said. "They're very good at spotting movement."

He swung his coat back and forth, the eagle's head followed it: left and right. Pagnell hurled the coat to the side as high and as far as possible, immediately standing perfectly still. The eagle's head followed the coat's trajectory to the ground. Tudu looked at the coat for a second and, unimpressed, back at Pagnell.

"Bugger," said the wizard very quietly.

One of the last remaining grimlocks attempted to spear Cope's back while no one was looking. How she saw it coming, Bez had no idea. Nonetheless, she sidestepped the thrust and gave the grimlock a hurt look.

"*Sethit tan*," it said, as though that made it all okay.

Cope slapped it aside with the flat of her blade and ran to assist Pagnell. Bez could see it was too far to run; she was too slow. Tudu snagged the wizard by the shoulder and tossed him screaming into the air before catching him in its open mouth. The eagle gulped. The scream died.

Cope yelled. The bird turned. The giant warrior did not hesitate. She leapt high and brought the sword round, over her head. Feathers sheared away, snapping like saplings in a storm. Tudu's head reared angrily before it lunged at the warrior. Cope's sword met its beak and bounced off. Tudu screeched – it didn't like food which fought back – but Cope stood her ground. Lorrika scurried in from the side, a bundle in her hand. Underneath the monster's head she ran, swinging up and over, and dropped the dead wizard's tattered coat across Tudu's eyes.

Tudu froze for a second. With a small exhalation it relaxed into a roosting position, stock still. It made some small, breathy sighs and settled slightly, as if ready for sleep.

Bez couldn't believe it. "What the...?"

Tudu's head turned sharply to face him.

"Damn."

It took a step forward.

Cope shuffled out of its way. The massive head turned blindly, head cocked. Cope stopped moving. The bird tilted its coat-draped head from side to side, listening with whatever passed for bird's ears. Cope remained still. Tudu screeched in her face. Cope held her nerve. She was brave, Bez had to give her that, although brave really was just another word for stupid.

Speaking of stupid...

The last of the grimlocks, with a veritable crown of feathers in its head and a pair of shell axes in it hands, charged. Its weapons whirling like windmills.

"*Pethita lethera*!" it screamed hoarsely. Even if there had been anyone else there to hear it (or translate it), they were hardly the most inspiring of final words.

Tudu wheeled on the grimlock, cutting off its death scream and more besides with a vicious nip of its beak.

Cope used the distraction to get to her feet. She ran to join Lorrika, but the blindfolded bird heard, turned and came after them. The two women were already sprinting. Lorrika veered to the far exit, saw it was pointless and angled towards one of the huge stone urns instead. She jumped, scrambled up the curved side and vaulted inside. Cope was a second behind her. She was far less nimble but grabbed the lip and hauled herself up and into the pot head first. Following the clatters and scrapes was no challenge for a visually impaired bird. Tudu was soon on top of them, jabbing and pecking at the urn. Its beak was too broad to get inside but only just. Bez couldn't see them, but he could picture them: cowering in the base of the huge pot, utterly cornered.

The grimlocks were all dead. There was no movement apart from the eagle's relentless efforts to get into the stone urn. Bez edged towards the entrance, eyes fixed on Tudu. Its blindfold might slip. It might just possibly hear him crawling. He prepared to play dead at any moment.

"Bez!" Lorrika's shout was muffled but carried. "Bez! Distract it!"

Bez smiled wryly. If by distract it she meant let it eat him then, sorry, he was going to have to pass. And really, what else could he do? Bez picked himself up with geriatric slowness and crept the last few yards to the door. Lorrika's shouting was only compelling the beast to even more frantic attacks on the urn. There were jagged scrape marks on the rim, but Tudu would have to work at it long and hard to crack it open.

"Bez! Help us!"

"Sorry, sweetheart," he murmured, and left. He actually meant it: he *was* sorry, in a deep and profound way that would stay with him forever, inspire him to great works of art, and which would give him an air of moody introspection when chatting up girls in taverns.

As he jogged up the dark steps, he visualised the way back out of the tomb. It was up the stairs, through the permanently broken Vice of the Infidels, across the grimlocks' makeshift bridge over the room of traps, then back through the grimlock cavern, collecting various treasures on the way and up through the chimney crack in the ceiling to fresh air and freedom. Easy, yeah?

He wondered what would happen to Cope and Lorrika in the end. Maybe they would simply wait it out until hunger and thirst got them. Maybe Tudu would eventually chip, bash and rip its way inside. Maybe they would attempt a bold last stand: a desperate bid for freedom. The giant warrior and the thief girl, side by side, fighting like heroes of old against impossible odds and dangers—

A shrill and agonised scream echoed up the stairs behind him. Lorrika.

"Gods! No! No! Don't!"

The scream went on a lot longer before abruptly, thankfully, it was over.

Bez shook his head ruefully and pressed on. When he

retold the tale, he would give Lorrika a better and nobler death than that, and she would be reborn as Ripped Leather Bikini Woman, celebrated heroine of the Nightly News. That would be a fitting tribute. She would appreciate it, he was sure. Would have. Would have appreciated it.

28

NEWPORT PAGNELL

The road from Qir to Ludens was well-tended, straight as a carpenter's rule, flat as a plate and as featureless as a hermit's diary. It was one of the fastest and safest roads this side of the sea, and made for mind-numbingly dull travel. There were no mighty rivers to ford, no wild creatures to fight off, and they had encountered no robbers on the road. There was almost nothing for robbers to hide behind, and the sheer tedium of the landscape was enough to make the average brigand give up on thievery and seek out a more interesting job.

Pagnell spotted Ludens when they were forty miles distant. It appeared as a brown pointy blemish on the equally brown horizon. The pointy bit was the temple of Buqit. If one was of a fanciful bent, one might imagine the peak of it glittered; that one could make out the bronzed statue which stood at the ziggurat's peak.

He leaned up against the driver's seat to get a better look.

"Another day and a half before we get there, sir," said Thedo the carter cheerfully.

Another day and half of sitting on the hard board in the back of Thedo's cart, having one's buttocks and spine hammered into jelly by the deceptively fine vibrations of the wheels on the road. Spirry was in the rear of the cart, sitting cross-legged on a grain sack in a little hidey-hole of crates and barrels she had created for herself. Her blonde hair was golden bright in the sunlight. With skin so pale, Spirry should have burned and peeled in this hot climate, but she seemed to thrive: a spring flower which craved only more and more sunshine. As Pagnell mopped his brow with the last of his clean handkerchiefs, and tried to shift himself so he could sit on a section of buttock which still had feeling left in it, he watched Spirry playing with a handful of grains of corn that had spilt from the sack.

"A day and a half," he said to her.

"I heard," said Spirry. "I have sharp ears and sharp teeth and—"

"A sharp tongue," said Pagnell.

Spirry stuck her tongue out to show Pagnell just how sharp it was. "Why did Buqit tell her people to build her city all the way out here?" she wondered.

"Who are we to question the will of the gods, little miss?" said Thedo.

"I'm sure if we do it very quietly so they can't hear, no one will mind," said Pagnell.

Spirry sniffed. "I'm all for asking questions, but there's no guarantee we'll get any answers. I ask myself things all the time. Like, why is Kestino the donkey pulling the cart and I'm the one riding it? Or, when people yawn, do deaf people think they're screaming? Or, why is it that to get to sleep you have to pretend to be asleep? You can ask these questions, but there aren't any answers."

"Competition," said Pagnell.

"What's that?" frowned Thedo.

"It's the same reason I chose a career in the fascinating world of oral hygiene and innovative dentistry."

"You said it was because there's enough suffering in the world already and it would be nice if someone could redress the balance," said Spirry.

"Yes, that, but also—"

"*And* that it's a better career than being a surgeon because, when dentists get it wrong, they get paid even more to try again; whereas surgeons are just left with the funeral bill."

"I think you're missing the keenly insightful point I was about to make, which—"

"*And* that there are hardly any other dentists in the world so you can charge what you like."

"Yes! That! Exactly that. I'm not saying the gods are into extorting money out of people for shining their general beneficence on us. Only a fool who wants to be struck down by divine fires would say it. Besides, spiritual extortion, that's what priests are for. Nonetheless, a temple to Buqit in a city of a dozen temples is only going to get one twelfth of the prayers but, in a city with just one temple..."

"I always stop by any shrines to Buqit, whatever the town," said Thedo. "Look." He reached into his grubby tunic and pulled out a pendant on a loop of string. Pagnell inspected it. A polished circle of wood with a pokerwork image of winged Buqit on one side and the words *Greetings from Qir* on the other.

"And how much did the priest charge you for this delightful piece?" asked Pagnell.

"He told me the Hierophant had bought one just like it the day before."

"How much?"

"It's not about price. Any self-respecting trader should make devotional offerings to the goddess of getting things done. See?"

Thedo passed Pagnell a notepad. It was composed of a dozen pieces of rough paper, tied together with string, with a stamped legend on the front: wonky, badly inked and already half-faded. *My List of Things To Be Done* it read, with a cheap representation of the eagle Tudu underneath.

"And you bought this too?" said Pagnell.

"The priest only charged me half price because I'd already bought the pendant. He threw in a quill and ink for free."

"We should stop paying you if this is what you're spending it on."

"It's an investment," insisted Thedo. "Anything I write in there is guaranteed to come true. And if it's not written down, it won't happen."

Pagnell opened the notepad. The first page was filled with bullet-pointed notes. It started with *Take NP and SH to Ludens* and ended with *Marry my True Love*. In the middle, squashed between *Stock Up on goods to sell* and *Return to Qir* was the item *Collect NP and the Quill of Truth in the Cornmarket.*

"We might have to play that by ear," said Pagnell. "You will pick me up somewhere, Thedo. There may be a lot of shouting and running by that point. Is the donkey going to be up to it?"

"Oh, you'd be surprised at Kestino's turn of speed when he's properly motivated."

"I'm sure I would."

The donkey tossed its head and brayed. Thedo tapped it with his long switch.

Spirry stirred the grains in her hand with a fingertip, flicking away the ones which did not please her. "When will the Amanni army arrive in Ludens?" she asked without looking up.

"In three days' time," said Pagnell, "if that sorcerer in Oopons was telling the truth. And it's not an army. General Handzame does not have enough men to call it an army."

Spirry flicked more grains. "How many men do you need to call them an army?"

"Lots."

"That's not a precise number. A hundred?"

"I suppose," said Pagnell. "Yes. You could have an army of one hundred."

"Ninety-nine?"

"I guess."

"Ninety-eight?"

Pagnell smiled tightly and bit down on a pithy response. Spirry was a fine travelling companion. She was small for one thing, and smallness was an often underrated quality in companions. She was certainly no idiot, and she definitely offered mental stimulation, but she *would* deconstruct every damnable thing she saw or heard. In Oopons, she had spent two hours arguing with a merchant, almost convincing him money was an imaginary concept.

"You can have an army of ninety-eight," said Pagnell. "You can't have an army of three. You can't have an army of twenty. Everything in between is up for debate."

"How many has General Handzame got?"

"Maybe twenty," said Pagnell. "She has her family name, enough gold for twenty men, the wizard Abington, and Rantallion Merken. It's those last two we need to worry about if anything. They may be old men, but they're dangerous."

Spirry laughed at that. "What do you lot know about old?"

"Fine. They're old for humans and they're clever."

Spirry whittled down her handful of grains to a final, perfect seed. "Cleverer than you?"

Pagnell twisted his mouth uncomfortably. "It's not enough to be clever. It's what you do with it. You know what Abington did during the plague in Dalarra, yes?"

Spirry nodded.

"Rantallion Merken is no better. Some years ago, he was paid to bring the bandit king, Lothwar, to heel. He had his lair up in the highlands where no one lived apart from the hill tribes to whom the Yarwish gave the rather disparaging nickname *mud hogs*. Merken bribed, cajoled and bullied the mud hog tribes into leading the charge against Lothwar's position. He didn't tell them Lothwar had laid concealed traps all around the area. Merken never intended the hill tribes to fight. He just needed them to spring the traps before his own men did."

"That was clever," said Spirry. "Horrible, but clever."

"And the lords who paid him were very pleased."

Spirry put a fingertip to the grain of corn and it unfurled into a green shoot, stretching like a man rising from his bed, growing and expanding until became a narrow stalk with a feathery head—

"*Spiriva! Stop it!*" whispered Pagnell harshly. He looked around to see if Thedo had noticed.

Spirry shrugged indifferently, and let the dry wind take the stalk up and away.

"If people knew who you are, what you are, life might suddenly get very difficult," murmured the wizard with nervous irritation.

Spirry smiled. "The sorcerer said Handzame was going to invade Ludens to get to the temple." It was as if the last ten seconds had never happened.

"That's the trick Merken is going to pull. They're going to use *Vanilli's Stoppered Voice.*"

"What's that?"

"Let me show you." He searched through his bags until he found a glass bottle with a cork stopper. "This is—" He pulled at the cork, grunting when it wouldn't come. He bit down on the cork and yanked, only succeeding in hurting his teeth.

"Is this the trick?" said Spirry.

Pagnell cursed silently and cast *Cowell's Frictionless Unguent* over the bottle. A clear and oily ooze appeared around the bottle neck. Pagnell gave the cork a twist and pulled it free. A blob of unguent clung to his fingertip and, without thinking, he licked it off. The unguent was shockingly bitter – the spell certainly needed some refinement – and he shuddered and spat.

"Okay," he said. "This is an empty bottle."

"It is," agreed Spirry.

Pagnell cast *Vanilli's Stoppered Voice* on it and passed it to Spirry.

"Now what?" she asked.

"Shout into it."

"Shout?"

"Into it. Yes. Anything."

Spirry took a deep breath and yelled. Her lips moved but no sound came out. She frowned and shouted some more. She produced nothing but silence.

Pagnell took the bottle back and pushed the cork into it.

"I don't see how that's going to help them invade a city with just twenty men," said Spirry.

Pagnell gave her a superior smile and smashed the bottle against the side of the cart.

"NEWPORT PAGNELL SMELLS OF SOUR YOGHURT!"

The donkey bucked in alarm at the sudden shout. "Gods' teeth!" said Thedo, equally alarmed.

"You see?" said Pagnell. "Now imagine that—"

"AND HE HAS QUESTIONABLE TASTE IN WOMEN!"

"Well, that's just not true," pouted the wizard.

Spirry snickered.

"Just imagine that – but with pots containing the war cries of a hundred men; a thousand. That's what the sorcerer sold to Merken."

"The sound of an army?"

"Throw in some fireworks – Sathean fire powder for preference: smoulders for an instant and the green smoke it produces is highly flammable – add an attack under cover of darkness and a city might think it's being invaded by an Amanni horde."

Spirry pulled an intrigued face. "That's impressive."

"Isn't it just?" said Pagnell. He lifted his coat and sniffed at his clothes. "And I don't smell of sour yoghurt. Thedo, I don't smell of yoghurt, do I?"

The cart driver tilted his head thoughtfully. "Ah, they do say northerners all smell of yoghurt, but I can't say I agree."

"Thank you, Thedo."

"I've always thought of it as a cheesy smell."

Spirry giggled, nodding.

"Yes, thank you, Thedo," said Pagnell curtly.

"You know, like it's been left out in the sun and it's gone all sweaty. Like a pair of old shoes, you know..."

"Yes. *Thank you*, Thedo!"

29

The rooms Pagnell had hired for Spirry and himself in a corner house on Cisterngate were more than adequate. They were spacious, clean, with few other occupants to pay the two travellers much attention. The only downside was the constant smell of jaffled cakes rising from the stall below their window. The smell was mouth-watering, but the cakes, which they had tried the day they arrived, weren't to Pagnell's liking. Spirry had declared a perverse fondness for them and insisted he buy her some every day.

"They're too dry," he complained, coming up the stairs with a full bag. "And not sweet enough."

"I like them," said Spirry.

"And proper jaffled cakes should be made with more butter. My grandmother used to make them with pig fat."

"Your people cook everything in fat."

"It's good for you," he said, mildly offended. "It's not a proper jaffled cake unless it's made with butter or pig fat. The Yarwish practically invented jaffling, so we should know."

"Will the Amanni invade tonight?" asked Spirry.

"Maybe. We'll go to the tavern and wait again."

Pagnell had asked around the city. Before his arrest, the wizard Abington frequented a number of alehouses and taverns, but returned to the one on Kidgate time and again. It had become a favourite. If he was going to make an appearance, it would be there.

"Do you think your plan is going to succeed?" said Spirry, which was Spirry-talk for, "*Your plan isn't going to succeed.*"

Pagnell produced a tiny bulging pouch. "Dried box moss. Smoke or ingest an ounce of this and you'll fall into a state of torpor which will last three to four days. Unbreakable. Abington is fond of carrying his pipe weed, flash powders, reagents and such on his belt. All I have to do is engage him in conversation—" he passed the bag of jaffled cakes to Spirry "—distract him – *Oh, my! What's that?* – and with a spot of my amazing sleight of hand he's stuffing box moss into his pipe."

Spirry made a doubtful noise. "And you think that will make them invite you to join their tomb expedition?"

"They need a wizard. Since I am the best wizard in town, I'm the obvious choice."

"The only wizard in town, you mean," said Spirry.

"And therefore the best."

Spirry opened the bag. She frowned, shaking it upside down to demonstrate it was empty.

Pagnell reached forward and pulled a dry jaffled cake from behind her ear. "Amazing sleight of hand," he said.

Spirry snatched the jaffled cake from him. "We need the Quill of Truth to stand any chance of completing our greater mission. Failure will be disastrous, Pagnell."

"Have faith," he said.

30

The Upgate market in Ludens was crowded and dusty. Pagnell and Spirry had wedged themselves in the small gap between a baker's stall and a cloth merchant's to watch a magician performing on a stage made from trestles laid over barrels. Spirry stood on an upturned crate to see over the crowd. The magician's robes were black and billowing, cobweb thin. Mystical shapes, embroidered in silver, hung on it like moonlit dew. He was doing a lot of talking and not a lot of magicking.

"Do you fear the gods?" asked Spirry.

"Where did that come from?" said Pagnell.

Spirry's eyebrows rose with a lazy thoughtfulness. "We're going to steal the Quill of Truth."

"Borrow."

"Without permission."

"Yes."

"I was thinking how the goddess Buqit might feel about that."

Pagnell gave the matter some thought. He was about to answer the question when Spirry asked, "Why's that woman on the stage not wearing any clothes?"

Pagnell tutted irritably. "You were asking me about the gods. And she is wearing clothes."

"Not many."

"Some."

"If I went out into the streets wearing as few clothes as that, you would have something to say about it."

An awkward uncomfortableness caught in Pagnell's throat. "I ... I certainly would. And I am grateful you've taken my advice regarding human clothing so seriously. It's okay for that woman to dress like that, with all the bangles and veils and whatnot, because it's part of her job."

Spirry wrinkled her nose. "Job? All she's doing is wandering up and down the stage, waving her arms about and winking at the men in the crowd."

"And that's her job. She's trying to add an air of ineffable mysticism to the act by appearing foreign and exotic; an alluring creature from some far off place."

"Where's she meant to be from?"

"She's not meant to *be* from anywhere. She's just trying to be foreign, in general."

"Ah. And what does *ineffable* mean?"

"Hmmm. It's hard to describe." He scratched his beard reflectively. "Of course, the magician's assistant's real job is to divert the audience's attention from noticing the trick he's about to pull."

"Trick?"

"The table he's using is clearly too thick, and there's a concealed compartment within it from which he's going to produce— What's he supposed to be doing?"

"Conjuring a banquet fit for the Hierophant's table."

"Yes. That."

Spirry stood on tiptoes to see better over the crowd. The crate she stood on wobbled. Pagnell put a foot on it to keep it steady.

"So, the magician is going to trick the onlookers into thinking he's performed magic," said Spirry. "He's making fools of them."

"We're all fools until we work out how it's done," said Pagnell.

"And the assistant is only there to distract the people from noticing how it's done?"

"Yes."

"By not wearing many clothes and appearing *alluring*."

"Yes."

Spirry thought about it. "Do you think she's alluring?"

Pagnell opened his mouth to answer. A thought struck him, and he hesitated. "I do not have questionable taste in women, Spiriva Handihaler."

She smirked.

Pagnell fumed silently for a minute while the magician produced pigeon and pineapple and pomegranate out of *nowhere*, announcing each with alliterative smugness.

"To answer your original question," Pagnell said coldly, "I believe Buqit will not object to our actions."

"You think she won't mind you stealing the Quill of Truth?"

"I think it's more of a case she won't notice, or won't bother to notice. I don't see the gods getting involved in the affairs of the world that often. Why meddle in the affairs of men when you've got priests to do it for you?"

He nudged her and pointed at a priest in the crowd. The round-faced man was watching the magician whilst hopping on one foot. He looked quite out of breath.

"What's he doing that for?" said Spirry.

"I think it's one of the items on their list of things to do."

"Or maybe he's just stubbed his toe and is keeping his weight off it."

"I don't think so."

"I could ask him."

"Don't ask him."

"He won't mind."

"*Don't* ask him," insisted Pagnell, but she was already gone.

31

The invasion came shortly after nightfall.

Pagnell and Spirry were already in the tavern on the corner of Kidgate and Mercer Row when it happened. Pagnell sipped at his tankard as shouts and roars and screams filled the streets outside. Spirry stared at her ale.

"Why do they do this?"

Pagnell looked at her. "Are you referring to beer or war?"

"Um. I was thinking of beer, but I suppose both."

"Well, beer is delicious and a good use of barley. War is stupid. Both are strangely irresistible to certain people with no consideration of how today's actions might have consequences tomorrow."

"I don't like it," said Spirry.

"Beer or war?"

The sounds of fighting faded as the hour passed. By seven bells, there were no more shouts from the streets. Those who had cowered in the tavern afraid to go home, did so. Those who had cowered at home and now needed a drink to settle their nerves took their place.

Spirry nudged Pagnell. Pagnell nodded: the wizard Abington had just walked in.

Pagnell had a hazy recollection of seeing him before, at a meeting of a wizardly order or some such in Yarwich. Tall, broad and swinging his beard about like it was his royal standard, Abington had argued with his fellow wizards, said something to upset Pagnell's friend and mentor, Tibshelf, and swanned out again. It was like having a disreputable and cantankerous uncle who no one saw except at funerals, and who only turned up to rekindle old family feuds and maybe start some new ones.

"Yep," said Pagnell softly.

"Who's the woman with him?" said Spirry.

"The one with dirt on her face?" He shrugged.

Abington and the grubby young woman took seats at a central table. He sent her off to fetch him beer.

"So, what now? When are you going to perform your amazing sleight of hand?" asked Spirry.

Pagnell squeezed the pouch of box moss in his hand, slowly flexing and unflexing his fingers. "I have to choose my moment carefully. First, I'll let him slake his thirst and—"

"Slake?" said Spirry.

"Yes, slake. It means to satisfy with drink."

"So, you're going to wait until he's had a drink or two."

"Yes."

"You should have just said that instead of using a fancy word."

"I'm going to wait until he's slaked his thirst—"

"Had a drink or two."

"—and then I've got a choice. I can charm my way into his confidence and get close to him. Or I can be generally obnoxious and grating and draw him in through confrontation, rather than ingratiation."

"The second one," said Spirry. "Definitely the second one."

Pagnell gave a joking sneer but she was right. Rubbing people up the wrong way came more easily.

So, as the two performers on their makeshift stage tried to entertain the clientele with their accounts of the day's doings, Pagnell interjected like the self-important know-it-all he knew himself to sometimes be, and criticised the quality of the artist's paintwork along with the logical consistency of their stories.

"Shut your jabber, fool!" called Abington with a scowl.

The storyteller struggled on with his tales, drawing some old chap at the back of the tavern into his account. Pagnell was about to throw some other unhelpful comments into the mix, maybe get Abington embroiled in an argument, when the tavern door was flung open and a giant of woman in Amanni armour stepped in. That she was here for Abington was certain.

While the performers stuttered in the presence of one of the supposed invaders, Pagnell leaned over to Spirry. "I want you to go back to the house. Now."

"Why?" said Spirry.

"I hadn't planned on doing this with one of Merken's soldiers watching."

"Does it make a difference?"

"She's been sent to fetch Abington. I'm out of time. Just go."

"But I haven't finished my beer," she said, looking at the pot which had stood untouched all evening.

Pagnell attempted to give her a stern look. It was easy to forget Spirry wasn't a child; stern looks just slid off her like peas from a knife. "Please," he said.

"This place is boring anyway," she replied.

"Stay in the rooms. Stay hidden."

She pouted. "You say it like I'm going to fly around the city, shouting 'Look at me!'"

He made a reproachful noise but reproachful noises were as effective as stern looks on Spirry.

As the Amanni warrior ploughed through the crowd, and the crowd nearly came to blows trying to get out of her way, Spirry slipped away.

The Amanni giantess sat at the table across from Abington and the grubby young woman. Pagnell watched their conversation, hoping to glean something of the tenor of their interactions; something to give him an edge; a way in when he approached. The wizard and the warrior weren't friends: that was as much as he could see.

He told himself he was just stalling now so, when the young woman went to the bar for more drinks, Pagnell tried to still his nervous innards, put on his best smile and crossed to their table.

"Go on then," he said, beaming as he sat down. "Tell me how it was done."

Abington was curtly angry. The woman was quizzical.

"The sneak attack on the city. Was it magic?" persisted Pagnell.

At that comment, the woman offered to put him to the sword. Well, at least he had their attention. He backtracked, made some bland comments, introduced himself, and offered a handshake which both of them pointedly ignored.

In response, Pagnell launched into his general spiel on his career in oral hygiene and tooth care, partly out of spite and partly because talk of dentistry either brought out the angry side in people or lulled them into a bored stupor. In the case of the warrior woman, Cope, it brought on wide-eyed terror. As far as Pagnell could work out, she feared he was a tooth-stealing sorcerer and in league with the fairies, which was only partially true. Offers to show her his dental tools did little to assuage her fears.

Abington was unimpressed with Pagnell's wizarding credentials and his offer to inspect Cope's teeth. Abington declared Pagnell's claims of dental prowess to be "Calumnious codswallop," and set about savagely scraping out his dead pipe. The older man had three pouches tied to the cord of his rope belt. The nearest was fringed with crumbs of pipe weed. Pagnell only needed a moment's distraction to add the box moss to it.

That distraction came almost at once with the return of the dirt-smeared woman from the bar, along with the handsome painter fellow about whose work Pagnell had been unnecessarily rude. While introductions were made and the artist chap, Bez, tried to engage Cope in some proposed artistic endeavour, Pagnell reached under the preoccupied Abington's arm, and thumbed a pinch of the box moss into the top of the pouch. What he hadn't planned for was the loop of twine holding the pouch to the belt coming loose, and the pouch dropping to the floor.

No one noticed it fall. Eyes were elsewhere as Cope rose to speak privately with Bez, and the young woman took her seat.

"Do me then," she said to Pagnell.

"Sorry?" said Pagnell. He saw her toothy grin and understood. "Yes, indeed. Open wide."

Pagnell ached to pick up the dropped pouch. It was now tainted with the narcotic box moss and if Abington saw it had fallen, he would be suspicious. He might check its contents before smoking them.

As he chit-chatted mindlessly about the young woman's dental history, he composed a plan of sorts. He would inflict a petty conjuring trick on Abington, a jaffled cake from behind the ear or something, a plainly obvious and entirely unmagical piece of legerdemain guaranteed to irk the self-important man. Behind that distraction he could bend down and retie the pouch to the belt. He even had a spell he could adapt to that end.

"You're from Carius, Lorrika," said Pagnell, espying the evidence of Carian dental work on one of her milling teeth. "Or thereabouts. Someone has tried to use beeswax to cure a rotten tooth. Failed, but tried."

"I'm amazed," said Lorrika.

"Then you're a fool!" muttered Abington.

"As I said, we're all fools until we work out how it's done," said Pagnell. "Half of magic is trickery."

"Trickery be damned," snorted Abington.

"For instance, if I was to do this..." He reached forward and was about to produce a previously palmed coin from out of Abington's beard when there was a loud metallic crunch from the corner of the room. Pagnell glanced over to see the artist chap, Bez, falling to the ground, Cope standing over him. Abington turned to look properly.

Quickly, Pagnell reached down, snagged the pouch between fingertips. At the mutter of *Nolan's Magic Thread* it secured itself tightly to Abington's belt in the space between the other two pouches. Even as he sat back, and Abington returned his attention to the conversation, Pagnell began to wonder if he'd reattached the pouch in the correct place. Abington looked down and seemed not to realise.

"So, what else can you tell about me?" said Lorrika as Abington filled his pipe with a furious energy. "What do my ears say? I've been told I've got ears like a fairy."

"That I wouldn't know," said Pagnell, smiling, relieved the tricky part of the job was done. "My experience of fairies is limited, and dentistry only extends to teeth and gums and the apparatus of the mouth. What would we be without our mouths and our voices, eh?"

"Quiet, perhaps," grumped Abington and rammed his pipe into the corner of his mouth.

Pagnell no longer cared for the old man's uncharitable mutterings. Abington just needed to take a few puffs of the pipe and he would be asleep and out of Pagnell's misery.

"Show me another tooth and I will speak all manner of truths," said Pagnell. Cope immediately placed a very recently removed cutting tooth on the table. "Well, I didn't mean it quite like that," he said.

"We're going now," Cope told Abington.

Not yet, pleaded Pagnell silently. Not just yet.

Abington extracted a bundle of fire-matches out of his robe sleeve.

"At a guess – and it is a guess," said Pagnell, looking at the tooth which had until very recently belonged to a young artist, "I'd say this is the tooth of an idiot."

Abington lit a match. "Toss a stone in this place," he said, putting it to his pipe, "and you'd hit a dozen brainless idiots."

Abington drew deeply on the pipe. Pagnell saw a curl of green smoke rise from the bowl. Green smoke? Sathean fire powder! But—

The flash of the explosion blinded Pagnell. Something hot sliced past his face. When he came groggily to his sense, his body was trying to stand, to get away from the table. The warrior woman, Cope, grabbed him firmly by the collar.

"You're going nowhere."

Pagnell blinked. "What?"

32

Pagnell blinked. "What?"

They were in the bowels of Foesen's tomb, in a hall littered with the dried, mingled remains of hundreds of individuals (most of which were now on fire). A mob of insanely tenacious grimlocks was charging at them through the room's only exit, and Bez had chosen that moment to mutter some nonsense about eagles descending from the abode of the gods.

Pagnell had no time to remonstrate with the artist or consider his words. The rock beneath his feet bucked and rose and the world twirled. Pagnell came down hard on his shoulder, the air knocked from his lungs.

A massive shape moved through a sudden cloud of dust which enveloped everything. The dust confused perspective and scale, but to Pagnell's eyes it looked like a giant bird was stalking across the room. Pagnell had a healthy dislike for birds. His mentor, Tibshelf, had owned a colourful caged bird which snapped at unwary fingers, and squawked constantly unless its cage was covered and the brainless creature was fooled into thinking it was night.

The giant bird screeched. It was like a fanfare from the world's most hateful orchestra.

A grimlock spear rebounded off the bird's flank.

Pagnell abruptly jumped to a working hypothesis. It was, as Bez had muttered, the divine eagle, Buqit's mount, Tudu. It made a certain illogical sense. The Quill of Truth was down here. No reason for it not to be guarded by the whole bloody bird.

Pagnell got to his feet. Tudu was chasing through the hall, not discriminating between humans and grimlocks. It snatched up a grimlock in its beak, flattening Lorrika on the backswing. Before it could spear her with its talons, Cope ran in and hacked at it with her longsword. Against the monster's hide the sword was only an irritant, a distraction, but it gave Lorrika opportunity to scramble away.

If they were to defeat the creature (rather than simply escape it), they would need something other than mundane weapons. Pagnell stuffed his hand in his pocket and found a small tightly-packed pouch. It contained enough box moss to put an army to sleep. He could only hope it worked on the physiology of gargantuan god-birds as well as humans.

Pagnell slipped off his outer coat, raised it to attract the bird's attention. He saw the vicious rips all along the bottom hem. "When the hell...?" he muttered. "I paid good money for this." He huffed in exasperation before waving it back and forth like a flag. "Here!" he shouted. "Over here!"

The giant eagle turned almost instantly. Pagnell's legs

trembled at the sight of its eyes. They were just like Tibshelf's vicious pet bird's: horrible beady things.

"What's the plan?" shouted Cope, helping Lorrika to her feet.

Pagnell didn't have a plan as such. It wasn't developed enough to be labelled a plan. "Plan? Well, I do have this pouch and—"

Tudu's beak jabbed down at Pagnell. It moved fast for such a huge animal. Pagnell jumped back. The beak struck the ground just in front of his feet, sending a waft of dust past his ankles.

"Birds of prey," he said, as much to himself as to anyone else. "They're very good at spotting movement." He swung the coat, left, right, left, right, left. And released.

The coat flew high, which was something; Pagnell was not one of life's great throwers. Tudu's eyes stayed on the coat as it flew up and down to the ground. Pagnell felt the weight of the box moss pouch in his hand. All he had to do was sneak round somehow, perhaps throw it into the bird's mouth...

Tudu snorted at the coat on the ground. Losing interest, it turned around and locked its eyes on Pagnell.

"Bugger," he said with feeling.

There was a grimlock yell from across the hall, but that was in a whole other world. His world was barrelling towards him on sword-like talons, a golden beak of certain death poised to strike him down no matter how he dodged. Pagnell turned to run but it was too late. The beak gripped his shoulder with vice-like pressure, forcing a scream of pain and fear from Pagnell's lungs. Tendons and muscles burned in agony. An instant later, Pagnell was up in the air: flung high and weightless.

There was no time for conscious decision making. Instinct told him to draw his arms and legs in, get the extremities out of the way. He slapped into something wet and spongy and all-enveloping; wrapped tightly about him like a blanket tucked in by an over-zealous housemaid.

It's a truth rarely aired, but generally acknowledged, that it's hard to think straight when being swallowed by a giant eagle. Images and hopes and emotions bombarded his mind. More than anything, he wanted to scream and cry and make it all go away, but he was squeezed inside a dark airlessness and had no voice. Part of his brain had retreated back in time to an anatomy lecture by some interminably dull wizard, and a diagram of a chicken's digestive system. There was a crop and gizzard and another stomach, the three of them in some sort of order: one was just a holding sack and one was where pellets were formed and from which indigestible food was expelled. It had been a really, really dull lecture and Pagnell's flailing mind wondered if he might be able to save himself if he'd paid more attention. While thoughts screamed and flashed back and chided his younger self, yet another part of his mind was working on a half-formed plan. His hands turned over each other in the confined space, found the ritual gestures to perform the spell of *Cowell's Frictionless Unguent*. Masses of bitter, oily slime poured from his hands. He forced himself to focus on the spell, to keep it going, feeling the jelly-like lubricant coat his body. His lungs ached dreadfully in the smothering confines, and he hoped he was giving the damned bird indigestion.

Tudu bucked. Even in the animal's cushioned innards Pagnell felt himself being swung from side to side and, most unpleasantly, forced upward, feet first. He had just enough presence of mind to squeeze open the box moss pouch and push it away before he was vomited out into stark light and the unforgiving hardness of stone. Cowell's Unguent poured from Tudu's open beak. Unaccountably, Pagnell's coat was draped over its eyes. If the expressionless face of a blindfolded bird showed anything, this one looked like it was experiencing a thousand hangovers, all at once.

Pagnell was exhausted and hurting enough to wish he could simply play dead and wait for the bird to go away. The drying slime covered his entire body, all but gluing him to the floor. However, it was increasingly clear nausea had brought out a rotten temper in the giant bird. It screeched and clawed the earth. All it had to do was stretch out and those talons would make pulled pork of the wizard's innards.

Pagnell reached for his pocket, nearly crying out at the pain in his shoulder. He groped instead with his good arm and hand. After a bit of awkward fumbling, he dragged out a bottle. He flung it as far away as possible. It smashed against a wall or a floor – Pagnell didn't bother to look – and Lorrika's previously bottled and stoppered screams of pain burst out.

"Gods! No! No! Don't!"

Tudu whirled and stomped blindly towards the screams. They went on at length. Either Lorrika had a low pain threshold or Pagnell wasn't half the field surgeon he thought he was.

Tudu snapped and clawed at the empty air, unable to

seize the source of the screams. The bird stumbled, walked into a wall, shook its head as though to clear it and then, very slowly, settled down to roost – before tipping over onto its side, unconscious.

"Hooray for box moss," said Pagnell, weakly. He started to peel his gooey, sticky body away from the floor.

A head popped out of the stone urn next to him. "What happened?" asked Cope.

"It ate me," said Pagnell.

"I saw that."

"And then I knocked it out with a sleeping draught."

"That's clever," came Lorrika's echoing voice from within the urn.

Pagnell frowned. "What are you two doing in there?"

"We were hiding," said Cope.

"Not much of a long-term strategy."

"Was getting eaten a better one?" said Lorrika as her head popped up next to Cope's.

Pagnell shook himself off. He whimpered at the pain in his shoulder. "I wouldn't recommend it," He looked across at the doorway which had been revealed when Tudu had risen from its slumber.

"The fifth threshold?" said Cope.

Pagnell nodded. "The final threshold. Foesen's Tomb and the Quill of Truth are through there."

Lorrika climbed nimbly from the giant pot. Cope followed, hauling herself out with a technique which could best be described as graceless but effective.

"Bez?" queried Pagnell.

"Turned tail and ran," said Lorrika.

"Left us to die," added Cope.

"Yes," said Lorrika. She sounded like she was trying to speak around a stone on her throat.

"He didn't choose to come here," said Cope. "Merken forced him."

"You don't blame him?" Pagnell was surprised.

Cope gave him a blank look. "Blame? What good will that do?"

"But if I try to run you're going to..."

"Damn well kill you. Merken's instructions."

"Good job I'm going nowhere but onward." He jerked his head towards the final gateway. "Shall we?"

Cope pointed to the sleeping eagle. "Should I kill it?"

Pagnell wiped unguent from his hair and flung it away. "Do you want to kill it?"

"Are we coming back this way once we have the Quill?"

"I imagine so."

"How long does the sleeping draught last?"

"That much would knock out a human for a month."

"And a giant eagle?"

Pagnell gave a one-shouldered shrug. "Couldn't say."

Cope strode towards the bird, sword ready.

"Although Buqit might not take kindly to you killing her pet," said the wizard.

Cope hesitated. "Pet?"

"Maybe."

In the heat of the battle, he would have had no problem with Cope beheading the beast or running it through; now it was fast asleep, he was suddenly squeamish about the idea. He could have spent an age wondering what moral difference there was between the two scenarios, but for now, he was happy to trust his squeamishness.

"Let's not ruffle any divine feathers," he said. "No more than we already have." He picked up one of the long feathers Cope had sheared off in her attack and twirled it meaningfully in his hand.

Cope lowered her sword and the three of them went to the final gateway. The corridor beyond the threshold was dark, but a yellow light flickered at its far end.

"Are there any more traps ahead?" asked Cope.

Pagnell could offer no assistance. "If Abington had notes or records of this section, we've lost them. I've got—" He ransacked his pockets. "—a very damp journal which is all stuck together and ... some diagrams for traps and devices we've already passed."

"I'll lead the way," said Lorrika. "Follow slowly."

Pagnell and Cope kept to the shadows while Lorrika tapped and prodded and stuck nasty sharp things in suspicious cracks. Death conspicuously failed to leap out and claim them.

"Maybe Kavda the Builder assumed an enormous death-eagle would weed out any final interlopers," Pagnell suggested.

Lorrika paused not far from the corridor's end.

"Problem?" said Pagnell.

"Does anyone else...?" She sniffed and frowned.

"What?"

"Does anyone else smell roast chicken?"

33

Pagnell, still trying to comb pernicious magical unguent from his hair and beard, failed to notice the step down as they entered the room, and stumbled. He thrust his hand against the edge of a table to stop catch himself, gasping at the stab of pain in his wounded shoulder.

"Are you hurt?" said Cope.

Lorrika, not half as clumsy as Pagnell, stepped cautiously down the step and inspected the room. "What the hell is this?" she said in soft wonderment.

The room was, in many senses, exactly what one would expect for the final resting place of a revered Hierophant. There was a large tomb chest, carved from onyx and alabaster. Across the top was a finely worked effigy of what could only be Hierophant Foesen, laid out as in death. The open braziers were very much in keeping with the tomb aesthetic, although the fact they were alight was mildly surprising. The other elements in the room were more difficult to comprehend.

There was a large bed in the corner, topped by a canopy of silks, and hung with fine curtains in peach and pink. There was an arrangement of plump cushions, and a small selection of musical instruments – a lute, a sacbut and a zither – leaned against a nearby wall. The table Pagnell had come up against was long and low, with bench seating either side, laid out for a banquet fit indeed for a Hierophant. There was roast chicken, but more besides. Glazed hams, dates in syrup, flat breads, tomatoes and aubergines in oil, oven-cooked goat, bowls of ripe fruit and thin-necked jugs of wine crowded the surface.

"Was someone expecting us?" said Lorrika suspiciously.

Pagnell stepped back from the table and tried to apply some rational thought. "Either this is all specifically for us," he said. "Or the room is always like this."

"I have never seen a tomb like this before," said Cope.

Pagnell considered the bed, and the cushions, and the steam rising off freshly cooked meats. "No," he agreed, slowly.

"Is it a trap?" asked Lorrika.

"I don't know. I don't see how."

"Because that's the Quill of Truth, right?" she said and pointed.

Pagnell had not previously noticed the carved effigy of Hierophant Foesen held a carved version of the Book of Truth under one hand and a long eagle feather in the other.

"So it is," he said.

"Maybe the food and that is just a distraction," said Lorrika. "To tempt people from taking the treasure."

"What? You think grave robbers might be diverted from their goal by juicy dates and the opportunity to play the sacbut."

"What's a sacbut?" asked Cope.

"The food could be poisoned," said Lorrika.

"It's that curly horn instrument," Pagnell said to Cope.

She nodded. "I ate some bad dates once. Couldn't leave the privy for three days."

"See?" said Lorrika.

Pagnell gawped. "See what? They're now trying to defeat us with poor food hygiene?"

"What's hy-giene?" asked Cope.

"The point is," said Pagnell, feeling the point had entirely escaped him, "I don't yet know the purpose of all this stuff."

"So, none of it's a trap?" said Lorrika.

"I said, I don't see how."

"Well, in that case..."

She stepped up to the tomb and reached for the Quill of Truth.

"Wait!" said Pagnell. "Let's just think—"

Lorrika's fingers touched the Quill.

34

Pagnell, still trying to comb pernicious magical unguent from his hair and beard, failed to notice the step down as they entered the room, and stumbled. He thrust his hand against the edge of a table to catch himself, gasping at the stab of pain in his wounded shoulder.

"Are you hurt?" said Cope and then stared about her in confusion. "Hang about..."

Lorrika cautiously trod down the step into the room. "What the hell just happened?"

Pagnell stepped back from the banqueting table. "That was weird."

"Did everyone else just have a vision of the future?" said Cope.

"Vision of the future? Was that what it was?"

"I recall us entering this room, and Lorrika looking at the food and wondering if it was a trap, and you explained the bent horn thing over there was a ... what was it, again?"

"A sacbut."

"Sacbut. And you were convinced none of these things were traps and then Lorrika went over here." She crossed to the tomb chest and held out her hand. "Then the vision ended on the moment Lorrika touched the—"

PAGNELL WAS SCRAPING Cowell's Unguent from his hair and didn't see the step in front of him. He stumbled clumsily forward and came up sharply against a table edge. He gasped.

"Are you—" Cope paused and frowned deeply. "—hurt?"

"Okay, it just happened again," said Lorrika.

"It did," said Pagnell, putting a hand to his painful shoulder. "And I don't think it was a vision of the future."

"Whatever it is, it's stopping us taking the feather," said Lorrika, approaching the tomb warily. "As soon as it sees us take the feather, it transports us back over there. So, maybe..."

Lorrika grabbed for the Quill of Truth, already turning away to run for the exit.

HIS HANDS FULL OF SLIME, Pagnell fell against the table and gasped in pain.

"Are—?" began Cope and fell silent.

With a roar, Lorrika sprinted to the tomb chest, clutched at the Quill—

. . .

Pagnell stumbled, collided with the table and gasped.

Cope said nothing.

Lorrika ran for the Quill of Truth.

Pagnell fell forward again, banged against the table again.

Lorrika was already running.

"Stop that!" he grunted in pain.

Lorrika skidded to a halt. "Why?"

Pagnell straightened slowly. "One, because it's clearly not working. Any time one of us touches the Quill, we get ... zapped back in time to the moment we entered the room."

"But if we were quick enough..." said Lorrika and snatched at the feather in Foesen's stone grasp.

Pagnell fell against the table and barked at the pain it drove through his injured shoulder.

"And two—!" he shouted, "—every time you do it, it hurts! It hurts a lot!"

"Fine," sniffed Lorrika, standing casually behind him by the entrance. "I was only trying. You know, a bit of experimentation."

"The point of experimentation is to try different things and maybe get an improved result," muttered Pagnell. "There's a name for people who repeat the same thing again and again, expecting something different to happen."

"What do you mean: *zapped back in time*?" said Cope.

"I meant exactly what I said." He tapped a brass goblet on

the food-filled table. "We arrived in the room at a certain moment in time, we stood around, we talked—" he traced his hand lightly over the table top "—Lorrika touched the Quill of Truth and – bam!" He tapped the goblet. "Time wound back to that first moment."

"Time does not wind back," said Cope.

"Not usually, no," agreed Pagnell.

Cope sounded cross. "The past is done and the future does not exist. There is now and that's it. Time is not a path you can wander up and down."

"Again, not usually."

"You've really confused me!"

"I can see that."

"If it helps," said Lorrika, "my old master, Rabo Poon, believed time was a conceptual, abstract framework which provides structure to the mental apprehension of events by the rational observer."

"It doesn't help, actually," said Pagnell.

Cope shook her head furiously. "Travel back in time? Travel *back* in time? No. It's not possible. It's not a thing. It's like asking someone how tall they weigh or whether they can remember what up was like. No." She kept shaking her head and it didn't look like she was going to stop.

Lorrika frowned. "Aurelion Pippo, the philosopher who claims to think for all men who do not think for themselves, argued the present was an infinitesimally small moment between the remembered past and the imagined future. The *now* is an invisible knife blade between two states of time which don't exist."

"Really not helping at all," said Pagnell.

"Essentially, time does not exist," said Lorrika cheerfully. "Which is handy because no one can ever accuse me of being late for anything."

Something worrying was happening to Cope's face. In the short time he had known her, Pagnell had come to accept Cope's face (and personality by extension) was like a sponge; by which he didn't mean it was brown and full of holes, but very much an absorber of thoughts and feelings. It projected very little. Now, Cope's genially open and accepting expression had tipped over into ghostly blank vacancy. A state normally achieved by a seasoned drunkard at the darkest moment of a five day bender: when the body was still moving, the lips perhaps still talking, but the soul within had been totally supplanted by alcohol.

"There is no time," she said. "There is no now."

Pagnell waved a hand in front of Cope's face. She didn't even blink.

Cope stepped backward with utmost care, as though heavy footfalls might put a crack in the universe, and pressed herself into a corner. "Are my memories even mine?" she whispered. "Am I my thoughts? What *is* thought?"

"Cope?" said Pagnell, clicking his fingers in front of her face. There was no response.

"Are we all just shadow puppets moved by an invisible puppeteer? Is anyone watching?"

Pagnell wagged a finger at Lorrika. "You did this."

"What?"

Cope curled up on the floor. "The shadows are imaginary. There is no one in the audience."

Pagnell blew out his lips, frustrated. "Well done, Lorrika. You broke Cope."

"I was just repeating what I'd been told by philosophers."

"Philosophers are dangerous things. You should know that. This is why the Carians are always getting invaded. No one likes a smart-arse. Right, now we have to figure out how to solve this problem."

"You think it's a riddle?"

"It's a puzzler," said Pagnell, scratching his beard, immediately regretting it as his fingers sank into fresh, oily unguent. He shuddered in disgust. "That's it!" He picked up a jug of drink, sniffed it, decided it was a dark wine, decided further he didn't care, poured a quantity into a shallow bowl and washed his face and beard vigorously.

"Solving it by sticking your face in wine?" said Lorrika. "Novel."

Pagnell ignored her and proceeded to tear off his equally oily tunic.

"And getting naked," Lorrika commented without judgement.

As he pulled the tunic away, Pagnell stretched his injured shoulder. He yelped.

"You're hurt," said Lorrika, looking at the blood-stained tear in his under shirt.

"An eagle bit me then ate me," he pointed out.

"Sit down and let me take a look at it."

Pagnell, who was slightly less slimed but definitely sticky, wine-scented and irritated, plonked himself down on a bench. While Lorrika peeled aside the ripped material around his shoulder, he angrily poured himself a cup of wine, downed it and ate a fig.

"How's the food?" said Lorrika.

"Delicious," he said miserably.

"At least that's something," she said. "You're not bleeding, but you've got one hell of a bruise coming up."

"Good," said Pagnell. "If I'm going to suffer, I want my body to put out the flags and bunting so everyone else knows it."

"I think you need a sling, though." She glanced around. Pagnell could see her considering taking down the curtains around the bed, but the material was too thick and unwieldy. Lorrika shrugged and undid the bandages around her hand. They'd grown brown and grubby, but would make a serviceable sling. Lorrika unwrapped them and inspected the scabbed bite mark between thumb and forefinger. It was sufficiently healed and, washed properly, would be nothing but a red mark in a few days.

She tied the bandage into a loop to form a sling and helped place it over Pagnell's head.

"What did you do with Spirry?" he said quietly.

Lorrika hesitated.

"I'm a dentist," he said. "Never forget a set of teeth. Or a bite pattern."

Lorrika's mouth framed several answers before she settled on, "I didn't hurt her."

"No?"

"She hurt me. Look."

"Good."

Lorrika adjusted the sling to support Pagnell's arm. She

clearly knew what she was doing. Pagnell watched her work. She was young, at least ten years his junior, barely more than a child, really. A thief by training or inclination, in service to philosophers and wizards, neither profession treating morality as anything other than an intellectual exercise or something which applied to other people. Did that excuse her being party to kidnapping and blackmail?

"General Handzame has her in the temple," said Lorrika. "Your little girl is safe. As long as you bring back the Quill of Truth."

Pagnell nodded and tested the sling. "She's not mine," he said.

"Oh, right," said Lorrika.

"And she's not a girl either."

Lorrika's brow creased.

"And how to get the Quill of Truth, eh?" said Pagnell, swivelling on the bench to regard the tomb.

"What do you mean, she's not a girl?" asked Lorrika.

"Come now," said Pagnell, "focus on the task in hand. There's the Quill of Truth in stony Foesen's hands. We need it but can't get it. What's the answer?"

Pagnell considered the black and white relief carving on the side of the tomb chest. The holy words *What will you do today?* were engraved among them. Below was a stylised representation of Tudu, the holy eagle, wings spread, cruel beak turned to one side. It was much like the one on the cover of the book Thedo the carter had bought in Qir. Apart from the gulf in artistry between this representation and Thedo's cheap souvenir. Was the image of Tudu meaningful? Was it a clue to the way forward?

"If we had some string or rope," said Lorrika, "we could tie it round the feather and then, standing in the doorway, yank it out and run for it."

"You're assuming the bit where we get zapped back in time only applies in this room?"

"I assumed, yes."

Pagnell gave it some thought. "Do we have string or rope?"

"We did have a big ball of string."

"Which grimlock Clive confiscated and turned into a natty knitted smock."

Lorrika poured herself a goblet of wine. "But *if* we had some string..."

"It might work," Pagnell conceded. "Or we might just reset the room."

"We might have to do that anyway if we want Cope back."

"This Aurelion Pippo..." murmured Cope from the floor.

"Hey, look who's back in the room," said Pagnell, turning to the warrior woman.

Cope got to her feet. "Who does his thinking?"

"What?" said Lorrika.

"You said he claims to think for all men who do not think for themselves. Does he do his own thinking, or does someone else do it for him? Either way, he's a liar."

Lorrika was perplexed.

"Oh, she's got you there," said Pagnell.

"And if he lies about *that*," said Cope, "how can we trust anything he says? Time not existing? *Pfff.*"

Pagnell laughed. "The philosophers of Carius outsmarted by our Cope. Excellent."

"What are we doing?" said Cope, hands on hips and ready to move into action.

"We're solving the conundrum which is this room," said Pagnell.

"It looks like you're eating and drinking."

"Ah, you should never solve conundrums on an empty stomach." He poured another goblet of wine. "Join us."

"We must return before the Hierophant's army gets here. We do not have the time."

"I think, in this place, time is the one thing we do have. We could eat and drink and stuff ourselves silly for hours on end, and if we so much as touch the Quill of Truth, we will be sent back to the moment of our arrival and—" He was silenced by a thought.

"Yes?" said Cope.

"Eat up," he said. "Eat up, drink, throw it on the floor."

"Why?" said Lorrika.

"We're making a change. We're making it different. Come now. You must be hungry."

Pagnell downed two cups of wine. Lorrika munched through a bunch of grapes. Cope, hesitant at first, picked at some rolls of what might have been pickled fish and then ate two chicken legs and a whole loaf of bread.

"I am hungry," she said. "How long is it since we had an actual meal?"

"Too long," said Pagnell, shoving four quail eggs in his mouth, one after the other. "Right. Right. That will do."

He got up and crossed to the tomb chest. He probed with his tongue at a fleck of egg caught between his teeth and looked at the effigy of Hierophant Foesen. The old priest looked very sombre, carved from a single piece of onyx. But then he was dead. It was probably the most appropriate time of life to look sombre. Pagnell gave the statue an amiable wink and picked up the Quill of Truth.

PAGNELL'S FOOT came down hard on the expected step at the entrance and he staggered into the table and swore.

"It's exactly as it was before," said Lorrika, coming into the room beside him.

"And I'm hungry again," said Cope.

They were correct. The banqueting table was fully laden as it had been when they'd first entered. Nothing remained as evidence of their previous appearance in the room. The headiness brought on by the wine had vanished, the crumb of egg no longer between Pagnell's teeth.

"So what does this teach us?" he said.

"That Kavda was a cunning fox," said Cope.

"Mmm. I suspect this particular device is beyond Kavda's genius abilities," said Pagnell. "I think this is the goddess herself at work."

"Is it?" said Cope. She looked around and gave a reverential nod towards the tomb chest. "Very impressive, your worshipfulness."

"What else?" said Pagnell. "What else can we infer?"

"It means we can eat and drink ourselves stupid and not need worry about a hangover. A dozen glasses of wine, a sing-song and then we just touch the feather and we're instantly sober."

"And we could do that as often as we like," said Pagnell.

"We could spend our entire lives enjoying day after day of food, drink and whatnot."

"Not just our entire lives," said Pagnell. "At the moment the feather is touched, our bodies are made as they were when we first arrived. We could theoretically enjoy a limitless age of gluttony, crapulence and indulgence of the senses."

"I'm not indulging in anything with you, wizard," said Cope firmly. "And I'm not sure about that whatnot you were on about either," she told Lorrika.

"Good food, good company," said Pagnell. He scuttled to the instruments in the corner and picked up the lute and the sacbut. "Music! We can have as much luting and sacbuttery as we could wish for. Again and again and again until we ... ah."

"Until we've had enough?" said Lorrika. "Because I think there's only so much sacbuttery I could stand."

"I understand now," said Pagnell slowly.

"Yes?" said Cope.

"It's the teachings of Buqit, only writ small."

"Is it?"

He crossed back to the tomb chest and placed a hand on the carved book under Foesen's hand. "*The Book of Truth* teaches us that after this life—"

"—we are reborn," said Cope, "and Buqit gives us the life we deserve: the good given better lives, the wicked punished with toil and misery."

"That's right," said Pagnell. "And we do it again and again and again until we get it right, until we have done everything on the *List of Things To Be Done*."

Lorrika gave him a worried look. "And that's what we have to do?"

"Maybe," he shrugged. "I'm really just grasping at straws."

"So," said Cope, "we do the right thing or things and then we will be allowed to take the Quill of Truth?"

Pagnell spread his hands. "Worth a try."

35

They ate all the food.

They drank all the wine.

They sat on all the cushions, individually and all at once.

They laid in the bed, singly and then together.

They played the instruments badly. Pagnell spent a length of time trying to get something resembling a tune out of the zither.

They sang along to the zither tune.

They smashed the instruments. Cope enjoyed smashing the zither.

They threw the food on the floor and ground it up with their heels.

They poured the wine onto the floor also and mixed it with the food with their hands.

They mopped up the mess with the bedsheets.

They tore open the cushions and threw feathers at each other. They hit each other with cushions.

Lorrika took hold of the Quill of Truth and they were at the door once more, Pagnell stumbling into a table and cursing his injury.

THEY PIOUSLY REFUSED to drink the wine.

They made a brief but devout show of fasting and refraining from food.

They prayed to Buqit.

They placed an offering of fruit at the foot of Foesen's tomb.

They recounted what few tales they knew of the Hierophants of Ludens.

They loudly praised the temple of Buqit as a shining beacon of spirituality.

They pleaded with Buqit to look kindly on them and, when there were no more pleas to be said, Cope took the Quill.

They found themselves at the door once more.

THEY OVERTURNED THE TABLE.

Cope hacked the bed apart.

They poured wine in the sacbut.

They stuffed bread inside the cushions.

They made a teetering pile of musical instruments, bread-stuffed cushions and topped it with dates and chicken legs.

Everything was moved. Nothing was as it once was.

Pagnell attempted to swap the Quill of Truth for the eagle feather he had brought from the previous room.

They were once again by the entrance. Everything was as it was before.

PAGNELL SPAT on Foesen's stony face.

Cope tried to prise the tomb chest open with her sword.

Lorrika screamed for a very long time.

Pagnell cast every spell he knew which wouldn't kill them.

Cope tore a brass plate in half with her bare hands.

Lorrika gave a spirited philosophical argument which disproved the existence of all gods.

Together they laid their hands on the Quill of Truth.

36

Pagnell poured himself another cup of wine.

"Try me again," he said. "Maybe the plan makes more sense with more alcohol inside me."

Cope continued polishing her sword. "We chop our hands off."

"Nope," he said. "Not making sense yet."

"Maybe it requires a physical sacrifice. And it strikes me the goddess Buqit doesn't like it when we touch the Quill with our hands."

"So," said Lorrika, munching on a nectarine, "we chop our hands off— All of them?"

"One, some, all," said Cope. "Does it matter?"

"I think it does, somehow," said Pagnell.

"If it doesn't work, we will be back as we were before with our hands reattached," said Cope.

"And if we succeed," said Lorrika, "we'll have the Quill of Truth but no hands."

"Correct," said Cope. Her face twitched as she considered whether this would be an ideal outcome.

"Yes, probably best we have a rethink of that one," said Pagnell and, fortified with a mouthful of wine, plucked disconsolately on the zither in his lap.

"I don't think that plan goes far enough," said Lorrika eventually.

"Not far enough?" said Pagnell and struck a sour note.

"We should kill one of us."

Cope bent to apply more buffing pressure to a dark mark on her blade. Pagnell looked at the sword and slid a short distance away along the bench.

"I don't think killing anyone is going to be help," he said.

"But it will," said Lorrika. "Think about it. We kill someone. You, for example."

"I don't want be the example," said Pagnell.

"You die and you go before Buqit for judgement and to be born into a new life."

"That's assuming the unique teachings of the *Book of Truth* are correct. It's generally accepted elsewhere that, upon our deaths, the gods will despatch us to one of various underworlds, blessed isles or mead halls to received our eternal reward, punishment or mindless oblivion – actually, if it's a mead hall, possibly all three at once."

"Whatever," said Lorrika. "While you're there, you ask Buqit or the gods or whoever what we must do to get the Quill of Truth. And then – this is the clever part—"

"I am so glad there is a clever part."

"—we touch the Quill of Truth and we're all transported

back to the door, alive as before, and you can tell us what the gods said."

Pagnell ruminated on the idea and, discovering his cup was empty, went to pour himself another. The wine jug was empty.

"It's a bold idea, I'll give you that."

"Are we doing it?" said Cope.

"We most certainly are not," said Pagnell. He reached for another wine jug. It sloshed emptily too.

"We're out of wine," he said, got up and touched the Quill of Truth.

THEY WERE by the door again.

Pagnell fell against the table, coughed at the pain it brought on and then immediately went to pour himself another goblet of wine.

"I was enjoying that nectarine," said Lorrika.

"And you will again," said Pagnell. "Pass me my zither, Cope, would you?"

Cope obligingly collected the zither from the corner and then, with a one-handed slam, smashed it to kindling against the wall. She smiled sweetly.

"I can just go touch the Quill again," said Pagnell.

"And I can break it again," said Cope.

Pagnell glared at her. Cope met his gaze and matched it.

"Abington said hell was other people," said Lorrika with a quiet emphasis.

Pagnell threw himself down on a bench. "Yeah, well he was a miserable old misanthrope," he said and immediately regretted it. The man had been dead for no more than a couple of days, killed by a mix up of pouches on a belt, but killed by Pagnell's hand nonetheless. "I'm sorry," he said.

Lorrika's attempt at a smile flickered for only an instant, like distant lightning. "It's okay," she said.

"No," said Pagnell. "I'm really sorry. I didn't mean ... he meant a lot to you."

Lorrika picked up a nectarine, the same nectarine she'd eaten in the last iteration of the room.

"He did mean a lot to me. But he was a miserable old misanthrope as you say, a horrible man. Everyone goes on about how he saved all the people in Dalarra from the plague."

"I heard about that," said Cope. "He found the cure."

"Drapim," said Pagnell.

"But what you need to know," said Lorrika, "is that a month before plague struck the city, Abington bought up or harvested every shoot, root and leaf of Drapim in a hundred mile radius. You see?"

Cope nodded in awe. "He could see the future."

Pagnell smiled charitably. "Cope, even for wizards, it's easier to make something happen than to predict it."

"You mean he made the plague happen?"

"And raised the price of Drapim to fifty times its ordinary value." Lorrika shook her head. "He cured the people, but at such a cost. Now, if I could just reach out and turn back time to *before* that moment..."

"The past is fixed," said Pagnell, "and full of regrets. None of us know what the right choice is until we look back and see if what we did was right or wrong. We're not all like the followers of Buqit with a written list of things to do."

Lorrika waved her half-eaten nectarine at Cope. "Cope's got her little cards to tell her what to do."

Cope placed a hand protectively over her jerkin pocket. "They're for me."

"I know they are," said Lorrika. "I'm just saying. Why do you have them anyway?"

Cautiously, Cope took the bundle of creased, soft-edged cards and held them in front of her on the table. "Sometimes, I don't understand people," she said. "They say one thing and do another. They talk with their eyes and not their mouths. They can say the same thing twice and it means something different each time. People can be very cruel if you don't understand their rules."

"Cruel? To you?" said Lorrika and laughed. "You're as big and scary as any man. You're an ogre."

"As I said. Cruel." Cope tapped the edge of her cards. "I was lucky to enter the service of Master Jarden Orre and he taught me what I needed to know. And those lessons I struggled with, I wrote down." She pulled one out at random and placed it on the table. Pagnell glanced at the heading: *How to join in with games, group activities, etc.* "What those lessons didn't tell me," said Cope, "was what to do with my life when Master Jarden Orre died. There was no card to tell me what to do next."

"Oh, yes," said Pagnell, "Lorrika mentioned you're on some sort of holy mission for the High Shepherdess to find out your true purpose in life."

"That is so. I heard people had visited the High

Shepherds and High Shepherdesses in search of the answers to life's great mysteries and so I travelled to the Aklan Plateau, through the forests of Gadzim, searching for High Shepherdess Gwell."

"And you found her?"

Cope nodded solemnly. "I walked for weeks in search of her. The High Shepherdess moves with her flock and does not stay in one place for long. I followed rumours and guesses and walked until my feet were sore and my spirits were low."

"You did a lot of walking. Got it. Move along," said Lorrika. "Tell him the bit where you met Gwell."

"I came upon a woman in a woodland clearing," said Cope. "She sat on a smooth boulder, her long-haired sheep milling around her. She carried a shepherd's crook and wore the cone-shaped headdress of the holy order of shepherdesses. Prayer ribbons were tied to every inch of her robes. And stitched to the front of her robes was the Aklan rune for the name *Gwell*."

"You'd found her," said Pagnell.

"So it would seem," said Cope. She sheathed her now clean sword. "I knelt before her and said, 'I have come a great distance, in search of guidance. I am ready to take on the challenges life has to offer and I hope you will lead me to my true purpose. I will undertake any labour required. I will complete any quest given to me. I will seek the answers to any question that is posed. Tell me, are you High Shepherdess Gwell?'"

"And was she?"

"She looked at her sheep, waggled her crook and tapped

the rune on her robe and then gave me what I think is called a *look* and said, 'Do bears shit in the wood?'"

"Well, I guess it was kind of obvious so..."

"So, I got up, thanked her and that was how my quest began."

Pagnell pursed his lips, perplexed. "Your quest began...? Began to what? Sorry, what quest?"

"I am on a sacred mission to answer the High Shepherdess's question."

"Question? You mean?" Pagnell looked to Lorrika for assistance. She had turned away, politely hiding the smirk on her face.

"You mean," said Pagnell, "*that* question?"

"Yes. I know it's a vulgar sort of question and, superficially, one might think it has a simple answer."

"—Yes."

"Exactly," said Cope. "But I know deep down there's a deeper, more profound truth."

Pagnell tried to pull a face which was anything other than mocking. "Cope, you know, sometimes, the deepest truth is the simplest truth. We think there is something more but the answer is the one staring you in the face."

Something clicked in Pagnell's mind. Thoughts fell into place and a door – not a big, or impressive, or exciting, but nonetheless very important door – swung open. He looked at the tomb chest. "Oh my good goddess," he said.

He stood.

"What is it?" said Lorrika.

"Ink. I need ink."

"What?"

"Ink, damn it!"

"There's no ink here."

He waved at the braziers. "Soot, wine, stuff. Make ink, Lorrika. Knife!" he said to Cope.

She passed him a butter knife.

"A sharp knife!"

Cope reached behind her and produced a short, whisper-edged blade.

"Where were you keeping that?" asked Lorrika.

"A friend of mine from the north told me you can never have too many knives. Always good to have a spare."

Pagnell took the knife and hurriedly cut the end of his eagle feather down into a point. Excitement made his hands shake and he had to start afresh twice.

"What are you doing?" said Lorrika.

"It's like the cards," said Pagnell. "Cope, your cards. It's what you've written down. A set of instructions. You write it, you do it. The carter who brought us to Ludens, he bought this stupid book in Qir. Cheap, tacky thing. He said to me—" Pagnell paused. He couldn't whittle a feather down into a quill and remember what Thedo said at the same time. As a wizard he knew his limits. "He said: 'If it's not written down, it won't happen.' It's just like that." He pointed at the tomb. "*The List of Things To Be Done*. The written word becomes the act."

"You are babbling," said Lorrika.

"No. Not this time. Ink!"

Lorrika had poured wood ash and wine into a shallow bowl and made a quantity of pasty grey paint. It was possibly the world's worst attempt at ink but it would do.

Pagnell scrabbled around for the last piece of dry paper on his person.

"I still don't understand," said Cope.

"It's not just you this time," said Lorrika.

"What are we here for?" said Pagnell. In truth, he shouted it. He had become manic. He knew it and didn't care. What maniac did? "Why did we come?"

"To ... to..."

"What," he demanded, "is the question before us?" Pagnell grinned and he probably looked like the biggest idiot in the world, but he was the world's biggest idiot with immaculate teeth. He capered over to the tomb chest with quill and ink and paper and pointed at Hierophant Foesen's own words carved into the side.

"What will you do today?"

He leaned on the tomb and took up his quill.

I will take the Quill of Truth and keep it.

He wrote it.

He said it.

He did it.

And then he giggled, which probably ruined the epicness of the moment but he really didn't care.

37

The journey back to the surface was quicker than the descent, but it was still long and— Pagnell would have used the word *arduous*, except he could hear Spirry declaring it to be a fancy word and entirely unnecessary when the word *difficult* worked just as well. He thought a great deal about Spirry as they tiptoed past a sleeping bird, climbed stairs, carefully crossed through broken traps and followed Lorrika's chalk arrows backward through the labyrinth. Cope drew her sword several times as unexpected sounds echoed ahead of them. They all feared remnants of the grimlock tribe, but none materialised. They stopped only to fashion fresh torches from discarded weapons and what materials they could spare. If they halted too long, the fatigued trio ran the risk of falling asleep and staying that way until the Hierophant's returning army found them, or some wandering horror ate them.

They were unsurprised by the Surprising Pit on the

reverse journey. A lip of stone ran along the edge of the pit at each side. Lorrika fairly scampered across the finger-thin ledge but Pagnell wasn't so confident.

He was halfway along, dividing his attention between shuffling his feet forward and merging his body with the wall, when Cope said, "You should give me the Quill to look after. In case you fall in."

"And you thought you'd mention this now?" huffed Pagnell with difficulty (his jaw was pressed right up against the rock face at the time).

"It just occurred to me," said Cope.

"Yeah? Well, you'll just have to wait, won't you?"

"I don't want it to get wet, that's all."

Pagnell laughed in mild hysteria and inched his feet along. "Wet, she says. Some of us are focusing on not dying!"

When he'd crossed, not died, and the Quill of Truth remained unwetted. Cope followed, with no more style or dignity than his effort, but with notably less whimpering.

"Maybe I should look after the Quill anyway," she said.

Pagnell looked up at her. "Don't you trust me, Cope?"

She tilted her head in thought and placed a hand unconsciously on the hilt of her sheathed sword. "No, I don't think I do."

Pagnell twisted his lips, gave her a mildly hurt look, produced the feather and passed it over.

38

They returned through the dusty, corpse-lined shelves of the crypt and out through the eagle's head archway. The Amanni guards in the great under hall of the temple spotted their approaching torchlight, and one dashed off to report their return. At once, the three tomb raiders were escorted up the many flights of stairs to the Hierophant's audience chamber, which General Handzame had made her base of occupation.

Pagnell felt oddly aggrieved they had been forced to suffer the trials and obstacles of Foesen's tomb only to be made to climb eight floors – eight floors! – to deliver the prize. Tired and a little giddy with hunger, he felt they should, if anything, be carried aloft like the triumphant heroes they clearly were. However, when he suggested this to the chap behind him, he was only offered a choice between walking or a knife to the kidneys. The chap wasn't overly clear on the matter, but since it seemed unlikely said knifing would be followed by being carried aloft like triumphant heroes, Pagnell decided not to pursue it further.

The Hierophant's audience chamber sat near the top of the temple's mighty ziggurat. Smooth walls angled inward, giving the room a sense of upward thrusting aspiration. It must be a devil to wallpaper, thought Pagnell. That thought alone made the wizard decide he'd better eat something soon, and maybe have a little nap, before he turned into a gibbering wreck. Beyond the wide balcony of the audience chamber lay the city of Ludens and the lands to the south. The sun was rising over the flat and featureless horizon.

In the light of day and in the company of Handzame's finest, Pagnell realised what a shambles the three of them must look. All of them had been soaked, dried, rolled in the dirt and lightly singed all over. All of them were wounded or scarred to some degree. Lorrika's arm was tightly bandaged; Cope had lost her armour in the tomb, received a bloody chest wound and a bunch of bruises; Pagnell had taken a nasty clout round the head from falling masonry, a painfully inconvenient eagle bite to the shoulder, and been thoroughly marinated in magic unguent and the digestive juices of a giant eagle.

He was gratified to see General Handzame didn't look much better. The Amanni woman sat ramrod straight on the Hierophant's throne, hands resting masterfully on the pommelled armrests: the very pose of a divinely appointed ruler in their seat of power. If Bez had been with them, he'd be committing the scene to paper already. However, despite her best efforts to appear magisterial and noble, worrisome days and sleepless nights were written deeply into the general's face. Her black, spiky plate mail looked more like a torture device she had been forced into than armour. The ridiculous helmet with the horsehair crest weighed heavily on her. She could just take it off, thought Pagnell. Why didn't she take it off? What was the point of being a conquering general if you couldn't take your helmet off when you wanted to?

"What did you say?" demanded Handzame.

Pagnell shook himself. Had he said that out loud? He slapped his cheeks rapidly to wake himself up. "We're here, general. We have returned."

"The Quill of Truth?"

Cope stepped forward and presented the large quill feather to her. Handzame took it and twirled it between her fingertips. "Is this it?"

"Yes, ma'am," said Cope.

Handzame pulled an expression, the sort which tried to be something other than disappointed, when disappointment was clearly the default option. "It's certainly big," she conceded. "I just imagined it would be a bit more..." She waved a vague hand.

"Magical?" suggested Pagnell.

"It is the Quill of Truth," insisted Cope.

"We met the bird it was taken from," added Lorrika.

In the shadows, there was an unhappy groan. Behind the row of Amanni soldiers, to one side of the chamber, stood a priest of Buqit: a round-faced (also bruised-faced) fellow in manacles. "What have you done?" he muttered despondently.

Handzame smiled. The condemnation of the priesthood gave it an additional air of authenticity.

"Where is Rantallion Merken?" she said. Demand the treasure first, notice your second-in-command was absent second. Setting your priorities the Handzame way.

"He's dead, ma'am," said Cope.

A ripple of disbelief and disquiet ran through the Amanni soldiers. Merken might have been a cruel and callous man, but he was a soldier's man. The men he'd led into the city would have respected him. They'd have put their lives in his hands; not necessarily Handzame's.

"How did he die?" she asked.

"We don't know," said Cope. "We think he stepped on a trap."

"Think?"

"There was no sign of him afterwards. No body."

Handzame gave a disgusted little sneer and ran her hand over the edge of the Quill. "And the artist? Where is he?"

Cope looked at Pagnell, who shrugged.

"He didn't come back?" asked Lorrika.

"Should he have?" said Handzame.

"He fled," said Cope. "We assumed..."

"Then he is still down there," said Handzame with a shrug. "Let him rot."

Pagnell imagined Bez wandering blindly through the twists and turns of the labyrinth, starving, dying by increments. The image didn't seem right. Bez was an intelligent man. It was a sly and narrow intelligence, but intelligence nonetheless.

"And so you three emerge victorious. You will be rewarded," spoke Handzame, attempting to sound magnanimous and, as with so many things, missing by a mile. "Gold, honours and a place in the sagas of the glorious Amanni."

"Right now I'd settle for a cup of water and a slice of toast," said Lorrika.

"Of course." Handzame clapped her hands. "You! A breakfast for our champions. Bread, fruit, the finest baked goods."

The Amanni warrior singled out by the command looked very much the picture of a soldier who had found himself demoted to kitchen maid and had no idea where the kitchen was, let alone the finest baked goods. He dithered and then scurried off.

"And you, wizard?" said Handzame. "Will it be gold, honours, or just a spot of a breakfast?"

"Where is Spirry?" asked Pagnell.

"Spirry? Oh, her." It wasn't pretence. For an instant, Handzame had forgotten she had Spirry as her prisoner.

If he had been a violent man, Pagnell might, at that moment, have decided to kill Handzame. He wasn't a violent man; even so he decided the general would suffer.

Handzame clapped her hands imperiously at one of her men. He looked at her quizzically. Pagnell detected a contemptuous aura to the man's expression, one he tried hard to conceal. Maybe two and bit days shut up with the general had soured any respect they might once have had for her.

"The girl," said Handzame. "Fetch her."

The man disappeared.

"And you?" Handzame said to Cope. "Your reward."

"An answer from the Quill of Truth, ma'am."

"Of course." Handzame nodded graciously, twirling the feather in her hand for a moment. "How does it work?"

Cope looked at her blankly.

"How does the Quill of Truth work?" said Handzame. "Wizard?"

"Yes?" said Pagnell.

"How do you make the Quill work?"

"You write with it, ma'am," he said with obsequious slowness. "Dip the point in ink and write."

"Is that it? Aren't there any magic words? No, *Magic quill, magic quill, reveal the truth and ... and...* whatever?"

"'Do my will,'" said Lorrika. Everyone stared at her. "You know, it rhymes. *Reveal the truth and do my will.* And I meant like *Do my bidding,* not write out my will and testament. Although you could. If you wanted."

"Yes," said Handzame uncertainly. She glanced at Pagnell. "Do you have to recite words, like that?"

"Only if you want to," he said. "I could give a demonstration."

He took a step forward. Handzame came to her feet, clutching the feather protectively.

"I'm not going to steal it," he said. "Or break it. I could have done either of those back in the tomb. Until I have Spirry, safe and sound, I am your obedient servant."

Handzame considered this. The childish reluctance to give up the feather played out on her face. And then she snapped into a pose of imperious authority which fooled no one.

"Indeed, you are," She held the feather out to Pagnell. At a third soldier she barked, "And you! Fetch parchment and ink."

39

Within a quarter hour, there was food, parchment and ink on the great stone table, and Spirry had been brought into the room. Pagnell went to her immediately; an Amanni warrior put out an arm to block him. The wizard tried to push past, receiving a punch in the mouth for his efforts.

"Fon of a bitff," he mumbled, clutching his lips.

"Show me how the Quill works," said Handzame.

Pagnell looked at Spirry: she appeared unhurt. Pagnell found himself almost physically overcome with relief. She was small, thin as an urchin and had a babyish cuteness about her. While there were plenty of people who would take one look and instinctively want to hug her, or tousle her hair, Pagnell knew there were also plenty who would see how small and cute she was, and immediately want to strike her; make her suffer. People were strange like that. People were idiots and monsters.

"They hurt you?" he asked, just loud enough for her to hear.

"No," she said.

"You hurt them?"

She looked at Lorrika.

"I meant anyone else," said Pagnell. Spirry made a see-saw motion with her hand and grinned.

Pagnell shook his head. "She'll be the death of me," he murmured, stepping up to the table where Cope and Lorrika waited beside Handzame. Cope watched intently as Pagnell took up the Quill of Truth. Lorrika pretended to watch intently, but her hands, mouth and brain were clearly intent on stuffing her face with food.

"Show me," said Handzame.

Pagnell dipped the Quill in the pot of ink. The round-faced priest gave a cry of "Blasphemy!" and was brutally silenced.

"As I understand it," said Pagnell, "the Quill is only capable of writing truths."

He put Quill to parchment and, with confident if scratchy strokes, wrote *The sky is blue* and *One plus one equals two.*

"All quills can write the truth," said Handzame. "You could have brought me another feather and shown me the same."

"So suspicious, general," said Pagnell, shaking his head.

"How does the Quill distinguish lies from truth?"

"Oh, like this," said Pagnell. Having no real idea of what would happen next, wrote *All sheep have wings.*

The moment Pagnell placed his full stop on the page, the writing crackled and smouldered. A flash of ember-red and the words burned from the page, leaving only a black mark which was cold to the touch.

"Tha's cool," said Lorrika around a mouthful of sugary pastry.

Handzame's eyes glittered at the possibilities. Pagnell suspected she'd not considered what all those possibilities were yet.

"So..." said Pagnell and bent to write a list:

The Yarwish king is asleep right now

There are apples on the table

Pagnell is the best wizard in town

Objects fall to the ground because the earth is breathing in

Bez is still alive

Yes, bears do shit in the wood

The Quill of Truth can identify ALL true statements

The number of hours until the Hierophant and his army reach Ludens is:

Pagnell scratched a tally of thirty-odd marks underneath this last statement.

The first and fourth lines burned out of existence instantly. The tally marks burned out, one by one, until there were twelve of them remaining. The other statements remained as they were.

Cope blinked.

"See?" Pagnell said. "They do."

"But, what does it mean?" said Cope.

Pagnell sniffed. "I think it means you need to go see High Shepherdess Gwell again. I'd go now if I were you. The Ludensian army is on its way here."

He reached forward and pushed a small bowl of apples off the table. It smashed. The second sentence burned to black.

"Oh," said Handzame, smiling uncontrollably. "This is good. This is so very good."

Another tally mark flared and vanished. Twelve hours until the city's army returned. Pagnell dipped the nib in ink and wrote three further statements:

No birds live at the bottom of the sea.
Beetroot is the first word in this statement
One possible anagram of fleas is false

They were peculiar but nonetheless true statements. At least, the first was true until Pagnell ripped away the corner of the paper and the first word. *Birds live at the bottom of the sea* smouldered and erased itself.

He quickly scribed something onto another sheet and stuffed it inside his shirt.

"My enemies' plans and deepest thoughts will be known to me!" cried Handzame. "The lost treasures and weapons of my ancestors will be mine again! I could bring the cities of the plains under my sway!"

"You could command dragons to do you bidding," suggested Pagnell.

"I could!"

"The greatest magic spells would be yours to cast."

"Would they? Yes, they would!"

"The fairy kingdoms of the deep forest would be yours to command!"

Handzame laughed. "Yes! Why not!"

"We should celebrate," said Pagnell, grabbing a goblet from the tablet. He was about to raise it in toast; instead he paused and examined the contents critically. "Water?" He whirled, Quill of Truth in hand. "Wine! We need wine! We need fine food! We need pigeon and pineapple and pomegranate!"

"You should just magic them up," said Spirry.

Pagnell gave a gasp of excitement – perhaps a bit too hammy a touch, but Handzame was too preoccupied by the possibilities of power. "Yes!" he said, pushing up his sleeves theatrically and trying to pretend his shoulder didn't hurt like hell. "One bona fide celebration feast coming up. Stand back, stand back—"

"Stop!" commanded Handzame. "Cope: restrain him."

Pagnell tried to step away, but there was already a long sword held beneath his chin.

"Miss Threemen," he sighed, "after all we've been through."

Handzame approached him cautiously. He supposed he should take some pleasure from seeing a fully armoured Amanni general look upon his ragged, filthy and thoroughly tenderised self with, if not fear, at least one of its weedier cousins.

"The Quill of Truth," said Handzame, holding out her hand.

"Of course, ma'am." He passed it to her, tickly end first.

"No spells please, wizard."

"I was only going to conjure up a celebratory feast. No less than you deserve."

Handzame's gaze was withering. It was mostly tired, but it was also withering. "My limited experience of wizards tells me they are not to be trusted."

"Generally so," agreed Pagnell, "and quite specifically in some cases. I'll never forgive old Tibshelf for telling me that damned pet bird of his was harmless. But, no, I'm one of the more harmless sort. I'm a pacifist myself; mostly anyway."

"Forgive me if I don't believe you," said Handzame.

"Oh, but you don't have to believe me," said Pagnell, gesticulating and almost slitting his own throat in the process. "You have the Quill of Truth, general. Write it down. Write *Newport Pagnell will not cause anyone physical harm with his spells*. Put *today* or *this week*. Can't guarantee I won't do a messy tooth extraction at some point. Throw in *Pagnell will tell no lies today* if you like."

Handzame wavered before going to the table and scrawling on the paper. Pagnell didn't see what it was but it was close enough. There were any number of variants – *I can trust Newport Pagnell* or *Newport Pagnell wishes me no harm* – which would have obliterated themselves instantly. Handzame seemed happy enough, though.

"Release him."

Cope lowered her sword. Pagnell ran his fingers across

his throat and checked for blood. "Ever considered barbering for a living?" he said.

"No," said Cope.

Pagnell pushed up his sleeves once more. "Right, now, a celebration feast as promised. I will need some assistance." He made a show of gazing around at his audience. "General, please, if you would. And, because I have questionable taste in women, Miss Spiriva Handihaler." He held out his hands to them.

"You want me to take your hand?" said Handzame.

"Only to help cast the spell."

Spirry stepped forward – no one stopped her – and, giving Pagnell a condescending eye-roll, put her tiny hand in his.

"General?" said Pagnell. "Please, if Spirry can do this, I'm sure you can."

Handzame was reluctant. She looked to her men and Pagnell knew he had her. "Of course," she said. "It's not ... dangerous, is it?"

"I assure you, it won't hurt at all, *but*—!" he yelled abruptly to the room, "—I advise no one to intervene whatsoever while the ritual spellcasting takes place." He attempted to make eye contact which each and every person. "I don't want to describe what might happen to you if you interrupt the spell at a critical point." He lowered his voice. "See you in Trezdigar, Lorrika. Trouble. That's what you should call yourself. And it was good to have known you, Cope."

He took hold of Handzame's hand.

There was an unmistakeable nervousness written on the

general's face. Let her men see that, Pagnell thought as he cast the spell, and uttered the opening incantation for *Quincy's Enchanting Gourmet.*

Pagnell recalled casting the spell only once before, as a training exercise when he was under the tutelage of Tibshelf. As with so many spells, the wonder wasn't in how to cast it but why bother casting it. The personal effort to conjure up a feast for one or more people was, at best, the same amount of time and effort one would normally need to find the food, cook it and lay the table. It was magic for magic's sake. Pagnell had Spirry and Handzame as willing (if, in one case, ignorant) assistants. The casting time would therefore be cut to a third. But a feast of sufficient size could take more than a day to prepare. Pagnell felt for the shape of things and poured his will into the spell...

40

He released his grip on Spirry and Handzame, and spread his arms wide. "Ta-dah!"

Along the wide table in the Hierophant's audience chamber, plates were stacked with juicy delights and delicate sweetmeats, pitchers of wine and foaming beer. Pagnell took a moment to catch his breath; his magical energies were spent and he was quite exhausted.

He waved a hand at the fabulous fare before them. "Now, *these* are drinks we can toast with."

Handzame laughed and picked up a goblet. "Come, let us fill our cups and drink to..."

The words trailed off as she turned to her men, or more precisely, to where her men had been. The room was empty, apart from the three of them.

"Where is everyone?" said Handzame.

"Um, gone, I should think," said Pagnell. He plucked a

gobbet of roast meat from a plate and popped it in his mouth.

"Gone where?"

"She hasn't noticed, has she?" whispered Spirry.

"No, she has not," agreed Pagnell.

Spirry leapt up onto the table with the grace and ease natural to her race and pointed out beyond the balcony, towards the sun. "Look at it!"

"What about it?" snapped Handzame.

"It's not rising. It's setting."

Handzame frowned furiously as though she could move the sun back to where it had been through the power of concentrated annoyance. She whirled on Pagnell. "What did you do?"

"Cast a spell," said Pagnell cheerily. "And spells take time."

"My men…?"

"Run away. No idea when. To them, we would have appeared frozen in a single elongated moment of utter concentration. As the hours trickled past, they probably realised time was growing short, and considered what might happen if they were still here when the Hierophant and his army returned."

"My men? Flee?"

"What else could they do? What else would they want to do? I warned them against interrupting the spell while it was being cast. I told them I'd not like describing what would happen if they interfered."

"Which is what?"

"Nothing?" suggested Spirry.

Pagnell nodded. "The spell would have just been cancelled."

"But you promised not to harm me!" said Handzame, lips tight with anger.

"And I haven't," said Pagnell. "Although, that doesn't mean you're *free* from harm..."

He picked up several pieces of parchment from the table and held one out to her.

THE NUMBER of hours until the Hierophant and his army reach Ludens is:

THE FINAL TALLY turned into an ash-black smudge. Pagnell smiled; sometimes the world matched one's dramatic expectations precisely.

"Your time is up, General Handzame. If we go to the balcony, we might be able to see the army approaching the gate. We might even hear them."

Handzame clutched the Quill of Truth with such furious intensity, Pagnell thought she might snap it. "You tricked me!"

"That's right. Accuse the wizard of being a conjurer with cheap tricks."

"You are, though," said Spirry.

Pagnell tutted. "General, I suggest your best course of action would be to ditch your armour, and the Quill, and run. Just run. One woman in a city this size ... you could make it."

Handzame gave him a bitterly incredulous look. "Leave the Quill of Truth? Abandon my destiny? Sacrifice the power I hold right now?"

"Ah," said Pagnell. "I feared you'd say that. So I do have one last *trick*." He glanced at the two pieces of paper he held, stuffed one away and held up the other.

General Handzame, already reaching for her sword, peered at Pagnell's writing. "*Beetroot is the first word in this statement*?"

"And, *One possible anagram of fleas is false*. Yes," said Pagnell.

"Nonsense," said Handzame and drew her weapon.

"Arguably. But then, if I do this—"

He tore the paper in half, shearing away the first half of each sentence and screwing up one half. Now the remaining sheet read:

THIS STATEMENT

is false.

"Cope reminded me, in the tomb," Pagnell told Spirry conversationally. "She's quite a thinker, but not in the conventional sense. We were talking about this philosopher who thinks for everyone who does not think for themselves and ... oh—"

The paper in Pagnell's hand began to smoulder. A red glow appeared among the letters.

"But then it's not false," Pagnell whispered, knowing full

well he was talking to the paper and, by extension, the Quill of Truth.

On the table, another piece of paper smoked sullenly. The sentence, *The Quill of Truth can identify ALL true statements*, was struggling with its own existence.

"But the Quill of Truth was made in order to distinguish truth from lie," he whispered.

The statement in his hand tried to erase itself again and wavered with the logical impossibility of it all.

"What's happening?" demanded Handzame.

"Pagnell's confused it," said Spirry. "He's good at confusing people."

Pinpoints of red holy fire flickered on parchment. On, off, on, off.

"I've really no idea what happens now," said Pagnell. "Although it might be worth taking cover."

The Quill of Truth burst into flames. Handzame yelled and dropped it. It drifted, burning, folding in on itself. Before it reached the ground it was a flake of ash, then a wisp of smoke, then...

"It's gone," said Handzame, dismayed.

"And probably for the best," said Pagnell.

"All my efforts ... all my gold...! For nothing!"

"Well, yes. Maybe that's why they say people who spend their money on experiences are happier than people who spend their money on *thiiiings*—!"

Pagnell threw his hips back, bending almost double to avoid being gutted by the general's sideswiping blade. He flung his head back to avoid being decapitated on the backswing. Even Pagnell, whose experience of fighting was limited to observer or as an occasional recipient, could see she wasn't much of a swordswoman. Yet Handzame was, nonetheless, a soldier with a sword.

He staggered back, up the short step to the balcony.

Spirry followed. "Send her to sleep!" she shouted.

"I'm out of oomph!" replied Pagnell, twisting away from a thrust. "That feast took it out of me."

Handzame gave an enraged cry, half yell and half snarl, which came out as a furious gargling sound. A blind swipe nicked Pagnell's knee and he fell back.

"A curse on all wizards!" screamed the Amanni.

"Yes! Yes! Definitely!" he said, hands raised in surrender. "Consider my lesson learned, ma'am."

"You will pay," sputtered Handzame. "Maybe I'll hack off some choice cuts of wizard flesh and consume your magic powers."

"Why does everyone persist in such outlandish beliefs?" sighed Pagnell.

Spirry leaped protectively in front of Pagnell. "Please!"

Handzame's sword was raised high. "You think I won't kill a child to get my revenge?"

"Despite the current evidence, I'd like to think the answer is yes," said Pagnell.

"I have a plan," said Spirry.

"No," begged the wizard.

"Move, girl!" cried Handzame. There were tears in her eyes. Handzame had shifted from vengeful fury into *tired-and-emotional, long-and-difficult-day, it's-my-party-and-I'll-cry-if-I-want-to* territory.

Spirry hauled Pagnell to his feet. The balcony rail was at his back.

"Don't think I won't do it!" yelled Handzame and swung.

Pagnell opened his mouth to protest. Spirry tried to shove him away from the wildly swung blade. Pagnell's thighs caught against the rail and he tipped. He certainly didn't mean to. He threw his hand out to grab something and his shoulder screamed in pain.

And then they were falling. They. Tiny hands gripped his undershirt. They were spinning.

Eight floors from the great audience chamber balcony to the hard ground of the lesser courtyard.

All Pagnell could think of was the sight of two plums striking the ground – what, two nights ago? – and flying messily apart on impact. Eight storeys was a long way. Time enough for one decent thought.

Small hands hugged him tightly.

They fell.

THE BARD

Bez tilted his face upward, raised his hand, and felt the warmth of the setting sun on his fingertips. He shifted his position, winced at the sound his feet made on the gritty ledge and glanced down to see if he had been heard. There was movement among the shadows below but what it meant, he couldn't say.

His plan had been ninety-five percent successful, which should have counted for something if there was any fairness in the world. He had climbed the stairs, crept through the crushing trap, tiptoed across the rickety timbers the grimlocks had laid across the hall of deadly tiles, and then, with barely a wrong turn, found his way back to the grimlock cavern. The cavern had been empty. The only grimlocks present were charred and speared bodies lying among the piles of accumulated rubbish and treasure.

The treasure. Bez had stuffed as much jewellery and coinage inside his clothes as he could. He placed a crown, all spikes and gems, on his head and tucked a gold statuette of Buqit under his arm before climbing the walls towards the chimney-like opening in the cavern ceiling high above.

Ninety-five percent successful. When Merken had told Bez the opening was too narrow for a man to climb through, Bez had measured it with thumb and brush and an artist's eye and judged it to be fine.Unfortunately, the damned old goat had been right, and that made Bez doubly glad the man was dead. The hole was, at its widest, two feet across, but narrowed sections and jagged stumps of rock made it impassable. Bez was facing the prospect of a night's squatting on the very cusp of freedom, on a ledge barely wide enough for him to sit on.

He couldn't climb down. While he'd been ascending, grimlocks had returned. He couldn't see how many, but he heard them and saw their fires. The smell of their cooking was, at once, repulsive and stomach-rumblingly good. Bez was able to reach his hand up through the hole and pluck some blades of grass from the surface outside. That had been his food. To drink, he licked the trickling moisture from the walls. He lips touched a beetle as he did so, and he recoiled in disgust; bursting into tears when he couldn't find it again. A beetle would have been delicious just about then.

Before the light faded completely, he took out the velvet bag he had snatched from Merken before killing him. This, he hoped, was going to be the big treasure prize. The way Merken had fondled it at every opportunity, it could only be something of immense value. Either that or dear old Grandma Merken's ashes.

It had transpired to be neither. If Bez was to guess – and

he had plenty of time to guess – he'd say the object inside the box was a mechanical biscuit. He couldn't be sure why anyone would want a mechanical biscuit, but that was what it looked like.

On the reverse, inscribed in a tiny script which was only legible in the full light of day, were the words:

Cnstnt Frce Tmpce
Manfcterd by H Gregnx, Carius

THIS OFFERED little help as to the object's purpose or value.

With his stomach growling and the light of day dying, Bez turned the device over in his hands, the hatred and bitterness inside him growing afresh. The bitterness he was used to: it went hand in hand with his natural cynicism; but anger? It was initially anger at Merken for dragging him on this stupid mission, gradually swelling to include the others – Pagnell, Lorrika and Cope – for not seeing his side of things; for not sharing in his anger. It was compounded by the failure of his plan and this frustratingly mysterious item. How dare Merken die and leave him with something so peculiar, so unhelpfully unique?! Layer and layer of hatred built up, like slimy deposits on a stalactite, until it was just a lump of shapeless hatred. He no longer hated anything in particular; he just hated.

There was a coiled spring in the back of the mechanical biscuit. He poked it, but it didn't seem to do anything. There were a number of wheels and little arms, but he couldn't divine their purpose. There was also a little nub of brass which looked a bit like a key. So he turned it. It made the tiniest of clicking sounds as it turned and there was a sense of growing resistance. So he turned it more, winding it round and round a handful of times.

The mechanical biscuit began to tick, like an insect in the grass.

"Right. A ticking biscuit. Of course it is," he murmured bitterly.

The ticking biscuit began to ring. Invisible bells, concealed artfully in its workings, rang out bright and clear and loud, a carillon which, if Bez hadn't been thrown into an utter panic, he might have recognised as the Carian civic anthem, *We Think So You Don't Have To*. He tried to unwind the key but it did not turn. He tried stuffing his fingers in the workings, only succeeding in cutting himself. He pressed the device to his chest to muffle the sounds. He tried *quietly* bashing it against a rock to kill it. All he managed was to knock the statuette of Buqit off the ledge. It fell, clattering and banging down into the cavern.

Bez whimpered.

There was a silence and then:

"Figgerik?"

"Leth a taner?"

"Yanera bumfit!"

"Bumfit?"

"Pimpera bumfit!"

They came for him. The grimlocks climbed at speed. Bez stood and clawed at the rocks around the opening. He punched at the edges. He jumped and thrust and squeezed and pushed his head and shoulders painfully through the gap. He could see grasses and reeds and a red sky. A long-legged wading bird flapped by: a majestic silhouette.

And then the grimlocks' clammy mitts were upon him. They hauled him kicking and screaming and spitting down the wall, passed from claw to claw, down into the darkness until he was lying, weeping and moaning on the cavern floor.

A shape loomed over him. It was stooped and twisted. Half its body was black and blistered. Its lower lip was a ragged and swollen mess. It was Queen Susan.

Beside her, Clive, his shamanistic robes of knitted string mostly burned away, inspected Bez closely.

"Figgadik tan?"

"Indeed, old friend. How's it going?"

"Sethada?"

"Stealing? No, no." Bez swallowed uncomfortably. "A misunderstanding. I can see how you might think that. But I was returning these treasures."

"Taner? Taner yan?"

"Certainly." He tried an appeasing smile at Queen Susan. "I was conscripted. I had nothing to do with them. I'm an artist. A creative type. We leave the fighting and the politics to other men."

"Dikada covit."

"No, an artist. Not a bard. So very different. See? No lute for one thing."

Over to one side, a little grimlock hauled something out of a rubbish pile. Its strings went *twoing* as it came free.

"Yes. No. Well, flattered though I am, drawing and painting is my metier. I could paint a picture – another picture, a better picture – of her noble majesty, Queen Susan."

Queen Susan jiggled happily and muttered something through her mangled lips that might have been '*Figg a tanad*' or '*Figger taner*' (which was something entirely different).

"Yes. Totally my pleasure. We will send images of you to all the grimlock tribes and they will repost them on their walls and they will bow before your very majesty."

"*Hov bumfada*!" cried Clive.

"Yes, indeed. And within that limited context I would be happy – no, delighted! – to be your *bard* for a while."

"*Ah, lethot yanada*," said Clive sternly.

"What?"

"*Lethot tanita*," agreed Susan, nodding vigorously.

"Bard for life?" Bez quailed, tears pricking his eyes again. "Right. Sure." Bez took the lute proffered him. "And what a life, eh?"

SPIRRY

Spirry had seen battles before and she'd certainly heard tell of them. While it was certainly not the most dramatic, the battle to retake Ludens from the Amanni horde was undoubtedly interesting to watch.

"Can you have a battle with only one army?" she asked.

Newport Pagnell stretched out in the back of the cart. For a moment, his face became that tight, scrunched up thing it became when she asked him questions. Then he relaxed, laid his head against a sack of goods and thought.

"It's a bit difficult," he said. "I think one of the defining qualities of any battle is the fighting."

Spirry looked at the Ludensian soldiers at the end of the street, going from door to door, searching buildings, poking around alleyways and even looking inside water barrels – just in case there might by an Amanni horde hiding in there.

"They are waving their spears about a lot," said Spirry. "It's a bit like fighting."

Pagnell made a doubtful noise. "Well, other features of a battle include there being a victor, which there clearly is, and, afterwards, some sort of celebration and the giving of medals. And – who knows? – that might happen. Anyway, some of us certainly got beaten."

The wizard did look like he'd just escaped from a battle. Spirry was certain that, after a suitable rest, he would bore everyone at length about he'd acquired each and every injury. The wounds she could understand; she didn't understand how he'd come to be so dirty. Humans she decided, particularly northerners, spent their entire lives finding new and inventive ways to get filthy. It was repugnant, really.

"There's something I don't get," said Thedo the carter from his position on the driver's board.

"Yes?" said Pagnell.

"I don't get how you escaped from the temple."

"Ah," said Pagnell. He offered nothing more.

The cart trundled towards the north gate, where all departing traffic was being stopped and searched.

"Because," persisted Thedo, "you got to me from off that roof top, didn't you?"

"We did," said Pagnell.

"And I heard a bloke on the stall across from where I was say he saw something flying down from the temple wall."

"Flying?"

"Yeah. With wings."

"Like a bird?"

"No," said Thedo. "Like a little flying person."

A soldier waved for the cart to stop. Two further fearsome

members of the Hierophant's army pointed their weapons, apparently prepared to spear Kestino the donkey if it looked like it was about to start a ruckus.

"Show your faces," said the soldier. "You. Sit up. This way."

Pagnell raised himself up with difficulty.

A guard, whose face was a big round bruise, as though someone has smashed the end of a pot into it, looked at the three of them in turn. "No, don't recognise any of them."

Another soldier peered suspiciously into the cart. "What are you carrying?"

"Grain, fruit, a bag of salt," said Thedo. "Got the whole inventory written in my little book." He passed his badly printed *My List of Things To Be Done* notebook to the soldier.

The soldier thumbed it without interest. Pagnell gave a little nervous squeak.

"Everything's in there," said Thedo. "Because if it's not written down it won't happen. Praise Buqit."

The soldier waved the book at Spirry and Pagnell. "And who are you?"

"I'm a dentist," said Pagnell.

"A what?"

"A tooth-puller. And this is Spirry, who I think our driver friend was about to accuse of being a fairy or something. You know, with the wings."

"And the sharp teeth," said Spirry, grinning.

"I was not," said Thedo.

The soldier sniffed. "As a dentist, do you get many dissatisfied customers?"

"What? Oh. This?" Pagnell pointed at his battered face. "Actually, there's a funny story behind this."

"I just bet there is." The soldier gave Thedo his notebook back and waved them through.

Beyond the north gate was the featureless plain and the dull straight road to Qir. The sun was a glowing semi-circle over the western horizon.

"You got any food on this cart?" Pagnell asked Thedo. The carter passed him a small sack.

Spirry watched the city to see if the entire Ludensian army had decided to give chase.

"Told you my plan would succeed," said Pagnell.

"So what have we got?" asked Spirry.

Pagnell pulled a crumpled sheet of parchment from his shirt and held it out to her. She opened it. Pagnell's penmanship was far from perfect, but it had been good enough for the Quill of Truth and Spirry could read it fine.

"This is it?" she asked.

"It is," he agreed. "The key to Urstar. And saving the world, of course."

"Never doubted you for an instant," she said.

"You so did."

She held her fist out and he gave her a celebratory fistbump with added finger sparkles.

"You know," said Pagnell, "no one round here does that."

"Savages," said Spirry.

Abruptly, Pagnell gave a little shout. Kestino the donkey brayed in surprise.

"What?" said Spirry.

"This is it!" Pagnell, pointed at the fruit he had just plucked from the sack. "This is it!"

Spirry looked at the light red fruit. "This is what?"

"The colour! I was talking to Merken about it, before he got exploded or something by a floor trap."

"You were talking about colours?"

"*This* colour!" Pagnell sat up straight, suddenly energised. "I said we needed a word to describe a light red colour, the one with a bit of yellow in it. I said there'd be a fruit which was that colour and it would revolutionise the way we think about it."

"Light red?" suggested Spirry.

"No, not anymore. Thedo! What do you call this?"

Thedo looked back. "Ah, they're new. Very sweet. Um, they're called kumquats."

Pagnell smiled broadly. "Kumquat," he said, savouring the word like it was the name of his beloved.

"What?" said Spirry, sure she'd missed something.

"Kumquat." He laid back. "Spirry, don't you think that kumquat sunset looks beautiful?"

"What are you on about?"

"It'll catch on. Trust me. I once knew a girl with kumquat hair."

"You're an idiot," said Spirry.

"Best wizard in town."

"We're not even in town anymore."

"Doesn't matter."

ABOUT THE AUTHORS

Heide Goody and Iain Grant are both married, but not to each other.

Heide lives in North Warwickshire with her husband and children.

Iain lives in South Birmingham with his wife and children.

ALSO BY HEIDE GOODY AND IAIN GRANT

Clovenhoof

Getting fired can ruin a day...

...especially when you were the Prince of Hell.

Will Satan survive in English suburbia?

Corporate life can be a soul draining experience, especially when the industry is Hell, and you're Lucifer. It isn't all torture and brimstone, though, for the Prince of Darkness, he's got an unhappy Board of Directors.

The numbers look bad.

They want him out.

Then came the corporate coup.

Banished to mortal earth as Jeremy Clovenhoof, Lucifer is going through a mid-immortality crisis of biblical proportion. Maybe if he just tries to blend in, it won't be so bad.

He's wrong.

If it isn't the murder, cannibalism, and armed robbery of everyday life in Birmingham, it's the fact that his heavy metal band isn't getting the respect it deserves, that's dampening his mood.

And the archangel Michael constantly snooping on him, doesn't help.

If you enjoy clever writing, then you'll adore this satirical tour de force, because a good laugh can make you have sympathy for the devil.

Get it now.

Clovenhoof

Oddjobs

Unstoppable horrors from beyond are poised to invade and literally create Hell on Earth.

It's the end of the world as we know it, but someone still needs to do the paperwork.

Morag Murray works for the secret government organisation responsible for making sure the apocalypse goes as smoothly and as quietly as possible.

Trouble is, Morag's got a temper problem and, after angering the wrong alien god, she's been sent to another city where she won't cause so much trouble.

But Morag's got her work cut out for her. She has to deal with a man-eating starfish, solve a supernatural murder and, if she's got time, prevent her own inevitable death.

If you like The Laundry Files, The Chronicles of St Mary's or Men in Black, you'll love the Oddjobs series."If Jodi Taylor wrote a Laundry Files novel set it in Birmingham... A hilarious dose of bleak existential despair. With added tentacles! And bureaucracy!" – Charles Stross, author of The Laundry Files series.

Oddjobs

Sealfinger

Meet Sam Applewhite, security consultant for DefCon4's east coast office. .

She's clever, inventive and adaptable. In her job she has to be.

Now, she's facing an impossible mystery.

A client has gone missing and no one else seems to care.

Who would want to kill an old and lonely woman whose only sins are having a sharp tongue and a belief in ghosts? Could her death be linked to the new building project out on the dunes?

Can Sam find out the truth, even if it puts her friends' and family's lives at risk?

Sealfinger

Printed in Great Britain
by Amazon

16224747R00202